Lost In The Wake

A ROMANTIC THRILLER INSPIRED BY THE MAGIC OF CRUISING

Linda S. Gunther

A Work of Fiction

Inspired by the lure of the ocean and the magic of cruising

This book is dedicated to the men and women who travel the world on cruise ships, working day and night, providing passengers with incredible experiences at sea.

Acknowledgements

Thank you all for generously giving me the gift of your precious time, your candid inputs, and your continuous encouragement.

Julie Tipton (cover illustrator)

Laurel Ornitz (editor)

Pam DeBarr

Colleen Fuller

Kathy Buchanan

Nico Swaan

Laury McInerney

Chapter One

The Promotion

When he was a young boy in Vouliagmeni, a seaside town south of Athens, Greece, he never imagined he would travel around the world on a cruise liner residing in a world of luxury at sea. Christian adored the nautical environment, even relished the occasionally rough ocean voyages, the regimentation of his daily cruise ship life, and meeting people from every corner of the world. He felt steadier at sea than he ever did in the dusty city.

At twenty-nine years old, he had just been promoted to assistant hotel manager of the 130,000-ton top-tier cruise ship christened *The Prism of the Deep Blue Sea,* the latest addition to Millennium Cruise Lines. Although not the largest in the fleet today, it was undoubtedly one of the most exclusive ships catering to high-end passengers who value excellent service, gourmet dining, and unparalleled entertainment.

Straighten up, Christian, he said to himself, as Captain Stavros Manzione sauntered by the reception desk. He glared at Christian and offered up a stiff nod, tipping his white cap, his typical version of good morning. Without a word, the captain clearly conveyed his message: Christian Stephanopoulos, just what are you doing to make this ship and my career the best they can possibly be? I am the captain. So, every day of your paltry little crewmember life, your mission is to please me, ensuring that I receive nothing but accolades for this elegant floating hotel that you now help run.

Just part of the job, Christian tried to convince himself. I chose this life, so I'd better suck it up, give the captain my most cordial, acquiescent smile, regardless of his approach with me.

"Good morning, sir," Christian said just as Ally approached the Reception area. She swept in beside Christian and jabbed him playfully below the counter while Manzione stared coldly into Christian's eyes.

Quickly distracted by two waitresses who wriggled by in their navy blue tight-skirted uniforms, the captain fell in behind them, watching their hips sway across the cruise ship's centrum and then down the promenade full of shops.

"Ally? What are you doing? Didn't you see the captain walk by?"

She nodded. "He doesn't notice me. I'm just part of the working class around here. The proletariat." She poked Christian in the ribs, saying in her Southern drawl, "Well, sharpen my pencil, what the devil are you daydreaming about now, Mr. Stephanopolous?" Surrendering to her teasing, he smiled at her. Ally continued, "Now that you're assistant manager, by golly, I think you've actually grown a couple of inches." She shot him a sheepish grin. "Okay, okay, I'm sorry. I didn't mean to almost get you in trouble with the boss."

"Hmm," he said, considering whether she was still playing with him.

"Christian, look at her. She's just adorable, a classic."

"What?" He kept his eyes glued to his computer screen. "Ally, I can't kid around anymore. We've got a lot to do this morning."

She moved close to him, tapped his shoulder, and looked up into his hazel eyes. "See that silver-haired woman sitting on the sofa?" Ally pointed discreetly. "It's her third consecutive cruise on this ship. I think she's been on board for well over a month. What a darling outfit she's wearing, all decked out in her pink Chanel suit."

Christian nodded, pretending to listen, but still focused on the data filling his computer screen. Ally nudged him again.

"Okay, okay, I'll have a look at her." He stopped working to look out at the sofa opposite Reception in the centrum area. "Actually, I *have* noticed her. She must love cruising, no question about that. And an added plus is the fact that she hasn't made one complaint or even had a front desk inquiry. I agree—she's quite a stylish little lady." He tilted his head, more fully appreciating Ally's fascination with the elderly woman.

"So precious—probably all of 4' 8" and she smells like flowers," Ally responded. "Yes, that's it, like roses. I notice it whenever I get near her, a light fragrance, not too overpowering. She's waiting for the string quartet to get started. I see her sitting in that same spot every evening eagerly awaiting the early evening concert. I love watching her. And when the music begins, she moves her head with such familiarity, like she was once a musician herself, maybe a violinist. I don't know exactly why I'm so taken with her, but I-I feel serene when she's nearby."

Christian didn't say it, but he acknowledged that the elderly woman's bright smile and warm demeanor reminded him of his mother, Althea. Like her, this sweet little woman seemed to view the world with nothing but love and appreciation.

Ally booted up her computer and refocused on the ship's business. "Well, I'm ready for an unforgettable fourteen-day cruise. How about you? Only three stops, today the cozy seaside town of Southampton, tomorrow the exotic city of Gibraltar, and then the ultimate thrill of New York City just days away. What a great itinerary!" In her deepest Southern accent, she raised her arms in the air and declared, "I feel as happy as a hungry boll weevil gettin' ready to snack on a cotton field. This journey will prove to be one hell of a work fest—I know that too."

Christian laughed and nodded in agreement. Although no guests stood at the hotel reception desk as yet, Ally anticipated that, as passengers boarded, dozens of them would soon be standing in the queue, anxious to run through their laundry list of disappointments and demands. The nonstop gripe party will erupt and not end until the final moments of the cruise, she told herself. It's the way of the world on cruise ships. Perturbed guests will say things like "Our stateroom is directly under the pool deck and we can hear people walking. It's horrible" or "My room attendant is nowhere to be seen and I need more hangers—NOW! What kind of cruise line is this?" Ally was ready. Her dimpled smile would remain pasted on her face regardless of how grumpy passengers might get or how absurd their complaints might be.

Feeling the heat of Christian standing by her side, her skin tingled with excitement, while he had no idea what was going on in her head, not a clue that Ally had fallen for him, partly because of his intelligence and quick wit, and also because she loved his ability to dream big, his child-like curiosity, his desire to explore the world (just like hers), and his commitment to excellence in his work. She was also attracted to his physical attributes—his dark olive skin, his sturdy body, his wavy dark hair, his sculpted cheekbones, and his hazel eyes—sometimes green, sometimes blue. At 5' 10" she thought him to be the perfect height for her petite 5' 3" frame. She often fantasized about how well the two of them might fit together, if it ever came to that. She even appreciated the signature bump on his long nose giving him that slight imperfection that endeared him to her. Ally's emotional defense was to playfully taunt him like a sibling, though at twenty-nine years old, he was actually almost seven years her senior. She masterfully hid her true emotions, enabling the two of them to become the best of friends. Recently, she thought about sharing her feelings with him, but it all seemed so complicated. He was her boss after all and that in itself established a forbidden territory. She treasured his friendship. She could sense that he didn't feel a physical attraction to her, yet they had grown close, very close. They started their service on *The Prism of the Deep Blue Sea* on the very same day, just fifteen months ago, the day before the ship was beginning its repositioning from South America to Europe. And here they were today ready to embark on another repositioning cruise, but this time, she was in love with him.

For Ally, working on *The Prism* was her first experience on a cruise ship. For Christian, it was his sixth year with Millennium Cruise Lines, having served on two of their lower-end cruise ships. Ally and Christian both typically worked nonstop 12- to 14-hour days, six days a week. Their friendship had blossomed quickly and easily, since they spent much of their limited time-off together, playing ping pong or Scrabble. Occasionally, they'd partner up to take in the sights at one of the ports of call, finding an out-of-the-way café, where they'd drink espresso with a side shot of Drambuie or Frangelico and talk for hours about their hopes and dreams until it was time to dash back to the ship and start their next work shift. From day one, she had reported directly to him.

But that didn't stop Christian from confiding his secrets to Ally, including his crush on Nadia, a striking twenty-six-year-old Russian girl whose primary responsibility was as hostess at the high-end Crystal Dining Experience. This trendy specialty restaurant was the place to be seen on the ship, where grand suite and platinum-level passengers gathered for breakfast or to gobble down $200 steaks and $20 cocktails at dinner, all gratis, because they'd just paid more than $25,000 per person for their cruise. Nadia had been blessed with a curvaceous shape and a breathtaking presence. No matter what she wore or the words she spoke, she exuded sex. She moved slowly when she walked, almost regally, taking each step with a pronounced elegance. So it was no surprise that men were instantly drawn to her and taken with her beauty. Christian could be just one of the pack blindly in lust with her. And for some reason he thought he had a good chance with her. Maybe that was true, Ally admitted, though that woman seemed to nonchalantly fend off scads of men who pursued her day after day. Hell, I'm probably in denial about the chances of them coming together, Ally thought, as she stood at Christian's side, blanking on the recently changed password for starting up her computer.

She sat down on the stool and looked at her screen. She would not dare reveal what was truly in her heart, especially since Christian's obsession with Nadia was at its peak. It was clear to her that he valued being able to share his feelings for Nadia openly with her. Ally could sense his trust in her, knowing that she would faithfully keep his secrets. He had confided to Ally that his plan was to wait until the time felt right to approach Nadia with his romantic intentions. Now that he'd been promoted and was becoming more confident, Ally knew that Christian was close to asking the Russian girl for a first date.

Only two nights ago, Ally had insisted that Christian role-play how he'd actually ask Nadia for that date. "Come on Christian," she said. "I'll pretend to be Nadia and you can practice." Relaxing in the crew's staff lounge on Deck 3, curled up on the shabby couch in her gray sweats, Ally elongated her body, stretched her neck up as long as she could, and spoke in a pretentious Russian accent and a deep sultry voice, caricaturing Nadia. "Vat do you vant to talk with me about then, Christian? You know that I do not have much time for frivolous banter. So be quick. Do you have something you vant to ask me, perhaps?" Christian and Ally had both collapsed into the sofa laughing, almost in tears. Now standing next to Christian at the front desk, Ally recalled their fits of laughter, their comfort level in each other's company. The more exhausted they were, the sillier they seemed to get during their free time together.

Remembering her password, Ally logged onto her computer system, ready to respond to the barrage of anticipated passenger issues. From just behind Ally and Christian, Packo Suarez, chief security officer, burst through the door of the hotel manager's office. Wearing a pair of dark Air Force–style sunglasses over his normally tan face, he didn't look as arrogant as usual, but instead flustered today, his complexion a pasty white, as if he had just received some shocking news.

In a stressed tone, he commanded, "Christian, get in here now. We have an urgent matter brewing."

Packo waved him into the office, but then slammed the office door behind him, before Christian had time to move from his computer. Raising his eyebrows, Christian swallowed hard, logged off, and placed the CLOSED sign on his section of the Reception countertop.

They don't consider you one of them yet, he reminded himself. Get used to it. Now two weeks since his promotion to assistant hotel manager he hadn't yet managed to gain the degree of respect he had hoped for from his superiors.

Ally chuckled. "No worries, Mr. Assistant Manager," she said. "I've got you covered. Go on, get in there."

"Thanks, Ms. Assistant to the Assistant Manager." He grinned and tickled her under the chin, unaware that he was simultaneously sending pleasurable chills up and down her spine. He looked into her eyes. What a pesky kid sister you would be, he thought. Lucky for me we're not related. He turned and pointed his index finger to the closed office door and imitated a marching toy soldier. "Wish me luck!"

When Christian entered the office, the security officer was on the phone with a worried look on his face. Christian listened as Packo twirled a lock of his unruly black hair around his large index finger, unaware that he was in fact exposing his frayed nerves to the underling who stood before him.

Packo was shouting into the phone with annoyance. "Yes, yes, I see, but the captain will be very unhappy with that news." He put his hand over the phone and looked over at Christian. "God damn, Southampton is becoming a difficult port for us to clear." He shouted again, "Maybe I need to go up your chain of command and speak with the Customs director." Realizing that his anger was becoming too apparent, Packo struggled to moderate his tone of voice. "Look, I-I'm sorry for my agitation. But you can understand how impossible this is for us. We have a committed schedule."

He stopped talking, forcing himself to listen without interrupting for what seemed like a long time to Christian, but Packo's face only contorted with increased frustration. Feeling awkward, Christian longed to demonstrate an increased air of confidence with senior officers. This is my opportunity to show it, he thought.

Packo continued shouting into the phone, now more heated: "I'll expect a call back within the next 10 minutes. Look, if you want Millennium's continuing business in this port … You have my cell phone number. Call me."

Packo hung up, shaking his fist in the air. "Snooty Brits, as if they rule the world! No chance that will happen again." He fidgeted with a pen on the desk and said, "We have trouble, my friend. That's what this Customs fuss is all about. A gun was found in a passenger's suitcase before it ever made it onboard. Some couple from Idaho." He looked down at a piece of crumpled paper and read his notes: "Matt and Sissy Caruthers. They've been on 43 Millennium cruises. Wife is 63. Husband is 67. He's a retired doctor. They have a German shepherd, called Sigmund, who is traveling with them." Then he went on to say, "Sissy's got 'anxiety' issues and the dog is her service companion. Can you imagine? The pooch has already created a ruckus by shitting on the carpets—the last time just steps away from the captain. I saw the whole episode. A disgusting mess! You should have seen Manzione's face ... Actually I kind of enjoyed it, though."

All Christian heard was the word *gun.* He knee-jerked a response, appearing unintentionally confident, surprising both himself and Packo: "So, are they being escorted off the ship then? Wouldn't that be your process from a security standpoint?"

Packo ignored the subordinate's question, still playing with his pen. "It's an AK-47, no less. Customs on shore want to throw the couple the hell off the ship. British bastards. I'm sure that gun was placed in their luggage by someone else. *A couple from Idaho?* Serial cruisers are not who you'd expect to be carrying a machine gun around. *Mierda!* Two weeks until I'm home for a three-month leave and this has to happen!" Packo removed his extra-large navy blue officer's coat, threw it down on the desk, and then started to pace behind the desk chair.

Christian stood alert and eager, hands down at his sides. "How can I help on this? Where is Lana? I haven't seen her today."

Packo unbuttoned the cuffs on his crisp white shirt and rolled up his sleeves. "Guess what, *you're* in charge now, *amigo.* Our hotel manager, your boss, has taken ill. Pneumonia, well that's what she says. She's on her way home to Spain for two weeks, where I wish I was right now. So, *you're* the man! You wanted it. Now, you got it." Packo's belly laugh swallowed up the small cubby-sized office. He shook his head, still laughing, and plunked down in the hotel manager's swivel chair. He reached behind him. "What is this? Ach, such an uncomfortable contraption. Look at this ergonomic crap." He grabbed the stiff back support from behind his back and tossed it onto the carpet.

Christian could sense the turmoil simmering inside his body but continued to fake officer-worthy confidence as he leaned against the door, his hands now in his pockets. He spoke with composure: "Well, it *could* actually be the doctor's AK-47. We can't rule it out, right? So, what's our next step?"

"Good question," Packo replied, shaking his head. "I informed the captain of the bloody problem just before coming in here. No surprise, he doesn't want to throw 'Dr. and Mrs. Millennium Cruise Lines' off the ship. The Caruthers are evidently two of our most valued customers. I also checked on how many friends and family members the couple has on board with them. Twenty-one of them are traveling together from the same place: Mink Creek, Idaho. They must have half the town in tow." Packo sighed and leaned back in the chair, twisting his black hair around his index finger, when the desk phone rang.

"Officer Suarez." Packo pressed a button to place it on speaker.

It was a familiar voice. "Captain Manzione speaking," the thick Italian accent spilled out from the phone. "Finally, I found you. Suarez, what's your update on our little situation? Are we leaving in 25 minutes as planned? I don't want that couple removed from this ship. You understand me? That better not be the solution," he barked.

Packo's voice softened as he responded in a manner just shy of a lilt. "Captain, sir. *Si,* I am working on this right now, just waiting for U.K. Customs to phone me back. I've made your request to them very clear. Confiscate the gun and we inform the couple what Customs has identified in their suitcase, but we communicate with them *after* the ship is underway, not before. Then we put the couple on some sort of surveillance during the duration of the cruise. You were right I'm sure—it's obvious someone else tried to smuggle the gun on board and stashed it in the Caruthers' suitcase. Perhaps we can catch the culprit when he attempts to retrieve the gun, *if* he does, but I'm—"

The captain cut him off: "Suarez, call Customs back again. I don't want any delays on my ship. You following me? *Fatelo!* Make it happen." He hung up.

"He wants what he wants," Packo said, facing Christian. "Our captain seems to be angry all the time." Packo got up, pulling his shirtsleeves back down, buttoning up the cuffs, and donned his uniform jacket, after sniffing each of his armpits. "Stay tuned. Despite the captain, I'm going to ferret out Dr. and Mrs. Caruthers and ask them a few questions about the contents of their suitcases. I'll get back with you Mr. (acting) Hotel Manager. Let's go, *amigo*."

Christian fell behind Packo as he opened the office door and watched him disappear into the sea of people lined up in the Reception area. Christian stepped back behind the desk next to Ally, who was now handling what looked like a pleased passenger. She's good at soothing their concerns. Smart as a whip, that girl, he thought. A cacophony of complaints blended together in the background from the array of disgruntled passengers waiting impatiently to beat up the hotel Reception staff. Ally shook the hand of a male passenger who left the counter with his satisfied wife, an appreciative smile on both their faces. Christian swiftly removed the CLOSED sign from his section of the counter, ready to take on the next simmering guest. Ally looked into his eyes and then noticed his serious expression.

"Did your toast get burnt in that office or what?" She wrinkled up her nose and looked closely at the dark hair at the nape of his neck. "Hell, I think I just spotted your first gray hair Mr. Assistant Hotel Manager." She reached up and faked plucking a hair from his head.

He could see her reflection in his computer screen. "You are one sassy Southern girl," he said under his breath. Although he knew Ally was barely twenty-two, at this moment she more closely resembled a cocky sixteen-year-old. She had that "girl next door" thing going on. "You're a brat and your precocious style is going to get us in big trouble one of these days." Yet he couldn't help but smile. "By the way, I'm now officially the cruise hotel manager for the next fourteen days. Our real boss has taken ill and is on her way home. So, get to work."

"What? Ooooo eeee, are you kidding? We're gonna have some fun on this boat ride with you in charge," she teased.

"You have no idea, Ally. No idea." He turned to her, gave her a wink, then looked up and graciously greeted an indignant young couple as they approached the counter. He spotted their gold cruise cards, which told him that they were top-tier passengers.

"Yes, and how can I help you folks today?" he said, smiling as if they just stepped into his private limousine and his only mission in life was to brighten their day with the sweetest strawberries and the finest champagne. He politely listened to their plight and then offered them a room upgrade, taking them from an inside stateroom plagued by a nasty stench to an outside stateroom with a wraparound balcony and no stench. He enjoyed the ability to actually please his customers, make them happy, something he learned from his mother.

Christian furnished the next couple in line with new cruise cards.

"Damn it son," the man complained. "Our cabin cards won't open our stateroom door. It's really irritating when we've traveled all day and night to get here."

Substandard check-in people on shore, Christian thought. We better give the port management some feedback. He made a note on a yellow Post-it and slapped it down on his desk by the keyboard. I'll bring this up in the captain's next staff meeting. I guess I'll be attending those now, he thought.

"Making notes to yourself now?" Ally joked.

"Ally, did you get any people asking for new cabin cards because they couldn't get into their staterooms?"

"Yep, three of them in the last 20 minutes, as a matter of fact, and the night's still younger than a preschooler."

Christian grimaced. "Those Southampton check-in people—I think most of them are well past retirement age and they frequently fail to key the cruise cards accurately." He scribbled, "U.K. Southampton Check-In—BAD KEY CARDING," on a yellow sticky note.

"Yeah, they're about as useful as a screen door on a submarine," Ally said, chuckling, and then shaking her head with disapproval. "But I guess it keeps us employed and anyway those retired people are always smiling, very cordial to our passengers. I mean, look at my favorite little old lady sitting over there. She's always in a great mood and seems to be sweet to whoever is near her. She must be at least eighty-five years old and is still charming and seems very intelligent."

Christian nodded. Ally could feel the heat of his breath on her body as he moved his computer mouse slowly in scrolling motions, searching for the list of "cabin card entry issues."

"Let me look at the last cruise out of this port and see how many cruise cards were keyed wrong before we had to make the corrections onboard." He quickly scanned the report. "Yes, just what I thought—over twenty inaccurate entries, which adds up to twenty useless key cards."

"What was going on in there with Packo, anyway?" she asked, her eyes staring at her screen, enjoying these moments with Christian, together commiserating about typical cruise hotel sail-away issues.

Christian taunted her. "As the American expression goes, 'if I told you then I'd have to kill you'."

"Well, bag my donuts, you best keep your hands to yourself, but come on, spill the secrets you heard in that office."

"I shouldn't breathe a word, but you are my closest friend on this ship." He looked around before he whispered, "A heavy-duty firearm was found in one of the guest's suitcases."

Her eyes widened, her expression losing its usual playfulness. She responded without a hint of her typically sardonic tone, "Christian, seriously? What's going on?"

Another obviously aggravated couple approached the counter. The man and woman were each outfitted in matching navy-and-white striped cruise wear. They were maybe in their late fifties, early sixties. It looked like the wife had a fair amount of face work done, her skin stretched tight around her eyes and cheekbones. Her mouth appeared fixed, like a wooden puppet's, barely moving when she spoke. Her makeup was overdone, thick black liner around her eyes, blushed red cheeks, and bright blue eye shadow.

With ease, Christian transitioned into his "most helpful" self. "How can I assist you today?" he asked. He noticed the platinum color of the two elite cruise cards as the husband slammed them down on the counter.

"We are Dr. and Mrs. Caruthers, in Cabin 9178. I hope you can solve our problem. If not, I want to see the hotel manager. Our suitcases are missing. We need them *now*." He huffed and puffed in dismay. "They still haven't made it to our cabin. We're elite premiere class for Christ's sake," he sputtered, as he pressed his fingers down on the two plastic cards. Christian noticed the German shepherd sitting obediently by the wife's feet. "So, what kind of room do we need to have to get our luggage delivered? We've been on board for well over three hours."

Ally creased her eyebrows and mischievously stepped on Christian's left foot, hoping to startle him into a smile. Instead, he glanced over at her just for a split second, pressing his lips together and narrowing his eyes with disapproval. Ally rolled her eyes before she looked away and then moved to the table behind them so they couldn't see the grin on her face. She listened carefully to the intense conversation, enjoying every syllable and nuance. She would tease Christian about it later.

Christian almost uttered *Skata* ("shit" in Greek) when he realized he was actually conversing with the couple from Idaho, the pair with the AK-47 in one of their suitcases. What should I say? He looked down at the service dog, the canine obediently positioned at the woman's side, wondering what was happening with Packo and U.K. Customs.

Responding politely, he said, "Dr. and Mrs. Caruthers, you are in luck. Actually, I am hotel management's senior officer for this cruise. If you'd like to have a seat on the sofa over there, I will immediately contact the staff member in charge of luggage delivery. I'll just be a few minutes and get back to you shortly with a solid answer. Please don't worry. You can depend on me."

Dr. Caruthers managed a quick nod in return, a little embarrassed at the antagonistic approach he had taken at the start of the conversation. Christian produced a half smile, wanting to duly acknowledge that the couple's late arriving luggage was indeed an important matter.

He turned to Ally, who had her back to them. "Excuse me, Ally, could you please get Dr. and Mrs. Caruthers some champagne from the bar while they wait for me to do a little digging into this problem?"

He's getting me back for stepping on his toe, she mused to herself. She'd do anything he asked of her. "Yes, of course. I can do that right now. Be right back with two glasses of our best bubbly." She flashed her most infectious smile, her dimples in the "on" position.

The middle-aged Dr. Caruthers seemed to perk up, intrigued by Ally's Southern accent and now noticing her petite shapely figure under the uniform. "Thank you kindly. We appreciate it." He took Ally's hand, holding it a little too long. "My dear, do you happen to have any Mumm's? That's our favorite champagne."

"Yes, yes of course, I guarantee we've got some Mumm's," she twanged back in response. "By the way, I love your dog." She reached over to pet the brown and black German shepherd.

Dr. Caruthers smiled. "Yes, that's our Sigmund."

Ally pet the dog again and then led the couple and their dog over to the centrum's sleek brown velvet sofa just opposite the elegant elderly woman in the pink suit. "And look at that, our very talented string quartet is just about to start their sail-away concert," she said. "You will have a bird's-eye view. Champagne and classical music, what more could you ask for while waiting for a problem to be solved?"

The ship's centrum was located mid-ship on Deck 4. Guests routinely gathered at the centrum meeting up with people before dinner and enjoying a variety of instrumental and sometimes vocal performances. A winding marble staircase led down to the centrum from the deck above, each step lit with changing colors of pastel blue, pink, and green. Photographs were often taken of couples and families posed and smiling at the foot of the impressive staircase.

Ally nodded hello to the poised older woman sitting on the other sofa. She took a sip of her tea, gracefully placing the cup on the table, and returned a warm smile. As Ally left the centrum on her quest for the champagne, she glanced back at the immaculately dressed woman and noticed her throwing a biscuit to the carpet. It landed right by Sigmund. What a sweetheart she is, Ally thought. She reminded her of a well-preserved Southern belle from back home.

Mrs. Caruthers shot the woman a disdainful look, as she tugged on the dog's leash, silently instructing Sigmund not to take the biscuit. At first the dog obeyed, but once his mistress turned back to look at the string quartet, he gobbled up the biscuit. Ally could see the elderly woman grin and nod to the dog, as if secretly communicating with him.

Chapter Two

Ally's Story

Ally hustled over to the opulent Centrum Bar, smiling at Jorge, the bartender. This ship's bars were also known as "Water World" to the crew, because the ship's chief bar manager encouraged his bartenders to water down the drinks, stretching a bottle of vodka or gin to its limit, continuously seeking to eek out the maximum possible profit.

Ally caught Jorge's eye as he threw a martini shaker into the air, impressing the two thirty-somethings eagerly waiting for their gin martinis. Like a skilled performer, he poured the drinks, and then with a pink, plastic, sword-shaped toothpick, pierced two green olives into each of the chilled glasses. After swiping the passenger's cruise card through the computer, he handed it back to the woman. He gave her a charming smile and then looked at the receipt in the tray, seeming pleased with the tip he just received.

Moving down the bar, Jorge greeted Ally: "The beautiful little *senorita, que pasa?*" he said. He was hoping that she was paying him a friendly visit to say hi. He'd had his eye on this pretty American crewmember for some time.

"Jorge, I need you to open a bottle of Mumm's and pour two glasses using your best-looking flutes. And I need those drinks faster than a hot knife can slide through butter."

He laughed at her choice of words. "*Si.* Happy to help out, but we don't have the Mumm's behind the bar, I'm afraid. I'll need to go get it from one of the specialty restaurants. It'll take me a few minutes."

"Okay, but please hurry as quickly as you can. We have a couple of very disgruntled elite-level passengers."

"Of course, *mi amiga*," Jorge said as he rushed off.

Ally stood by the bar and from afar watched groups of passengers strolling around the magnificent centrum, delighting in their first look at the *Titanic*-era staircase. Cameras flashed nonstop as guests captured shot after shot of their relatives and friends at the foot of the retro-looking staircase.

The string quartet had started, opening with Beethoven's Opus 18, Number 4. Ally recognized the melody with bittersweet memories. She could see herself playing the piece over and over again in the parlor of her father's great Southern plantation. It was his favorite. Her private music teacher, Ms. Candy Adcock, would tap her tapered wooden baton against the polished table, helping Ally to stay on point. Once a month, Randolph Collette would hold a mini concert at his mansion, where he'd feature his young daughter, Allison Rebecca Collette, usually as the opening act to a renowned opera singer or an esteemed ballet dance troupe, fully impressing the guests at his grand parties. People would come in droves just to be seen at one of Randolph Collette's splashy shindigs.

The well-known mogul of a prosperous Savannah, Georgia, cotton plantation, Randolph owned a billion dollar business, which had been in his family for over 125 years. He required Ally to practice the violin for two hours each day and to go to ballet lessons three times a week. She was additionally trained in dressage and became a highly rated champion at her prestigious private school. Other than music and horses, her father expected her to read and study every waking moment of her childhood. Every four weeks, he'd freeze her activities, take her out of school for the day, and escort her to his corporate offices, where he'd teach Ally everything about cotton, from seeds to fabric. She learned about the history of cotton, the intricacies of the various agricultural techniques, and the secrets to her father's manufacturing processes. She listened and learned like an obedient child, absorbing it all.

Allison didn't need to study much for school, being able to achieve A's in every class without much effort. She was a gifted child. Her IQ was assessed at 143. Once this was measured through testing, she was immediately accepted as a member of Junior Mensa when she turned twelve. Hearing this news, Randolph Collette arranged for a performance similar to the caliber of a mini Cirque de Soleil. A circus tent with all the high-wire accoutrements was raised on their expansive back lawn. He wanted a celebration commensurate with Ally's impressive Mensa achievement. Allison told her father that she enjoyed the extravagant celebrations but was secretly embarrassed by the whole scene, hiding out for chunks of party time in the rooms upstairs. Her favorite place for escaping the crowd during big parties was her father's cherry-wood-paneled office.

She would head straight for the free-standing antique world globe. She'd close her eyes and without peeking, spin the orb really fast, then poke her finger out to stop its turn. When she opened her eyes, she'd excitedly dream of being at her blindly selected destination. She imagined the planes, trains, and ships that could transport her to these wonderful faraway places. Sometimes she'd even fantasize flying on her father's intricately patterned Egyptian carpet that sat under his dark mahogany desk. She'd feel it whisk her off her feet, over the rooftops of the spacious Savannah mansion, flying her swiftly to Guatemala, or India, or China, or even Africa. She'd stare at herself in the gold-framed wall mirror hanging behind her father's massive desk. She'd make funny faces and speak in the accent that matched the country where her finger landed on the globe.

At nineteen years old, when she graduated early with top honors from Georgia Technical Institute, with a degree in biotechnical engineering, her father was extremely proud. He arranged for a famous Italian diva to headline her well-attended graduation party at the family mansion. He wanted to brag about his daughter.

Unlike the pride he had in his daughter, he was disappointed with his son, Edward, who was four years older than Ally. Edward seemed to wander through the world with half a brain and spent a lot of his time partaking in drugs, his preferences being marijuana and cocaine. At six years old, he had been diagnosed with attention deficit disorder (ADD). He'd often spit out his medication, his silent rebellion against his father. His ADD got in the way of his education, causing him to hate being in class, often skipping school and roaming the country roads looking for adventure. Randolph was made aware of Edward's truancy but decided to ignore him and avoid being around him.

Ally's mother, Abigail, wasn't much more satisfying to Randolph than his son. She spent hours each day hibernating in her private bedroom suite tucked away in the upstairs corner of the twenty-four-room mansion. She had been a striking beauty in her youth, although educated only through the tenth grade. Randolph met her in the Hyatt Hotel bar at the annual National Cotton Convention. She was just eighteen years old. He instantly fell madly in love with Abigail's perfect snow-white skin, her sculpted cheekbones, the delicate line of her narrow chin, and her long slender legs that seemed to never end. Randolph wanted to own this beauty, so he pulled the lovely, but unsophisticated Abigail into his life, fitting her in like a round peg in a square hole. Within less than a year of marriage, Mrs. Collette sank into a deep depression with periods of mania. She would drink endless glasses of iced tea spiked with expensive scotch whiskey, while she played nonstop gin rummy with a group of imaginary friends, almost never leaving her bedroom suite before late afternoon. Sometimes Ally would wander up near her mother's room, although the sign hanging on the door read, "NO CHILDREN BEYOND THIS POINT. THANK YOU KINDLY, ALLISON AND RANDOLPH."

Occasionally, young Allison would press her ear to the door, hear her mother vigorously dealing cards, shuffling them like a professional, and speaking to her imaginary friends.

"Y'all ready for me to wipe your asses?" she'd sing out in her drunken voice. "I got my game on today, ladies." Then she would explode with laughter and single out each individual imaginary player. "Aw, come on Cecily, you ain't got no gin rummy. I know that! Mavis, you want some more iced tea? I'll put something extra special in your glass. Ruby, I can see your cards. You best sit up straight. No slouching." Then there would be silence, just the slapping down of playing cards on the table, and Abigail screeching and howling with laughter. She'd poke more fun at each invisible competitor around the table. "Three aces, four jacks, and three queens. Now, that's gin rummy. Y'all lose again!" Abigail's glass, full of clinking ice cubes and whiskey, would sometimes crash down on the table with a clatter. "Well, dang it Tilly. You done knocked over your drink, you bumbling old biddy. That's not very ladylike now, is it? No, no, leave it be. I'll clean it up after I fix you another gimlet. Let me put on some music for y'all."

Forties big band Benny Goodman music would play out from Abigail's antique record player. Ally wanted to burst in, climb up onto her mother's bed, and enjoy the card game with her, even talk to her imaginary friends if that would make her mother happy. It would be fun, if her mother would just let her come in. But she never got the chance. The door was always locked.

Nanette, the pretty maid, would walk by, find Ally listening at the bedroom door, and shake her head at the little girl. "Your ma, she got some mental problems. But she's okay. Leave her be, honey. Nothing for you to worry your head about. Run along, Allison Rebecca. Go practice your violin, girl. That's what your father thinks you're doing right now, anyway."

All through her childhood and into her teens, Allison generally saw her mother only at dinner, where Mrs. Abigail Collette would be decked out in some flowing, pastel-colored, chiffon dress. She'd appear, already marinated in whiskey, her makeup smeared, but obediently sit on the high-back chair, like a pale white plaster mannequin, a stupefied smile pasted on her face, faithfully listening to her husband report on his day. He would tell his captive audience about his day as CEO of the cotton company, usually with a detailed overview of his activities in board meetings or how he successfully influenced some important megabucks customer.

His son, Edward, would sit at the table playing with his food, waiting for the moment when he could either be excused or slip away unnoticed.

Sometimes Ally would catch her brother sneaking off to a bathroom where he would smoke half a joint of marijuana to help him make it through dessert, where his father would either ignore him completely or berate him for some small thing that didn't even really happen.

Ally would feel guilty about her unconditional status with her father as the only truly respected family member. He seemed to also like Nanette, the maid, the only other person in the household that he showed any interest in other than his daughter. Ally had noticed him brushing Nanette's shoulder as he passed her on the staircase each day. She also noticed the long stares they'd give each other without speaking any words.

As head of the household, the tall, slim Randolph Collette would make sure he was home every night for formal dinner at 7 o'clock. He expected the whole family to be present. It was the only slice of family normalcy that he required. At dinner he would engage with his daughter and ask her about her day, while the servants served the food and topped off his wife's wine glass. Each night, after dinner, he dedicated himself to further educating Allison Rebecca about the world of cotton, leading her out of the back door of their mansion. He'd take her by the hand down the lighted magnolia-tree-lined path out into the cotton fields, where he'd passionately lecture her about the "magic" of cotton. To him, cotton was something sacred. He revered everything about it. "Allison Rebecca," he would say, "you will follow in my footsteps and one day replace me as CEO of this company. Yes my darling, when I'm too old to get out of bed anymore, you will take the reins."

"But Daddy, what about Edward?" Allison asked one day. "Won't he be the CEO with me? He's a boy."

Her father would first grumble, and then be amused by her innocent and candid question. "You can't spend what you ain't got! And your brother ain't got nothin' upstairs. You know what I mean, Allison Rebecca? He's just not near your caliber."

Of course she understood what he said about Edward but she felt sorry for her brother. Her father seemed to detest him. Randolph wanted to forget about Edward there in the field, swatting the air to sweep away his thoughts about his disappointing son. This happened every time Ally would bring up her brother in conversation. "Forget about your lazy brother," he'd say. Randolph would then bend down on his knees. "Close your eyes sweetheart." He'd brush her tiny upturned nose with a silky puff of cotton. That was the one tender ritual he'd typically add to his field tutorials. She'd giggle, thankful for that special moment when he'd cease his lecturing and make contact with her in a more playful way. He'd tickle her and run after her, initiating a game of tag. But just as quickly, he'd transition back to his hard-shelled demeanor. He'd pull her down on the grass and look her sternly in the eyes. "You are destined to become a leader. Do you realize this, Allison?" he'd ask her over and over, holding the ball of cotton out in the palm of his hand. "This is nature's miracle, my little princess! Nature's miracle." Sometimes he'd even respectfully kiss the cotton ball like it was a deity.

Like Alice in Wonderland, Allison wanted to disappear down one of the rabbit holes in the cotton field. She could see that her father took great pride in his achievements. She could also see that he was lonely and sometimes even showed signs of depression. Although just a young child, she recognized the symptoms. He talked a big story, but she was sure he had regrets about his choices in life. Big and powerful, yes, and intimidating to all those around him. Although compliant and respectful, Ally longed to run away from this life, but she was too overwhelmed by her father's expectations to let her thoughts spill out of the bag. She never said a word about her anxieties, her distaste for the prospect of running his cotton business in the future. Her greatest fear was falling into depression, like her mother, her brother, and her father. She needed to escape— it was the only way to save herself.

Two days after her college graduation, she showed up, unannounced, at her father's corporate offices in downtown Savannah.

"Allison Rebecca. What a happy surprise. I thought you were rehearsing at the mansion for tonight's concert."

"Daddy, let's go to lunch, just you and me."

She took him by the arm, flashing her dimpled smile. He raised his eyebrows and nodded his head, dropping everything, more than happy to leave it all for an hour or so to spend time with his lovely daughter.

"Hot diggity dog. Yes, I'm hungry. Let's get outta here." He beamed, flattered to have his daughter show up like this.

Over seafood and salad, Ally delicately announced that she was leaving Savannah for a different life. She spoke quickly, spitting out her words, more nervous than she'd ever been before. "Maybe someday I'll return here Daddy, but right now the cotton business will have to wait. I love you very much. You know that I'll miss both the plantation and the whole family. I'm so sorry, but I have to live my dream, *my own* dream."

Randolph struggled to stay composed, sitting there in the middle of the chic restaurant. "Is it a boy? Some fool you've fallen for?" her father sadly inquired.

She could see a few tears drizzling down his already ashen cheeks, one teardrop sliding and then dripping onto his toasted-almond-covered asparagus. He probably didn't even know that he was crying.

"No Daddy. No, nothing like that. My plan is to explore the world. I actually have a job that will enable me to do that. Once I get settled, I'll write you all about it. I'm sorry to say this, but I'll be leaving home in three days."

She wanted to hug him, tell him she knew that he was lonely too, and that she understood sometimes he, himself, probably thought of escaping the plantation life. Ally was just about to reach across the table and tenderly touch her father's hand, apologize for how she felt, what she was about to do, when his sadness suddenly vanished and his fierce anger erupted. He slammed his knife down on the white tablecloth, almost sending his salmon off the plate.

"God damn it girl. You're not even telling me where you plan to go, and I'm your father."

"Daddy, I'll give you all the details as soon as I get there. I promise. I-I just want to ..."

"First, I have a fucking son walking around in a trance most of the time, and now this! You're no daughter of mine. You're cut off. You've given up a fortune. I hope you're happy! You've got 24 hours to change your mind about this nonsensical whim. Allison Rebecca, do you understand me? Otherwise, you can kiss your inheritance goodbye. The limo is outside. Take it home. Right now, I just want to be alone. I'll find my own way home."

Those were the last words he said to his daughter. He stood up, slapping the black cloth napkin down, onto his unfinished plate of food. She had expected her father to be disappointed, upset, but not have such an emotional negative reaction, especially in public.

Sitting there alone at the table, she was embarrassed, all eyes staring at her. She realized that she had been stupidly naïve. Of course, her father would be outraged by this news. How could she not see his extreme disapproval coming? This news must be hurting him so badly, ripping his insides apart. In his eyes, she was the next prodigy, the only hope for the family. Maybe I should have introduced this subject months ago, but I just didn't have the guts, she thought, noticing the waiter approaching her with trepidation.

His voice was shaky. "The check has been taken care of by your father, Miss Collette."

The top echelon of Savannah society watched and whispered as she slithered out of the restaurant.

Early the next morning, Randolph left Savannah, off on a sudden business trip, she heard her brother say. Three days later, when Ally was about to depart for her great adventure, she desperately wanted to say goodbye to her mother, who had listlessly received the news from Randolph about her daughter's imminent departure. Her brother, Edward, didn't flinch when Ally told him that she was leaving home. Since Randolph was out of town, Edward was fogged out on drugs most of the time, knowing that he could practically walk around the mansion smoking a joint without anyone saying a word about it.

Ally approached her mother's suite on the morning of her departure. She waited outside, listening for her mother's usual fantasy card game ramblings, but, surprisingly, there wasn't a sound. Ally turned the handle on the bedroom door. It was unlocked. She opened it as quietly as she could to find her mother spread out on the canopy bed, sound asleep, her face buried in her feather pillow. Her slender arms seemed to be twisted up in strange contortions, her flowered silk negligee hiked up above her thighs, an empty glass of whiskey turned on its side by her pillow. Ally listened for her breathing. She was relieved when she noticed her mother's foot twitch a little. The room smelled like a mixture of lavender and whiskey. She tiptoed over to the bed and tapped her mother's arm. Abigail flinched again but remained passed out. Sweeping an auburn wisp of hair away from her face, Ally gently kissed her cheek. She picked up the highball glass from the sticky bed sheets and placed it on the nightstand. Then she left, walked down the long hallway to her own room, grabbed her black Louis Vuitton suitcase, and fled the mansion.

Ally wrote her father a letter twice during her first month working on *The Prism of the Deep Blue Sea,* but he didn't respond. During the second and third months, she called him three times from different European ports of call, but he didn't answer his cell phone. She left him a few voicemails requesting that he email her back, but he never did. It had been sixteen months now since she left Savannah. She had to admit that she felt happy and free, unchained, although she knew that she had given up her financial security, abandoned her potential bio technical career, throwing away her higher education, and had lost the love of her powerful, yet at the same time, powerless father. She felt as though she had never had an intimate conversation with him, never really knew his inner thoughts, having often daydreamed about what it would have been like if they had those deeper conversations with each other about real feelings. What if he had cared enough to listen to her hopes, dreams, and plans for the future? How would her life have been different at home? Even now, she still loved him despite his tunnel-vision approach to life and his cantankerous behavior. She was sure there was something good inside her father, suppressed but yearning to get out in the open. Still, she had no desire to return to Savannah.

Chapter Three

Confrontation with the Caruthers

Jorge finally returned to the Centrum Bar holding a bottle of Mumm's champagne. "Not so easy to find this stuff. They got all kinds back there— Veuve Cliquot, Moet Chandon, even Dom Perignon—but the Mumm's was hard to locate. For you, the most adorable girl on this ship, I pursued it like a mad man."

"Jorge, you are my hero. Thank you. The hotel management owes you one. Let me take the whole bottle. It will help appease the grumpy couple for having to wait so long."

As Ally rushed back to the centrum area to deliver the champagne, she could hear the string quartet starting up. The ship was moving, which meant they must have resolved the issue regarding the gun. What a situation, she thought.

Damn, the captain is standing there with the Caruthers and their service dog. I'm sure they're complaining about me and their nonexistent champagne. Now they're leaving the centrum and following the captain. Looks like he's schmoozing them.

Sprinting to catch up with them, Ally said, "Excuse me Captain. I-I have the champagne for Dr. and Mrs. Caruthers. Sorry, it took me awhile."

She smiled at the middle-aged Dr. Caruthers. He winked, wanting to recognize her efforts.

"Yes Captain," said Dr. Caruthers, "this young lady was getting us some champagne while we waited to hear about our luggage. I'm up for having a drink, I can tell you that."

The captain stopped in his tracks, thrown off guard by Ally breaking in with the champagne. He quickly recovered his charming veneer and flashed his most suave smile.

"Yes, of course, your champagne." He looked down at Ally's uniform to catch her name, staring a little too long at her breast pocket. He remembered watching her at the gangway as the boat docked yesterday in Southampton. Nice ass, he had mused to himself. "Ally, can you please take the Mumm's over to my office so I can chat with the Caruthers while they sip our favorite onboard champagne?"

He stared coldly into her eyes. She could feel him thinking you stupid girl. You dare to interrupt my interactions here.

As they moved down the promenade, they saw dozens of passengers starting to celebrate the start of their trip. People were enjoying pizza and beer at the pub; others were drinking cappuccinos and munching on elaborate pastries in the café bar; still others were waiting outside the promenade shops for them to open.

The captain led them to his special meeting room, a combination of an office and a lounge for elite guests or weekly staff meetings with his top officers. Packo Suarez stood in the doorway, ready to greet them. Ally followed in silence, the tray of glasses and champagne now feeling heavy and awkward. I wonder why Security is involved here, she thought.

Captain Manzione spoke as they approached Packo. "Dr. and Mrs. Caruthers, let me introduce our chief security officer, Packo Suarez."

Packo reached out to shake the man's hand. The dog growled in return. Ally glided around them and rushed into the office, carefully placing the tray down on the table, then fled the office. She could clearly sense that the captain wanted her out of the way. No ambiguity there. The captain took a moment to watch her ass disappear into the crowd. He refocused back on the Caruthers.

"We know that you're very concerned about your missing luggage and we'd very much like to talk with you about it."

Mrs. Caruthers seemed to panic. "Are our bags lost? What's going on? Did you leave Southampton without our luggage? And if that's the case, why didn't you tell us before we left the port? What's wrong with this cruise line?" The German shepherd growled again, locking eyes with the captain.

"No, no. We have your luggage on the ship. But we actually have some security questions for you. You see, there is a problem. As captain, I wanted to personally connect with you." The dog snarled. The captain cringed inside but kept his professional face intact. "Please sit down."

He pulled a chair out for Mrs. Caruthers. The dog bore his teeth and made a deep guttural sound, appearing ready to rip into the captain at any moment.

Dr. Caruthers grabbed the leash from his wife and yanked it. "Sigmund, cut it out," he commanded, snapping at the dog. "Stop growling!" The doctor looked over at the officers. "He doesn't usually do this. He's a service dog." Another growl. "Stop it, Sigmund."

"Matt," Mrs. Caruthers reacted. "Can't you see that Sigmund is upset? So am I! Don't chastise the dog. He's protecting me." She turned her head to look at Packo. "What is this hogwash about? What's the security problem? This is outrageous. W-we just want our luggage." Her hands began to shake. She quivered anxiously and looked as if about to faint. The dog moved closer to his mistress without taking his eyes off the captain.

"Look, my wife needs to go lie down and get some rest. She's traumatized by all this dramatic mumbo jumbo about our luggage."

Packo took the reins. "Sorry Dr. Caruthers, but for this discussion, we need to have both you and your wife here. This will most likely take just a few minutes."

A knock at the door. The captain peered across the conference table at Packo.

"It's okay. I asked our assistant..." He caught himself. "Sorry, I mean, I asked our hotel manager to join us. I believe that this is him now." Packo opened the door. "Yes, Dr. and Mrs. Caruthers, I'd like you to meet Officer Christian Stephanopolous."

Christian recognized the couple from the hotel reception desk. "Yes, yes, we've met." Christian shook the doctor's hand. He looked over at the table. "Splendid. I see that the champagne arrived then."

The captain was annoyed at this intrusion but stayed composed and amiable. He wondered why the hell this junior crewmember was invited to sit in his office. What value could he possibly add to this troubling situation?

"Yes. Yes. Let's get to the point for the doctor and his wife," the captain said.

Sigmund whipped his long tail back and forth, and started to wander around the room, settling down by Christian's feet. He would prefer not to have the canine's attention. He could feel the captain's disdain for him just being there. He sat down at the table. Unexpectedly, Sigmund placed his dribbling snout on Christian's knee, looking up at him. His automatic response was to pet the dog. Sigmund was pleased.

The doctor touched his wife's hand. "You okay, Sissy?" She looked away, biting her lip. "My wife gets nervous, upset ... very easily. Sissy, it will all be fine."

The captain dropped his head, assuming a humble, apologetic persona. "Let me first say, Dr. and Mrs. Caruthers, we have appreciated your loyalty, cruising with Millennium Cruise Lines so many times. You are, indeed, our most valued passengers. And we understand that you have several relatives and friends from Idaho sailing along with you on this cruise. But, unfortunately, we need to talk with you because a weapon was found in your luggage. We need to inquire as to whether you have knowledge of this weapon?"

"Lord, your accusation is outrageous. What weapon? Just what the hell are you talking about? Why would we have a weapon? Do you mean a penknife?" The doctor elevated his voice, angered by such an accusation. "The scissors in my bathroom kit? What? What?"

Packo responded, "No, not a penknife, not a pair of scissors. A gun, an automatic weapon, Dr. Caruthers, an AK-47 to be precise. It was found in your black Samsonite suitcase, the one with the yellow-and-green striped ribbon tied around the handle, the same color ribbon that is tied to all your other black Samsonite suitcases." He paused and then softened his voice, realizing the captain was now leering at him. Maybe Manzione would have preferred to break the details of the discovery, instead of him doing it. He can feel his superior's frosty gaze on him. "Please, Doctor, if you can shed any light for us? We are not accusing either of you of anything, rest assured, but we need your input here."

Dr. Caruthers leapt off his chair and moved to the porthole behind the desk. He looked out through the small circle of glass, down at the frothy waves. The ship seemed to be cutting through the ocean at a fast pace. His shoulders stiffened. He didn't turn around.

In an angry whisper, he said, "There is no way we would ever travel with a gun, let alone an automatic weapon." He turned back around and lashed out. "Are you insane? You're a bunch of imbeciles to think that we would ever hide or potentially brandish a weapon. I'm going to sue for this! I have a brother who's a prominent lawyer and he's travelling with us. First thing I will do when we leave here is alert him."

Packo broke in. "So, you don't know about the AK-47. Okay, we understand. I am very sorry to add more fuel to this fire, but a taser gun was also found in one of your other suitcases."

"What the devil? That's ridiculous. We don't own a god-damn taser gun. I'm going to sue!"

The dog kept his head on Christian's knee, ignoring the heated exchange. Christian could no longer keep his silence. He looked into Packo's tired eyes and then addressed the captain: "Is it possible that these weapons were *planted* in their suitcases?"

Packo nodded and sighed. "*Si. Si.* This is what I think, too. Someone else planted these items. Even though we suspected this from the beginning, you must realize, Dr. Caruthers, we needed to talk with you both about this situation. We're on a ship headed out into the middle of the ocean. Any weapons on board are serious business and must be thoroughly investigated."

Dr. Caruthers picked up his glass of now flat champagne. "God, I need this!" He downed it in one gulp.

Sissy Caruthers turned red. She shook with anxiety. "Matt, the last thing you need is a drink right now," she exclaimed. Her dog left Christian's side and moved over to her. She continued, "I brought the taser gun with me," she admitted. "It's mine. I know it was crazy, but I'm always scared."

Mrs. Caruthers jumped up and catapulted herself over to the captain's desk. She swept her arms in a rage across the mahogany surface, sending everything on it crashing to the floor. The dog remained calm, his head slightly tilted in wonder at his mistress's actions. Manzione had the urge to hurdle himself across the room and wring the woman's neck when he saw her destroying the order on his desk. Packo noticed his boss's reaction, and placed his hand on the captain's shoulder, signaling him to stay unruffled. Christian walked over to Mrs. Caruthers, sliding a chair across the paisley carpet so she could sit down. She dropped into the cushion, her body sagging, the energy sucked out of her.

She spoke in a husky whisper. "We don't own an AK-47. We don't own any type of gun. We are against guns. Period. I brought the taser for protection. That's all! I bought it in the hotel in Soho. Believe it or not, the hotel gift shop carried some protection devices for travelers. The taser was one of them. They said it was legal in the U.K."

Dr. Caruthers stood and moved to the mess on the carpet, bending down to pick up the desk pad and a now chipped coffee cup.

Packo said, "Please, leave it all. We will take care of that."

The doctor put his hands on his wife's shoulders and looked over at the three officers, shocked by the admission that just came out of his wife's mouth.

"Clearly, gentlemen, we did not bring an automatic weapon on board. I am sorry for the taser. I had no idea. You can keep it. But you didn't have to treat us like criminals. We don't deserve that."

The captain glanced across the table at the bottle of champagne. He wanted to grab it and take a slug, but instead rose and offered his hand to Dr. Caruthers. "Please go back to your stateroom and relax. We will get all your suitcases to you in the next 15 minutes. I promise that." He raised his eyebrows and looked in Packo's direction.

Christian jumped in. "Dr. and Mrs. Caruthers, can I have a special dinner brought to your cabin for tonight?"

The captain nodded in agreement. "Yes, yes our best filet mignon and the baked Alaska."

Dr. Caruthers felt exhausted. "That would be good. We're tired."

All he could think about was getting his wife and her dog out of this office. Christian started to retrieve a business card from his uniform jacket pocket, but realized it said Assistant Hotel Manager, not Hotel Manager. He grabbed one of the captain's business cards and a pen from the carpet, quickly writing his name and phone extension on the back of the card. He handed the card to Dr. Caruthers.

"Please call me any time with any requests you may have. We want you to be comfortable, to enjoy your cabin and our fantastic cruise itinerary. We promise you a world-class experience from this point on."

"Yes, yes," the captain quickly added. "The AK-47 debacle will be thoroughly investigated and we will find out how it got placed in your suitcase. Don't worry. We will find the culprit. Our number one priority is to keep our passengers safe." Those were the captain's famous last words on the subject. What would happen in the next 72 hours would turn his words inside out.

The captain opened the office door for the couple and their dog. The doctor helped his wife off the chair and out into the busy promenade area. It was a party mood out there.

Chapter Four

The Officers' Plan of Action

The captain released his bottled frustrations. "What the fuck is the game plan, Packo? We're not any closer to knowing where that AK-47 came from."

"First time for this. I guess we need to try to catch the gun stasher in action when he comes to retrieve the gun from the Caruthers' stateroom. I'll have a security man watching their cabin 24/7. It's our only chance."

"Well, you better call your man and get him to the door right away. But for God's sake, make sure that couple never sees a crewmember stationed outside their door. They will hit the roof and definitely sue us."

While Packo made a quick call, Christian shifted uncomfortably, not exactly sure how the captain expected him to participate in the discussion. But Christian was a logical thinker. He sat there considering what else could be done proactively to catch the perpetrator. "Captain, excuse me, but can I offer some ideas here?" he ventured forth.

The captain nodded. "Go ahead. By the way, Mr. Stephanopolous, you handled yourself well with the Caruthers couple, especially with the psycho wife. Well done. You helped calm things down." He sat back in his chair, then sipped some champagne out of one of the glasses and said, "So, what do you suggest? I hope you have some brains in addition to your accommodating style."

"I'm thinking maybe we should do security checks on at least all the male passengers." He looked at Packo. "Is there a way to do that? Find out if they have any record of gun crimes or some other criminally violent background? Maybe I'm off base and it's a long and challenging process since our guests are from all over the world." He shook his head, puzzled by what their next move should be.

Packo pressed his lips together, his unblinking eyes staring out toward the porthole window, in thought. "It's not impossible, but it's a 24–48 hour process to tap all the countries represented by passengers and crew. I could make it happen. But time is of the essence here. We only have one stop before we're scheduled to cross the Atlantic Ocean. I have no idea what is being planned here, whether it is to involve our ship or it is earmarked for something at one of our upcoming ports."

"Make it happen, Suarez. And good input Stephanopolous." The captain glanced down at his wafer-thin gold watch. "I need to get to the passenger muster in 15 minutes and make my announcements. Christian, is that your first name?"

"Yes sir."

"Right. Christian, will you stay behind for a few minutes and pick up all this crap from the carpet? Much appreciated. Do the best you can at placing everything back on my desk in some degree of order. I like things neat. Yes?"

"Of course, sir. Glad to help with that."

Packo chuckled as he stood and stretched, looking over at Christian, who began to gather up the items from the carpet. "What a twist with that taser. The woman's crazy! I think now we've seen everything."

"Well, let's make sure we don't see any more guns." The captain scowled. "We need to treat that couple with kid gloves. We can't lose them as future cash cows. And they have a lot of clout on that despicable Cruise Critic website. People from all parts of the globe follow their reviews."

Into his cell phone, Packo commanded, "Marco, meet me in the hotel manager's office. I want to talk to you about watching a cabin 24 hours a day, without the guests suspecting anything. Be there in three minutes." He disconnected.

Chapter Five

Nadia, the Detached Hostess

Leopold mopped the floor in the grand buffet kitchen. He was assigned to this task for three hours in the morning and two hours in the late afternoon. For the rest of his 11–12 hour workday, he did laundry on Deck 8. Sheets, pillowcases, towels, and guest's garments trickled into the small hot room full of stainless-steel washers and dryers all hours of the day and night. It was a nonstop operation. He hated the job, but he had bigger fish to fry, so he put up with it.

He looked up. His coworker, Ashok, dropped another basket of laundry down in front of the giant washer. "Another load, Leopold. They are coming in fast. We're still catching up on the cabin laundry from the last cruise. Agh, this smell is awful. I miss my old job on the pool deck. This sucks," the Indian coworker complained.

"I agree, Ashok. This job sucks."

As Leopold rushed out to retrieve the next load of soiled towels from the pool area, his sister's name appeared on his cell phone. It beckoned him to answer, but not before he pushed another heavy load into the cavernous washing machine.

"Da?" he answered the phone. "A screw-up. That's what it was. The gun. What a fuck-up all around!"

Nadia winced. "What do you mean? Is Gorby okay?"

"Gorby. Gorby. That's the only one you care about. He's a baby, Nadia. A brat. He's in the water in his boat waiting. He's fine! *Nyet. Nyet.* That's not the screw-up. What I mean is the AK-47. I had stashed the gun in some overstuffed black Samsonite suitcase, a yellow-and-green ribbon tied to the handle. Then I managed to drag it past Security out of the way. But some idiot security ape pulled it back again. They found the god-damn gun. I watched it right in front of me. The asshole security guard's eyes were as big as cow patties. His neck stretched straight up like a skinny chicken. I disappeared quickly onto the ship right after that. I never liked the idea of an AK-47. We didn't need it, Nadia. What the hell for?"

"What for?" She mimicked her brother. "What for?" Her eyes darted around to double-check that she wasn't being listened to or watched by some waiter lingering outside the kitchen stealing an unscheduled break from the suffocating humidity of the hot kitchen.

She noticed Christian rushing past her, the one who worked at the hotel front desk. He looked over in her direction. *"Chyort voz' mi!"* she swore under her breath. Such a fool, that Christian. He must do this "drive-by" routine at least five times a day, hoping to catch a glimpse of me. She ducked down, feigning to be searching for something in the elaborately handcrafted mahogany hostess station. Stupid Greek. But she admitted to herself that she was flattered to be able to attract every man's eye on the ship, including the Goody Two- Shoes, Christian Stephanopolous. For now, I want to keep him on a string. It may be useful to keep him distracted as our sideline activities unfold, especially since I hear that he's been made the hotel manager for this cruise. Who knows what information I may need out of him.

Her brother impatiently yelled into the phone, "Nadia. So, did you identify the first mark?"

"Don't yell at me, Leo! You're the dummy who has now put the ship's officers on alert. I'm sure word about the AK-47 has reached the ship's captain by now. You should have been more careful in getting it through Security. We might have needed a weapon like that."

"It's done Nadia. Done! There is no connection with us to the AK-47. What about the mark? Do you have a girl for us yet?" Leopold detested it when she played her commanding "big sister" routine.

"*Nyet.* I need to work on this."

Andre, The Crystal Dining Experience's head chef, wearing his tall white hat, appeared before her, ready for the usual pre-dinner chat, more than eager to go over the dinner specials for the evening. She flashed her enchanting smile. Her full red lips curled to greet him. She ran her tongue across her top lip to the corner of her mouth and threw her head back, sending her gold hoop earrings dangling. A few long raven black curls fell over her left breast, which peeked out from her fitted gold lamé gown. She disconnected, placing the cell phone back into her small satin purse, which was tucked on the hidden top shelf of the hostess station.

"Andre, you look like a lost sheep looking for the rest of his flock." She laughed and touched his perfectly trimmed beard with her long crimson fingernails. Nadia Zelnikov stood sleek and tall, pulling him in with her dark almond-shaped eyes. "Andre, you want to tell me about your specials, don't you? I can't wait to hear what you're cooking up for the passengers tonight."

His ego immediately stroked, he poured out his words with passion, his description of each culinary creation vivid, hoping to titillate this beauty with his unique trademark dishes. Maybe I can bed her before this cruise is over, he thought. He imagined feeding her his Viennese dark chocolate soufflé with his fingers, then moving them nimbly down to her delectable breasts, and licking the creamy fudge off her nipples slowly with his tongue. She was aware that he was probably fantasizing about her as he babbled on about Parisian Sole Almandine and Stuffed Creole Shrimp wrapped in peppered bacon.

He bored her with his patter. She ate very little and thought of food as something the body needs to live but not to be savored or revered in any way. Her personal passion was not for food but for making as much money as possible on the black market. That's how it was for her in Russia and that still remains her priority wherever she travels with her two brothers. She has them do the dirty work while she does the real thinking. Lately Leopold has been vying for equal power. Very annoying, she thought. As the oldest of the three siblings, she naturally took control from the beginning, although Leopold was only eleven months younger and Gorby was almost two years his junior.

Their youngest sibling, Yelena, now only sixteen years old, was still at home with their abusive father. Yelena was to be married in two weeks. Nadia and her brothers were not going to make it home for the wedding. It was to be merely a civil service ceremony held in the gray offices of the council building, maybe followed by a brief family get-together in the town hall's basement. Nadia didn't have any true feelings of love for her siblings. Her sister, Yelena, was a stupid girl, Nadia thought. Nothing would make me get married even at twenty-six years old. I want to make a lot of money and stay free while I am young, perhaps never marry. Who needs it? She couldn't imagine falling in love, generally despising all men. She didn't trust them and she had no need for romance.

Nadia grew up in a small village in Russia, just a 20-minute bus ride from St. Catherine's Palace. Throughout her childhood years, her mother, Liv, worked all hours of the night at a factory that made fur hats. Liv was the cleaning woman and was continuously ailing from a variety of breathing problems. The fur would get up her nose, into her throat, and crawl down her esophagus, as she mopped and scrubbed the floors and polished the assembly line machinery. But she would never dare miss a day of work for fear that she'd lose her job. Nadia barely saw her mother, who was the sole breadwinner in the household.

Her father, Ivan Zelnikov, a handsome man, with an accounting education, was often too drunk on cheap vodka to keep a job very long. He had a wandering eye for the Russian village's young women who flirtatiously followed him with their eyes as he walked across the street or while he drank and cajoled with his buddies all afternoon at the corner bar. He'd have a number of dalliances during any given year, picking the prettiest girl under the age of twenty-one whom he had yet to bed. They stood in line for Ivan, as he had become known as a ravenous lover. The local girls would place bets on who would be next to snag the notorious village stud.

When Ivan drank at home, which was usually each night, he exhibited other bad habits. During Nadia's childhood, starting just after her eighth birthday, he was repeatedly guilty of inappropriately touching his daughter, his fingers trailing up into her private area while he sat on her bed, pretending at first to be reading the newspaper. She would be thumbing through a book or finishing up the last bit of homework. This was his ritual almost every evening, her mother still at work in the factory, her father slugging down vodka in their tiny kitchen before fondling his young daughter.

He'd swagger into her room at about 9:00 each night and plunk himself down on the bed with his paper, throwing it to the floor after a few minutes. Then he'd reach out and tenderly brush the dark curls from her forehead. "You are a beautiful girl, Nadia. Beautiful. You will make many men crazy. I am already going crazy for you, and I am your father." He'd slide his hand down her arm, lingering at the bare delicate flesh on the inside of her elbow. Then he'd make believe that his two fingers were a little man walking about heading for her wrist. Then the fingers skipped down to her stomach, and finally under the blanket, inched up her nightgown, strolling with curiosity up her inner thigh and settling on the opening leading to her vagina. "*Da*, it's good Nadia. Very nice." He'd stroke her cheeks, stare into her eyes, while he pushed those fingers inside her. His eyes would open and then slowly close, feeling his pleasure, dreaming about the potential of entering her. But he pledged to himself never to sink to that level. For him, the evenings with his stunning daughter far surpassed screwing any silly local girl. Sometimes he'd kiss Nadia's cheek and then rest his head on her chest while he enjoyed the increased moisture that he knew he had generated inside her. "Ah, nice and wet," he'd whisper in her ear, his voice raspy and his speech slurred. Nadia would sometimes slip on her headphones while all this was happening and listen to some ballet etudes while her father probed her body. She'd turn out the tableside lamp, trying anything to escape the real darkness enveloping her creaking bed and invading her young body. She'd imagine herself far away, thousands of miles away.

When she turned thirteen years old, there were several occasions when she felt stimulated by the bulky fingers. She didn't want to admit it to herself. She didn't want to feel any sensation whatsoever from her drunken father's touch. But she'd find herself yielding, responsively moving her lower body rhythmically down into the two digits wiggling around deep inside her. When she'd finally shudder, her body stiff, he would lift his head from her chest and turn to look at her. A heroic grin sat on his unshaven face, excited that he could satisfy her as he had done with so many young girls in the village. She could smell his rank breath, feel where his dribble had wet her skin under the thin nightgown. He was like a sugar-coated poison to her. She'd find herself not wanting it, then wanting it, then not wanting it, then completely disgusted with her reluctant yet abandoned submission. It was her circle of hell. She hated him for it and began to hate herself whenever she could not resist arousal. He'd end the ritualistic scene with a gentle kiss on her forehead. Then he'd leave the room, often bumping into the door before exiting.

Did he feel guilty? She often asked herself this question. Did he feel anything? She never knew. Nadia developed a distinct hatred for all things men. Was her father doing the same thing to Yelena while Nadia was out in the middle of the ocean on this giant ship? She had no idea and had never asked her sister about it. Maybe that was why Yelena was getting married so young, Nadia thought.

From the time she was five years old, Nadia studied the art of dance. Ballet and sexual abuse were what defined her childhood. Her mother wanted her graceful, willowy daughter to become a famous ballerina. Liv would save a little money from each paycheck for Nadia's three lessons per week with Madame Peroushka.

Nadia excelled in ballet, her body perfect for dancing. Her pirouettes were appraised as exquisite, her arabesques long and elegant, her skills and abilities far beyond that of any of her classmates. Ballet was Nadia's escape from her life at home. But when Madame Peroushka hit her stick on the wood floor as Nadia danced the pas de deux across the mirrored studio with her assigned boy partner, all Nadia could hear in her head were her father's pathetic utterances as he violated her body. She'd smell his liquored breath all over again each time the Russian boy touched her body during the duet. The boy only wanted to hold the captivating Nadia. When she danced solo, she was in heaven. If she had to dance with a boy, it was pure torture for her.

The day after Nadia's thirteenth birthday, her sister, Yelena, was born, an accidental pregnancy for Liv. That was when Ivan put his foot down. "No more ballet lessons for Nadia. We need the money for the new baby. Anyway, Nadia needs to be at home taking care of her little sister instead of spending time on useless dance lessons." That day was the end of Nadia's hopes of a classical dance career and her dreams of stardom.

Her neighbor, who lived upstairs with his family in Apt. 302, was a dark, swarthy, older teenage boy named Karl and the child of a single mother. His mother was poor, with only a part-time housecleaning job, but the boy seemed well-dressed and always had cigarettes, while his mother wore winter boots with gaping holes. Often he'd appear suddenly without warning as if he'd been tracking Nadia's every movement without her being aware of it. Then he'd just stare at her, saying nothing. He liked the control he experienced when sneaking up on people and catching them by surprise. One day when Nadia was walking baby Yelena in her pram just outside their apartment building Karl approached. He slithered up close behind her.

"What, no more ballet lessons, Nadia?" He laughed in her ear. She was startled but kept her calm demeanor. He continued, "Just baby wailing for you now, *nyet* Nadia? I heard all about it from your brothers. Such a pity."

"My family can't afford ballet lessons," she snapped. "And I need to watch Yelena every afternoon, as soon as I'm home from school. I'll be fine. What's it to you?" She wanted him to disappear. She hated boys, and this one seemed suspiciously manipulative.

"Do you want to make some rubles, Nadia Zelnikov? A lot of rubles? I could get you a good job. You could make a lot of money, just a couple of hours a day three days a week. Then you could take ballet lessons in the evening. I could probably get you 4,000 rubles for each of these two-hour sessions. Interested Nadia? You could give some of your earnings to your family. I think they would greatly appreciate that."

She stumbled, almost falling down onto the pavement. "Four thousand rubles?"

Karl smiled. "*Da,* that's 12,000 rubles per week for you. Of course, I get a little kickback, too. I charge an even higher price to the customer. But you would clear 12,000 a week, guaranteed. Are you interested?" He sang out the word again to her. "*Interested?* I know you must be. I'll even watch the baby while you're working."

"You're crazy Karl. Go home." The baby started to cry out. Nadia became angry. "Leave me alone. I need to get Yelena to take her afternoon nap."

He rushed up in front of her and blocked her from pushing the pram further down the street. "Aren't you curious about this job? Just a little?"

"Okay Karl, what is this job that pays a fortune?"

"Well, it's a little odd, and you would need to be with an old man, Mr. Yeschenko. He's really old, maybe sixty-five or seventy. He lives in the next building. He's seen you many times and he's hungry for you, Nadia. He loves your slender body, especially your long, graceful neck. He told me this."

"You're an imbecile, Karl. I don't think he would pay that much money. Why would he do that?"

"He's in love with you, and he's very rich. Filthy rich. He has a huge inheritance from his dead wife. He lives on the top floor over there." Karl pointed. "The man owns the whole building. I'll repeat it. Twelve thousand rubles a week for you. Who knows, maybe you could get more once he starts to really know you, and like you even more."

"Karl, you want me to be a prostitute?"

"Okay, *da,* but only with this one old man. That's it! Anyway, you'd be more like a friendly escort."

The baby started wailing. "Yelena needs her bottle. Leave now. Let me think about it. I'll tell you tomorrow."

Karl didn't respond with words. He nodded, clicked his heels together, then turned and walked away, snapping his fingers to some imaginary tune. She heard him climb the stairs to the entrance of their brick apartment building.

Within less than 24 hours, Nadia decided that she would indeed do it. She knocked on Karl's door the next afternoon, right after school.

"Good, I knew you'd come," he grinned. "You start tomorrow at 3 o'clock, right after school. I'll come to your door to get baby Yelena and take you over there. Wear something nice, and be clean! Mr. Yeschenko is in love with you, but love can fade instantly if a man is disgusted with a woman's hygiene."

It was Nadia's way of getting even—fucking an old man while her father continued his nightly fingering game. She began to fake having responsive sensations as he probed her. The more she showed her pleasure, the quicker he'd release himself and leave her bedroom.

Nadia started making a lot of money selling her body to Mr. Yeschenko. The man was gentle but surprisingly sensuous and made her feel like a beautiful princess. He bought her expensive gifts on many occasions and gave her extra money well beyond their agreement. Her father and mother asked no questions about her new afternoon job. They knew she had one and that a neighbor named Karl watched Yelena while she worked. They were thankful for the extra rubles each week. They could savor a steak now and then, pay the bills, and even buy some pretty clothes for the baby. But the nights of abuse from her father continued. Nadia never resumed her ballet lessons. Her intentions were there, but it didn't happen. Instead, she bought pricey clothes, designer shoes, handbags, and jewelry. She even bought some skimpy negligees to titillate Mr. Yeschenko, who had become obsessed with his little whore. This arrangement went on for three years after which Mr. Yeschenko became gravely ill with colon cancer and was barely able to move from his bed. Yet he continued to pay her until his death at seventy-three.

Nadia's brothers, Gorby and Leopold, started hanging out with Karl, her upstairs pimp. The boys would drink and gamble together. One night Karl invited the three Zelnikov siblings out to the corner bar for a drink. He wanted to talk to Nadia and her brothers regarding something important. In hushed tones in the ripped-up red leather upholstered booth at the back corner, he asked Nadia and her brothers to consider influencing the neighborhood girls to sell their bodies for money, maybe even entice them to go to other neighboring communities where lots of rich men lived. "I have some good connections," Karl said. "We could all go into business together. I have big plans. Nadia, you would become my lead recruiter, a businesswoman."

The old Mr. Yeschenko had only been dead for a month. Nadia was missing the money—that was for sure. She was about to ask Karl for another client, but had been stalling. Hearing Karl's new scheme did indeed interest her.

Her brothers seemed alarmed for just a moment at Karl's provocative proposition, sitting silent with big eyes. Then, as if in unison, they both nodded to each other, grinning, their eyebrows raised at each other. They were in agreement. *"Da. Da.* We are intrigued, Karl." Leopold spoke for both of them, eager to hear more. Gorby also listened closely, fantasizing about his new life.

Karl described his vision: "You have a lot of nice-looking girlfriends, Nadia, several who may be interested, and I can see you have a natural charisma, excellent for getting girls to work for us." He turned to look at her brothers. "Gorby, Leo, I see those ratty girls you hang out with at the pool hall. Lots of them might be thrilled to make some fast money in return for sex. They would just need to clean themselves up a little. Each girl you attract and sign for six months will bring you each 30,000 rubles. Nadia, as our lead recruiter, you would get a generous additional bonus on top of that, based on the collective output of the three of you. What a team we would be!"

Nadia gave further consideration to Karl's plan, calculating her potential annual income. That's how the Zelnikov family sex trade and trafficking career got started. The brothers were delighted, eager to get out there and start recruiting the local girls.

Leopold smiled. *"Da,* they're sluts anyway. They put out every night for free. Those girls would love to have sex for money and maybe get to travel, buy nice things." Gorby nodded, agreeing with his brother. The deal was sealed.

Sitting next to him in the bar that night, she carefully watched Karl, how he lured her brothers in, how he painted the picture of their future prosperity. He was a nasty piece of work, Nadia thought, but Karl had been honest with her from the start, and as a result, she had made a pretty penny with Mr. Yeschenko. She was ready to expand without having to further prostitute herself. She could concentrate on using her primary power, her greatest gift—her brain.

Their new prostitution business blossomed, which translated into the rubles rolling in. Nadia showed her appreciation to Karl. He had become attractive to her. She liked his way of thinking and gradually realized that she wanted to fuck him, to achieve some degree of control over this over-confident young man. He was like her in so many ways. Over the next couple of years, she found that Karl was wrapped nicely around her finger when it came to sex. He had a couple of girlfriends he spent time with, but he would always end up on Nadia's doorstep, even late at night, just after many of his dates. Karl was very careful never to verbally confess his attachment to Nadia, keeping some emotional distance between them. His primary goal was to have Nadia stay on board and stay successful in the sex business. It would make him a pretty penny.

One prostitution activity morphed into another and Karl gradually managed to get the Zelnikov siblings plugged into the international sex slave trade, where young teenage girls, usually virgins, would be abducted and sold on the black market. They would go for extremely high prices to rich Asian men or to Saudi Arabian royalty. Each girl was worth hundreds of thousands of rubles. Business went well for about three years. Karl pointed out that Nadia and her brothers were in need of a new inventive channel to connect the right girls to their rich clients. South American,

European, and even American teens would be ideal. It was Nadia who came up with the cruise ship plan.

And now Nadia and Leo were respected crewmembers on *The Prism of the Deep Blue Sea* while Gorby worked behind the scenes in a small motorboat. Tonight, just outside of Gibraltar, Gorby sat in his small craft, drinking beer and waiting until the ship's arrival, which was scheduled for the following day. This was their second cruise line. Escapade Cruise Lines, their first employer, took them to places on the other side of the world in South America where they had successfully abducted five young girls and then sold them to Asian clients who wanted gorgeous young Latino teens for their private harems. They made the equivalent of $985,000, a splendid booty to supposedly split between the three siblings and their leader, Karl, or so Leo and Gorby were led to believe. Karl was the glue, connecting them to underground buyers, negotiating the price at a private auction, and making the hands-off arrangements.

Chapter Six

The Arrangement

Nadia played her role perfectly, the consummate hostess. Just snooty enough to be respected and beautiful enough to excite the husbands who sometimes slipped her an extra $20 if she seated the couple or accompanying family at a window table where sunsets were breathtaking. She'd come by later in the meal to say "Hello" and "How's your food tonight?" Then she'd touch the husband's shoulder while she looked deep into his eyes, flirtatiously beaming, satisfying the man's three-second fantasy, invisible to his wife, who was busy perusing the elegant dessert menu.

At about 9:30 in the evening, the restaurant slowed down. A few guests were finishing up their late dinners. Nadia was anxious about tonight. She would be assisting Verena Keppler, a dull girl from Munich, Germany, who was the director of the Teen Scene, the organized teen club on board for girls and boys between the ages of fourteen and seventeen.

This was Nadia's second job on *The Prism of the Deep Blue Sea.* In most cases, cruise ship employees have multiple jobs on a daily basis. Nadia assisted Verena and the teens each morning from 8–11 a.m. and then in the evenings from 10:00–midnight, where they spent most of their time dancing or singing karaoke. They were long workdays for Nadia, with small chunks of time to get some rest between her hours hostessing each day and then as fashion, hair, and makeup advisor to the teenage girls, the niche she had carved out for herself with the teen club. Every morning, Nadia would coach the excited, wriggly teenage girls, bringing along a box full of glittery eye shadow, colorful eyeliner pencils, and sometimes fake strands of neon hair, which she would fasten to a girl's head, furnishing her with a special glow for later that evening. Nadia's engagement with the girls allowed Verena time to stage athletic activities like water volleyball tournaments for the high-testosterone boys who needed an ongoing physical release. The girls idolized Nadia and couldn't wait to see her each day and night, sucking up her expert counsel on how to look gorgeous and desirable. For Nadia, it was her opportunity to scout out the likely targets for sex trading.

It was almost 10 p.m. Nadia closed up her hostess station and rushed from the restaurant down to Deck 5, where the teens were anxiously waiting for the discotheque called The Haven to open for the first sail-away teen party. A long line was forming, with Verena at the head, now chatting with a couple of pretty teenage girls from Italy. They spotted Nadia coming their way, her long black hair swaying as she walked, her evening dress sparkling with her every move, her makeup immaculate, and her perfect figure admired by all the young girls. The frenzied teenage boys stared at her, their mouths hanging open, wishing they could just spend a few minutes in her presence or maybe have their photo taken by her side, which would guarantee their bragging rights once back at home.

One of the Italian girls yelled out, "Nadia, you look gorgeous. *Bella! Bella!*"

Nadia waved and smiled as she walked up to them and kissed them both on each cheek, giving her European-style greeting. Verena beamed, excited to have this ravishing woman by her side. Verena, a shy lesbian, had instantly developed a silent crush on Nadia, which the Russian could sense from the first few times they worked together.

"Nadia, you look stunning tonight!" Verena hugged her, pressing a little too long in her embrace.

Nadia laughed to herself, allowing Verena to partake of a fleeting feel of her bosoms as she pressed back into the young German's chest.

Bursts of laughter and noise came from the more than forty teens already in the queue, eager to dance the night away on the moving ship, hopefully hook up with a teen of the opposite sex, and perhaps later have their first kiss under the stars on the windy pool deck.

Short skirts or tight dresses and high heels adorned each girl in the chattering group who were now screaming in reaction to some joke between them, their hearts racing at the possibilities the night might bring, in hopeful anticipation of having something juicy to record in their journals.

A few gawky thirteen- and fourteen-year-old girls were whispering about one of the older teenage boys who stood near the back of the growing line, his hands in his pockets, his hair hanging in his face, half covering his deeply set steel-blue eyes.

"He looks like a rich bad boy,'" one of the Italian girls whispered to her friend.

Nadia was somewhat amused by the variety of teenage behaviors as she scouted for a potential target. It was always challenging to identify a girl who fit the desired profile for their needs. She had to be beautiful, naturally striking, have a slender body type, and be fourteen or fifteen years old, the prime age range requested by the richest men of the world. And she must be lacking self-confidence, with an obedient, innocent, and submissive aura about her. This combination of qualities put the girl in the "sweet spot" for their purposes.

Nadia gazed down the line, doing an initial scoping out of the female prospects, ferreting out a prime pick. Halfway down the line, she noticed a tall girl, maybe 5' 7", with long legs and shoulder-length, thick, red hair. The girl was bending down, searching in her purse for something. Nadia couldn't quite see her face. When the girl looked up, Nadia saw the bluest, pure crystalline eyes. She had a sprinkle of brown freckles across her nose and a wide-eyed look of innocence about her, and Nadia assessed her to be around fifteen years old. Her clothing appeared somewhat old-fashioned compared to the way the rest of the crowd was dressed, and she didn't seem to be mingling much with the others.

Nadia remarked to Verena: "Nice group. Lovely girls! They appear to be having a good time already. Well, except for that one over there," she said in a hushed tone. "See the one with the red hair. She seems kind of withdrawn, awkward. We should get her to dance with one of these handsome boys." Nadia laughed.

"That's Amy Skyler," Verena said. "I talked to her earlier today at the Teen Scene Meet and Greet. *"Ja,* she's definitely more introverted than the others. But I know she wants to make friends. She just lacks confidence and a bit of social flair. A loner for sure, but you should see her run track. She is fast, a remarkable sprinter. I'm already calling her our Prism 'speed demon.' Look at her long legs. I had the girls race this afternoon, and Amy was yards in front, first to the finish line every time. She even beat the boys, who weren't too pleased about it, but I could also see that they were in awe of her raw beauty. Right after the races, Amy seemed embarrassed by her string of wins' and went off to the sidelines, away from the group and all the attention."

"Da, Verena. I can imagine her doing that. Look at her, her eyes down and pretending that she's searching for something in her purse. I think she's insecure with this discotheque scene." Nadia stopped herself, realizing that she was spending too much time making comments to Verena about Amy Skyler. "What about those three screeching girls over there?" She pointed to the end of the line. "Look at them. Ah, they're just teenage girls, I guess. Like an illness, *da*? And the very worst kind—rich and spoiled." Both crewmembers laughed.

"I love that dress, Nadia. You should be modeling on a Paris runway instead of working on a cruise ship. I could look at you all night."

Nadia smiled, understanding perfectly what Verena meant. She winked at the German with a knowing look.

Verena felt a little embarrassed by this interaction, but at the same time she was mesmerized by Nadia. She also couldn't help but notice that Nadia was often cold to her except when they were formally working together in the teen club. Otherwise, when she'd run into Nadia in the staff cafeteria or in the employee lounge area, the Russian basically ignored her, distancing herself and acting as if she didn't know Verena or care to know her. Verena couldn't figure her out. Nadia was a puzzle, hot in one arena and icy in the other. Maybe it's a cultural thing. I would love to get closer to her in many ways, Verena thought. Ah, stop fantasizing, she told herself.

As the arched gold doors opened to the discotheque, Nadia's phone vibrated inside her purse. Must be Leopold checking in. What's his problem? I'm the one directing this plot, not him. He seems to have an inaccurate view of his actual influence on what we do and how we do it. Doesn't he realize that he takes his orders from me? I make the calls to him, not the other way around. It's all Karl's doing, inflating Leo's ego before each job in order to motivate him, not just for the money but for the bogus power he perceives he'll get by thinking he's leading the next malicious venture. Such a fool! Both of her brothers, Leo and Gorby, had no idea that Nadia was getting paid double their take each time they had success abducting and transporting a victim into the arms of a billionaire. That was her sideline agreement with Karl from the start. She was the "brains" under Karl and she would be duly rewarded for her co-leadership role.

She answered the call. "What do you want, Leo? I'm engaged with important activities here."

"It's 10 o'clock, Nadia. Have you found our target yet?"

"Leave me to my business, Leo. I'm still working this out. I'm just about to talk to the targeted girl. She's fifteen years old. From the U.K. Pretty. Fair skin. Red hair. Very, very shy. A perfect target for us. She will go for a fortune. I need to go now. I'll contact you with the selected girl's name and remind you of her description again. I can guarantee that she'll be on Deck 6, back of the ship, at the start of the running track, at exactly 11:30 tonight. Gorby knows exactly what to do. He'll be out there in the boat waiting. Stop worrying, Leo."

She hung up and made her way inside the discotheque. Standing at the bar, where many teens were already sipping their Shirley Temples and nonalcoholic Long Island Iced Teas, Nadia watched the group intently as she sipped a martini. She located Amy Skyler, who stood in a corner at the far end of the club. What a lovely vision, she thought. Alone and looking self-conscious. Perfect.

Nadia wandered across the dimly lit, low-ceilinged room through the mob of noisy, dancing teens. The music was blaring. A group of older boys watched as Nadia crossed the room. She could hear one of them as she passed by.

"Nice ass. Look at that sexy woman."

"Her name is Nadia," another boy commented.

"Shit man, she's Russian. Is that hot, or what?"

Another one said, "Yeah, she works on board at that fancy restaurant. I think my dad is in love with her."

"Hello there," Nadia said, sliding up against the wall next to Amy. "Aren't you going to dance?"

"N-no. I'm just watching." Amy looked down at her feet.

"Yes, sometimes that is more fun. *Da.* Your name is Amy, isn't it?"

"Yes, I'm Amy Skyler. You might know my mum—she's an actress on a soap opera in the U.K. Her name is Wendy Skyler.

Nadia sipped her martini. "No. I'm sorry, but I never heard of your mother. She must be beautiful because I can see that you've inherited someone's good looks. Do you know how pretty you are, Amy? Those boys over there would die to dance with you." Amy offered up a faint smile but seemed to disbelieve the idea of boys dying to dance with her. "So, Amy, tell me about both your parents. What are they like?"

"They're always fighting about my mum's TV career. My dad doesn't like it." She hesitated, "I-I'm tired of hearing them argue. He's American and my mum was born and bred in England. She's constantly annoyed with me because I-I've turned out the opposite of her. I'm just not outgoing like she is with people."

Nadia nodded and touched the girl's hand. "Tell me more about you."

"I-I didn't want to be here tonight. But my mum and dad forced me to come out and mingle. I like the daytime teen sports activities on the ship, but I'm not very good at these nighttime social events. I-I don't know. I guess it's silly of me, but…"

Nadia threw her arm around the girl. "Listen, *I* think you're lovely. Can I offer you some advice on how to feel more comfortable with the other girls and maybe even how to flirt with some of these handsome boys? I know a few things." She squeezed Amy's hand. "I can teach you a lot. *Da?* I like you Amy and I'd be flattered if you let me help you."

"Really? Well, y-yes. How? Thank you. You are beautiful and when you talk, everyone turns to listen. Maybe it's your Russian accent. You're Russian, right?"

"Very Russian. *Da.*"

They both smiled.

Amy looked down at the floor. "Oh, I just wish—I wish ..."

Nadia squeezed her hand again. "You can break out of this, Amy. I'm a very good teacher. But I don't want to embarrass you, me giving all my attention to you when we're with the rest of the group. You can understand that. *Da?* So, I will give you some of my private time, off the record. Nobody needs to know. Some private tips on makeup, maybe coach you on how to comfortably chat with other girls, how to look your best, and of course, how to hypnotize boys. You certainly have what it takes." She looked her over. "How does that sound to you?"

"Amazing. But why would you do that for me?"

"It's simple. You are a stunning girl and you don't even know it." She laughed. "You see this brooch on my dress. Sparkles, doesn't it? You do the same thing—stand out like a diamond in a box of gray marbles. Look at those other girls. They are dull gray marbles. I like to see raw diamonds like you get their opportunity to sparkle."

Amy admired the brooch. "Is that a real diamond? It's bigger than anything my mum owns."

"Yes, it is genuine," she lied. "Later, I'll tell you how I acquired it. It's an interesting story. I was once a girl just like you. So, tell me, are you fifteen or sixteen years old? You seem quite mature."

"I just turned fifteen."

"Ah, that's a good age to be. Listen Amy, how about if we meet later tonight? At 11:30 on Deck 6, right at the starting line of the running track, on the very back of the ship. You know this place? Isn't that where the Teen Scene did the races earlier today? Would it be okay with your parents if you were out that late?"

Amy nodded. "Yes, I raced on that track this afternoon. There's no worry about my parents," she said now with more excitement. "They're hoping that I'll be partying at the pool after this disco dancing."

"Perfect. Then we can easily go from the track to a private space I know where we will have our first coaching session. Just for an hour tonight. We'll do the same each evening at about the same time, if that works for you. But you mustn't tell a soul. It must be kept confidential, only between us. Can you keep our agreement a secret? Not tell your parents or Verena or anyone else? I could get in a lot of trouble spending so much time with one guest, showing this kind of favoritism."

"Um, yes. Okay. I can meet you later at 11:30, and each night after that. My parents want me out of the cabin having fun. I won't tell anyone about my time with you."

"Perfect." Nadia pat her hand and glanced down at her watch. "Oh my goodness, our meeting is just a little over an hour from now." She grinned at the girl. "Our secret arrangement—I like the sound of that. Don't you?" Amy smiled. Nadia had closed the deal. "Well, I better leave you. I must mingle with the others. I'll do a little dancing with those hungry boys over there," she whispered. "Watch me. I will be subtle but instantly capture their attention. It's called 'presence.' *Da,* it is your first lesson. We can talk about it later. See you at the track on Deck 6."

Nadia winked goodbye and glided over to the dance floor, taking one of the geeky boys by the hand. She started dancing. The other boys stopped and gasped, wrapped in envy. Nadia moved her hips just slightly, gracefully sweeping her hands up in the air, like the ballerina she was before. Amy watched her, smiling to herself. What a nice woman, she thought. I can learn so much from her.

Christian and Ally entered the discotheque. Both good friends with Verena, they waved over at her. Nadia smirked, mocking them inside her head. Those two, why were they still wearing their uniforms? Trying to score points with young people dressed like policemen, so unsophisticated. You'd think they'd have the sense to change into more elegant evening attire, she thought, criticizing them in her head.

Christian quickly eyed Nadia on the dance floor. He was captivated by what he saw—her slender silhouette shimmering as the strobe lights blinked on and off catching the light of the huge disco ball hanging above them. He had hoped that he'd find Nadia here, knowing that she was assisting Verena with the Teen Scene club that night. God, he thought, she looks gorgeous. I just want to touch her.

"Stop your gawking. You're like a lovesick dog in heat." Ally elbowed him gently in the ribs. "Come on, let's you and I dance."

"W-what? All right, Ally. You caught me out. Let's dance."

He grabbed Ally's hand, whisking her out on to the dance floor, situating them only inches away from Nadia. From the corner of his eye, he watched the Russian twirl around with the skinny teenage boy who couldn't seem to keep to the beat of the music. She seemed to be off in another world, not even acknowledging her teenage dance partner. She was feeling the rhythm of the music with her body and soul, he thought. I want to be in that world with her. Nadia spiraled down sensually and then slowly wriggled up again, her eyes still closed, her hips swaying erotically as she bent her knees and repeated the move up and down several times.

Ally pretended not to be annoyed with Christian's gawking at the Russian, as she bounced around the dance floor, giggling with the teenage girls, who have automatically connected with her. To avoid getting more annoyed with Christian, she started to choreograph a dance with a group of teens, guiding them to move together in a circular formation and encouraging them to sing along to the well-known John Legend tune. Catching himself too obviously absorbed with Nadia, Christian followed suit, forcing himself to shift his eyes away from her and instead back to Ally. He joined in the dance with Ally. The adolescent boys kept their eyes glued to Nadia as she continued her hypnotic dance with her awkward young partner. Her long, dark, wavy hair swung from side to side, her hips moving with the rhythm of the music.

From the corner of the room, fifteen-year-old Amy also watched Nadia. God, I really want to be like her, she thought. I'm not sure why she's being so nice to me. For some weird reason she likes me.

The music paused and Nadia finished her dance. She hugged several of the teenage girls goodbye and moved to leave, brushing Christian's sleeve as she passed him. He smiled at her just as she had hoped. Nadia stopped and touched him, running her index finger from the top of his right shoulder down to where the cuff of his uniform jacket met his wrist. She bit her lip as she connected with his hazel eyes.

"Christian, so wonderful to see you out having some fun on your off-time," Nadia said. You're quite the dancer, aren't you? I didn't know that about you before now."

She glanced over at Ally, shooting nonverbal bullets of physical superiority at the petite blonde. Christian sizzled just hearing her Russian accent, the seduction in her voice. Her touch sent an automatic message to his lower body. He attempted to gain control of his reflexive physical reaction.

Nadia moved her long fingers, waving an intimate goodbye. "Have a good night then, my friend." She smiled and rushed out through the gold-arched doors of the discotheque.

Ally rolled her eyes. "I guess you won't be cleaning *that* jacket any time soon." She pulled him toward her as another popular song played. "Okay Mr. Jack Rabbit, time to shake it off."

A little embarrassed by what just happened, how he must have looked, Christian danced with Ally to the beat of Bruno Mars.

Once she left the club, Nadia tapped in her brother's number on her cell phone.

He answered. "*Da.* I was waiting for your call." Leo sounded annoyed. "You took long enough, Nadia."

"I'm confirming that it's all set, Leo. The girl's name is Amy Skyler. I've confirmed that she's fifteen years old. Very pretty. Long red hair. You'll know her when you see her. She will be there at the start of the running track at 11:30. That's what I told her."

"*Da.* I'll be there."

"Let me know when the handoff is done," Nadia said.

She disconnected and shoved the phone back in her buxom cleavage. She needed to be seen in a crowd for the next hour in case there was any need for an alibi. She wanted credible witnesses who could attest that she was nowhere near Deck 6, not anywhere in the vicinity of the running track at the back of the ship. She stepped into the elevator, pressing the button for Deck 12, heading for the pool deck party. Wait. What about Christian? Yes, yes it couldn't be more perfect. I knew his silly crush would come in handy. As the door opened to Deck 12, she could hear the laughs and shouts coming from the pool area beyond the sliding glass door. The rock band played—the party in full swing. Two couples stood behind her as she left the elevator. Both middle-aged men turned around and stared in Nadia's direction. She got out and then pushed the button to immediately go back down to the discotheque on Deck 5. She needed to hurry before Christian disappeared from the disco with Ally, that blonde with the annoying accent.

As she entered the club for the second time tonight, her eyes searched for Christian. He had his back to her. He was shaking it up on the dance floor with Ally and several young teens. Ally was leading them all in the old-fashioned Locomotion. Hmm, Nadia thought. Not too bad of a body on that man. Maybe not a Greek god, but he's got a fine physique. She tapped him on the shoulder.

He was startled to see her back in the discotheque. Slow dance music filled the club. He wanted to kiss the DJ for playing the Billy Joel classic, "The Way You Look Tonight." He held out his hand to take Nadia's. She accepted his offer. Oh my God, he thought. I'm going to hold her. "You came back, Nadia? I thought you had disappeared for the night."

"Yes Christian. I'm here in the flesh. I changed my mind and wanted to spend some time with you. Maybe we can check out the pool party upstairs. It's already 10:30. The festivities have started. I scouted it out for us. They are rocking up there. Interested?" She wrapped her long arms around his neck. He is a bit taller than me, she thought, but *so* skinny. In any case, he's a good alibi for me tonight.

"I'm beginning to get a little too hot," Nadia said, grinning at him. The song ended. She was about to lead him to the door just as Lionel Richie started the next song. She hugged him closer and sang along, the timbre of her seductive Russian accent a perfect counterpart to the tender lyrics. She whispered the singer's words into Christian's ear: "I can see it in your eyes. I can see it in your smile. You're all I've ever wanted." Nadia laughed. "Wait, wait. We must dance to this one before we go."

He nodded and beamed. "Sure. I have no problem whatsoever with that."

"Christian, I love how you hold me when we dance. You've definitely got some talent. Believe me, I recognize excellent technique when I see it. I was a ballerina, you know. *Da!* In Mother Russia." She kissed him sweetly on the cheek.

"That is not surprising," he said, his throat suddenly becoming dry.

Ally watched from the sidelines as she feigned meaningful chatter with the teenage girls who nervously waited to be asked to dance. Her heartstrings strained as her eyes followed the clinging couple out on the dance floor. This is not fun to watch, she thought. She was never confident with the opposite sex, having spent most of her young Southern life buried in books or practicing the violin. Yet she always had other children, both boys and girls, admiring her and wanting to be friends with her. But she had little time for them, leading the structured life her father had designed for her. Her father, who smothered her with attention anytime he wasn't working. If Daddy were here now, she thought, he'd probably offer Christian a thousand bucks to have the next dance with me. What does he see in that phony Russian, anyway? She's stunning. I'll give her that. But there's something fake about her. Am I the only one who sees it? There's an eerie strangeness to her. Before the song ended, Nadia pulled Christian from the polished wooden dance floor and escorted him out of the nightclub. Ally felt deserted by her close friend, the man she was in love with.

Chapter Seven

The Sea at Midnight

It's chilly, Amy thought as she walked out through the sliding doors onto Deck 6, heading to the running track, which wrapped all the way around the immense cruise liner. It was 11:25, approaching midnight. The navy blue sea looked choppy. She could see the ship's wake just below her as she stood by the railing and looked out at the sea. Wow, that's beautiful, a bubbly, perfect wake like you see in the movies or in the cruise ship ads. But in the distance she could also see scary-looking whitecaps. Kind of a strange place to meet up with Nadia, but she said we'd go off to some private place.

Amy's excitement soared, anticipating having the best time with this worldly and fashionable woman. She sat down on one of the two wooden deck chairs, placed just off the track, facing out to the sea, a popular daytime rest spot for fatigued runners. The quiet scared her a little; not a soul was about.

He crept up on her, hoping to lift her off the chair and toss her overboard without her seeing his face. But she jerked and turned around when she heard his footsteps behind her.

"Nadia?"

"*Nyet,* but she's on her way. No worry." Shit, Leo thought, now I'll need to play along, not frighten the girl. Otherwise she might scream. He swiftly transitioned into a soft-spoken friend of Nadia. "You are Amy, *da?*" he said, holding out his hand. She nodded. "Nadia told me to tell you she was held up and would be here in a few minutes. She asked if I would meet you and wait with you. It is kind of spooky here, *da?*"

Amy was nervous, feeling a little creeped out. It must be my imagination, she thought. Her trusting nature then seemed to override her fearful knee-jerk reaction.

"It's a nice evening," he said, smiling. "Although look at that sea. Ooh, a little rough I'd say. Very dense fog out there tonight."

Who is this man? He has a distinct Russian accent, identical to Nadia's, Amy thought.

"Look down there, Amy," he exclaimed. "Do you see that big object protruding from the surface of the sea? It looks like some kind of boat wreck. Look, there, just below us." Leo pointed down to the left of the white, frothy wake. Amy glanced down at the water, but didn't see anything unusual, only giant whitecaps that appeared to be increasing in size. He touched her arm gently. "Amy, stretch your neck out a little. It's really something. Difficult to spot, but once you see it, you will be amazed." He helped her up to the ship's wooden railing, supporting her like a little girl. For a moment, she enjoyed his gentle touch, like her father used to do when they'd go sailing on his yacht, The Kincaid. "Da. I think you will be able to see it now," he told her.

She was suddenly flying overboard. She twisted like a pretzel in the air before finally hitting the water like a heavy sack, the freezing water an icy shock to her system. Her lungs seemed to fill up with water. She was overcome. I can't breathe, she thought. I'm going to die. How could that man …? Her legs were heavy, weighing her down, taking her down into the deep black of the ocean. The sensation of sinking fast was overwhelming. No, I want to live. Her limbs struggled to get some degree of control. Reaching both arms upward and kicking her legs fiercely in utter desperation, she moved up, finally breaking the surface and breathing. Treading water, she blinked her eyes open and shut, the salty water stinging her eyes. Furiously dog-paddling, she felt something touch her arm. It was the bottle of her Paxil pills she had put in her pocket floating away. The medication that soothed her when she got extremely nervous, felt like she was going out of her mind. She gurgled, trying to keep the water out of her mouth. She was not a trained swimmer and could barely make it across the length of a swimming pool without having to stop and catch her breath. She wiped her eyes and looked around. A cloak of blackness surrounded her, the lights on the fading ship, which was speeding away, becoming less and less visible in the soupy fog. As if rising from her body, she saw herself fighting for her life, floundering just at the edge of the ship's disappearing wake, wriggling around in a dark sea of torture.

That man shoved me. I know that it was no accident. Why? Why did he do it? She yelled out, "Help me. Someone help me." She prayed that just one person on that ship would have noticed the girl pushed overboard and now lost in the sea. But it was late at night. It was very quiet on Deck 6, at the back of the ship. Nadia should have been there waiting for me. Why wasn't she?

Amy cried out again. "Help. Help." That man, if he didn't intentionally push me, then maybe he will get the crew to find me out here. He will get help. He will get help for me. She repeated this over and over like a mantra in her head. If I think good thoughts, I'll get rescued. But she couldn't manage to wrap her mind around anything remotely positive. She panicked, her body freezing up. I'm going to die. God, please! Please help me now.

A light. Something shined. She could see it out of the corner of her eye. She paddled around to face the opposite direction. It's a boat, a small boat. Oh God. Thank you. "Over here. Please, help me!" she screamed. "Help me!" It was coming toward her, whisking around in a half circle, making its way to save her. The light brightened, almost half-blinding her. "Thank you. Thank you. Over here!" she screamed louder. Her arms reached as high as she could stretch herself above the rolling waves, beckoning the boat.

"I'm coming. I'm coming to you," a man yelled out. He had a dark brown, scraggly beard. His hair looked long and wavy, much of it escaping from his black knit cap. She saw his long crooked nose and ruddy weather-beaten cheeks. He's not very old, maybe late twenties, Amy thought. "Here grab this," the man called out. "Grab this, Amy Skyler."

How does he know my name? Are they looking for me? They must be. She felt safer now. She lunged for the orange life preserver. With three tugs on the rope, Gorby grasped her hand, hoisting her out of the angry sea and onto the slippery boat deck. He slid down and fell on the deck, then sat up and looked at her. He smiled at her, his hands folded across his chest.

"*Da*. Very nice, though you look like a drowned rat."

Her red hair hung in thick, long, tangled strands. He could make out the carrot color even in the dark night. She felt relieved. Her life was saved.

"Thank you. Thank you so much. You know my name? How?"

"Ach. I know a lot of things," he chuckled. "Okay, let me help you up. You need to dry off. Yes, you are a beautiful little chickadee." He got a closer look at the girl as he helped her to her feet. The wind was up and the boat violently rocked, almost knocking them to the deck. A wave crashed against the bow, spraying them both with freezing salt water. "Let's dry you off." He opened the door to the cabin below. "Down there! Go down there and grab that towel just under the sink."

Amy stepped down the three wooden steps. The door slammed shut behind her. She could hear him quickly latch it. No. No. She couldn't believe what was happening. She tried to twist the door handle. No use.

"Why? Why are you doing this?" she cried.

The small boat rocked. She rolled from one corner to another corner of the small cabin. She could hear him yelling, swearing in another language, as the waves crashed against the hull. The seesaw motion continued. Suddenly, the bulky man unlocked the door. He entered, his husky shape barreling down the steps. Was he just protecting me, getting me inside to a safe, dry place? He must just have a gruff manner. He grinned and came close to her, then bent down, putting his hand on her leg.

"It's okay little beauty," he told the petrified girl.

He grabbed hold of her leg, yanked her to him, dragging her across the cabin floor, her wet body ending up near the bed. She hit her head hard on the wooden frame. The man reached with his other hand into a metal box while still keeping a firm hold on her right ankle. She began to sob. He's bad. A very bad man! Exhausted, she found it difficult to yell out or fight him.

"Stop your whimpering, girl. It unnerves me. "

Gorby removed a heavy metal chain from the box and wrapped it around her leg, clicking the lock into place. She felt helpless. The waves, the cold ocean, and this repulsive monster of a man who helped her at first and now was imprisoning her—someone help me. Mummy. Daddy. Please, she hopelessly cried inside her head as she trembled, more afraid than she'd ever been in her young life. With all of her might, she mustered a weak kick.

"Nyet. Nyet." He laughed amused, realizing that she had very little energy or will to fight. "You can't get away. Gotcha, my little chickadee."

"Why? Tell me why you are doing this? What do you want?" She gave one final pull on the bulky chain in desperation. Then she noticed that her left arm was bleeding at the elbow. Something sliced it open as he was dragging her.

"Ach, use this." He threw her a towel so she could hold it to her injured arm. She hesitated, but then picked it up, the dirty fabric crusty. "Use it. It will stop the bleeding. We want you alive, mostly unmarked." He laughed.

He moved to the sink and filled a bowl full of water, then placed the plastic bowl down on the gritty floor beside her.

"Drink. Drink. I have the pleasure of treating you like a dog for now until you become a princess again. But then you will only be a slut. A princess slut. *Da,* we will get thousands and thousands of rubles for your sweet young behind."

Amy quieted down, no strength left in her wet, tired body. She stopped struggling, almost passed out, her head dropping down on her chest. What did he mean, "princess slut"?

"Good. You're calming down." He stroked her chained leg, fantasizing about taking advantage of her, then shook a finger in her face. "My advice to you—don't be a pain in my ass. You will regret it, chickadee."

He got up and closed the door behind him. The click of the door lock broke any spirit she had left in her. Dizzy with eerie thoughts, she sat up, her back to the metal sink cabinet.

It was Nadia. She did this to me, that woman who was pretending to be so nice to me. I'm such an idiot. I deserve this, she thought, as she dropped her throbbing head on the wet gritty floor, which smelled like dead fish. She reached for the bowl of water, held it with trembling hands, and took a sip, then gagged and threw up in the bowl, her vomit shooting out onto her legs and down her wet clothes. She started to shake, her anxiety settling in and no medication. She stared at the locked door, which blurred, the rectangular room spinning around her, the hammer inside her head banging, banging. She prayed to God for help.

For the next 30 minutes, Gorby battled to keep control of the small motorized craft, fighting the blustery wind gusts and the wall of 15-foot waves. Suddenly, the weather conditions shifted. Out of nowhere, smooth water returned to the open seas. A few stars peeked out from behind the dark clouds, while the glow of the three-quarter moon lit up the surf.

He maneuvered the boat closer to land, and headed for the decayed, half-eaten, wooden dock just below the dilapidated lighthouse. Let me get this girl inside, off my hands. I need a beer. He imagined sipping it. I'll jump in the truck. It's only 13 miles to the closest bar. He pulled her up the short flight of stone steps and opened the door to the base of the abandoned lighthouse, nudging her in, then throwing her onto the cement floor.

"Ack. You smell bad." He looked down at her. "You smell like a hog from my grandmother's pigpen."

"Why? Why? T-tell me ... w-why are you doing this? Wh-wh." She could barely form words.

Chapter Eight

Pool Deck Party

Nadia led Christian to the dance floor on Deck 12. She swept one arm high in the air, lifting her hair, moving to the rhythm of the band's version of the rock 'n' roll classic, "(I Can't Get No) Satisfaction." In the other hand, she held a Dirty Martini. Now and then she took a slow sip, the vodka relaxing her, warming her inside. She had the Greek's complete attention, which was precisely her plan. To Christian, she seemed abandoned, like a wild child, lovely, fascinating, unpredictable. Before tonight, she had been typically cold to him, occasionally saying hello but usually passing him by without even a nod. But right now she seemed to be on fire. Electric, like her soul is reaching out to me, he mused, her sensuality oozing from her every movement.

It might take some work, she thought, to get him irreversibly hooked on me, but I see that he's already more than halfway there. She needed that alibi until the early morning, just in case anything went wrong with Leo grabbing the girl.

"Oh Christian, I feel *so good*. After an exhausting day, I can finally let myself go. It's you who brings this out in me."

I should say something, but what, he thought. I just want to look at her. Scrambling, he commented, "I hear the captain will close this party with another one of his Italian arias. He's quite good. Have you heard him sing?"

"*Da*. I think it's been over five times now that I hear him sing the same sad aria. So dismal. He's too uptight, our captain. But his voice *is* trained, very good. I don't know if I want to stay that long at this party, even though we would miss out on the captain's aria." She winked and slid her long nails down his jacket sleeve, signaling for him to come closer and move his hips in synch with hers.

"You like dirty dancing like I do?" She smiled. "Come on, try it with me." She put her martini down on a table. As she pressed into him, he let her take the lead, enjoying her body's erotic motion. "*Da. Da.* You are already decent at this dance," she whispered in his ear as they almost grind to the music.

He could feel her heat, imagining what this might be like without clothes. He thought twice about his behavior, usually carefully conservative when out mingling with the passengers. He couldn't help himself tonight, though.

The pool deck was packed with guests of all ages, partying, singing along to the classics. The drinks were flowing and the excitement of this "once in a lifetime" cruise was now a reality for many who will never do something as extravagant again. The band transitioned into another popular tune: the Beatles' "Hey Jude." Nadia stole the show on the dance floor with her sultry gyrations.

Ally and Verena entered the pool area, passing through the automatic glass doors, accompanied by a sizable crowd of teenagers following just behind them. A few of the teenage girls were already paired off with their cruise romances, likely to endure for the rest of the fourteen-day journey. Ally spotted Christian and Nadia. There he is, off in a dream world with the woman he's admired for months but never had the confidence to pursue. She watched him move to the music with the tall, slender woman. Nadia caught Ally's eye and instantly took Christian's hands and placed them on her swaying hips, then got closer, nuzzling his neck, her eyes still on Ally.

There is something about Nadia that I cannot stomach, Ally thought and turned away. She's like a fox in the hen house. Am I jealous? Certainly. I'm hopelessly insecure. Geez! Christian, that jack rabbit. He didn't even excuse himself in the discotheque, just left me there without offering even a word of goodbye. Look at him. He's deluded. I'm such a mule. Why do I waste my time? I have more brains than this—at least I thought I did once upon a time.

Ally reconnected with Verena. The teenage girls pulled each other onto the dance floor in small groups. Everyone knew the words to "Hey Jude." Most of them sang along, while many of the boys hung back and watched, picking out their favorite females until they spotted Nadia. The teenage girls became invisible as they gawked at the Russian's languid body. Noticing the obvious reaction of the young boys, Ally shrugged her shoulders and headed to the crowded bar with Verena, who had also spotted Nadia and was instantaneously dazzled by the way her body moved so seductively to the Beatles' music.

Leopold hung by the edge of the dance floor, signaling his presence to his sister. Nadia was startled to see him. Leo, the fool! What is he doing here? He was supposed to leave me a message once he grabbed the girl. Stupid brother! At 6' 5", he was plainly visible in the crowd. He locked eyes with Nadia and jerked his head for her to come over and talk to him by the elevator.

Christian couldn't help but notice Nadia gazing over at the tall uniformed deck hand. He recognized the man as one of the mechanics on board. I think he also works in the hotel laundry room. Looks like she knows him, maybe quite well. He's handsome enough and obviously into fitness. Looks Russian or maybe German. Nadia turned Christian away from direct line of sight with her brother, taking his hands and placing them around her lower back, as the band transitioned into "Under My Thumb." Christian got lost in the texture of her gold lamé dress, wishing he were touching the skin beneath the fabric. Leo stood there, gesturing a second time for her to break away. Nadia's annoyance mounted. She had always been careful to avoid any face-to-face contact with Leo on the ship. No interaction whatsoever except a brief conversation every now and then on the cell phone.

Christian couldn't help but ask, "Who is that guy? Do you need to go talk to him?"

"Who's who?" she laughed.

"Is he a jealous boyfriend? He looks upset and determined to get your attention. I bet every straight male on this ship is interested in you. I can't blame them. Seriously, it's okay if you need to talk with him."

Nadia had truly forgotten herself for a moment, feeling loose and relaxed after her second Dirty Martini. My imbecile brother. He spoils everything. "*Nyet.* No. Christian, he's my broth…" She quickly caught herself. "I mean, he's just some silly deck hand who's been plotting to date me since the first week we started working on this ship. He's Russian, from some town I never heard of. He was in my initial orientation session. Ever since then … well, you know!" She ran her hands down her shapely body, grinning. "He works in the restaurant kitchen, always tries to grab me. I ignore him." Shit, she thought. I need to change the subject away from my idiot brother. "Oh Christian, I think I'm feeling a little tipsy." She danced slower and feigned dizziness. "M-maybe I just drank too much." She giggled.

Christian was momentarily confused as to what to do. She noticed his puzzled expression. Damn it, she thought. I told a wasteful lie, responded reactively. Now he's caught me. Why didn't I just say Leo's a mechanic and a laundry worker? The truth. Shit! Christian took her in his arms.

"Okay, I confess," she said. "That man over there is, in fact, my lover." Christian's face went pale. She giggled. "I got you good this time! Didn't I? I was kidding, *Nyet, nyet.* That man is *not* my lover, nor anyone I want to know. Like I said, he's just some lame admirer. Christian, *you* are the man I've been waiting for."

Christian pulled her to him, whispering in her ear: "I'm not sure I believe that. You sound more than a *little* tipsy. What should we do with you?" I like her playfulness, he thought, but he couldn't deny she was a trickster.

"Dancing with me like *this* is a good start." She raised her eyebrows suggesting that maybe something more might happen later.

"I love dancing with you, Nadia, but despite what you say, that man over there *really* wants to talk with you. By the way, I've never seen a taller man on this ship, either crewmember or guest. " Christian turned Nadia around a full 360 degrees to face the tall man. "Look how persistent he is. He won't stop waving to you."

Skata, she thought. He's still on the subject of Leo. Nadia reached over her shoulders and yanked firmly on her two dress straps that held her comely breasts in place. The spaghetti-thin straps flopped down in front of her, both breasts flopping out and almost fully exposed. "Oh no," she gasped. Christian reacted. Like a knight in shining armor, he stopped dancing, removed his uniform jacket, wrapped it around her bare shoulders, and then hastily fastened the top buttons to immediately conceal her ravishing breasts. The men around them didn't miss a beat, instantly gawking over to get a peek at her chest. Christian was proud of his graceful and automatic sashay into the role of a dashing young prince, for a moment visualizing himself sitting high upon a white stallion and reaching down to sweep Nadia up into the gem-studded saddle, then galloping off into the sunset, her stunning breasts pressed up against his back.

"Christian. Thank you. I almost lost my dress," she gushed. I owe you something for saving me. Don't I?" She snuggled up to him, giving him a long, soft kiss on the lips.

He felt lightheaded. As he looked around, he noticed that the unusually tall man had vanished from sight. Was he gone? He scanned the wider pool deck area. No sign of the man. Christian's eyes unexpectedly rested on Ally who was at the bar just opposite the hot tub. The bartender was leaning across the polished bar top. Ally sat on a stool and appeared to be telling him some funny story. The bartender looked amused and touched her arm as he threw his head back and laughed at her joke. Ally, she loved to tease, probably made some smartass remark to the guy. Well, he appeared to be enjoying it. She's a high-spirited girl, a firecracker, he thought.

Nadia brushed Christian's cheek with the palm of her hand, a gesture expressing her appreciation for his demonstrated chivalry. He felt shivers move up and down his spine as she pressed her unhinged breasts to his chest. Is she going to bless me with another kiss before she leaves me tonight? More long, hot kisses. His expectations for the evening had already been far exceeded. And it happened so inexplicably—her coming back to the teen disco, seeking him out, luring him away, and now offering him a promising kiss with more to come. Was she just feeling lonely and was he just the lucky one to be selected? He didn't care and was grateful for this turn of events, this serendipity.

"Christian, can we talk alone? How about on one of those lounge chairs facing out to sea? There?" She pointed to a chair somewhat isolated from the party crowd.

He nodded. "Of course."

She took his hand, leading him. As they sat down, she gently pushed him back on the headrest, opened the two buttons of the jacket she now wore, and moved his left hand onto her left breast. Her skin is like velvet, he thought. She moaned softly.

"Nadia, this is very nice."

"Tonight is special, isn't it?" she purred. He adored her Russian accent. "Ah, I love this breeze," she said, "and how you are touching me. We have a spark, Christian."

Now moving to the other breast, he gently kissed her ear. Life is good, he thought, here at sea on this spectacular ship and in the company of this voluptuous woman. He continued kissing her, moving down to her neck. He didn't notice the Caruthers standing above them, only a few steps from their lounge chair, their eyes wide, gazing down at the steamy couple, Sigmund the dog obediently by their side. After a few moments, they strolled away.

"Getting chilly out here," Christian whispered. "I wonder if we're going into some kind of storm." When he looked up, he noticed the little old lady from the Reception area, the one in the pink suit who Ally had pointed out. She passed by, walking carefully, stepping along with the support of a pretty blue sparkly cane. She met eyes with Christian and smiled.

Nadia tickled him with her tongue behind his ear. She felt satisfied with the drama she was able to create, finally distracting Christian from the subject of Leo. I can skillfully think on my feet and do it very well, she complimented herself. Her only mission right now was to seduce the innocent Greek. Damn it. How could I have foolishly almost uttered the word *brother*? Rarely am I loose-lipped, especially when it counts. Leopold, he's inept. Why was he here, anyway? Did something go wrong with Amy Skyler? She worried, but she had to persist, accomplish her immediate goal, which was to bed Christian Stephanopoulos, securing a very credible alibi. She moved her hand inside his shirt, feeling his skin. "Hmm." Nice abs, but he's so naïve. She knew men and understood how to make them feel like lions when they were merely empty-headed little sheep.

Her cell phone buzzed. Shit. It's Leo. He can wait! N-no, I must talk to him. Find out what happened with the girl. Christian felt the phone's vibration on his chest. The device was still buried in her bra cup under her left breast. He chuckled.

"I think you're getting a call down there and it's not me." He grinned.

"Da." She reached inside the jacket and pulled the phone out of her dress and glanced at it. "Oh, it's the restaurant manager, Lazarus. I'm sorry, I must call him back. Christian, how about if I meet you in your cabin in 30 minutes? Anyway, I want to put on something more comfortable. I promise you will like it." Her eyes closed for a moment as she sighed, encouraging him to think how much he would enjoy her visit to his cabin.

He was somewhat surprised but undeniably thrilled to hear her say those words: "How about if I meet you in your cabin?" Did he hear that right? Could there possibly be any more divine invitation?

He nodded. "Do you know my cabin number? Or are you a Russian psychic with a magic crystal ball?"

"Da!" She closed her eyes as if in a trance and held her hands in the air stroking an imaginary round object. "I can see us on the bed, our bodies bare, wrapped together in the dark. How do you like my crystal ball?" She stared at him. Her eyes were hypnotic. "So, your cabin number?" She eased back into his arms and giggled.

"It's 2210, if I recall correctly. Recalling numbers is not easy for me at this moment, in fact, nearly impossible with you so close."

She smiled and rose from the chair. "I will be there in less than 30 minutes. Christian, do you happen to have a candle in your cabin?" He shook his head. "I know we're not supposed to have such things on board, but I am a bad girl. I would like us to see our bodies in candlelight as we play together. I will bring one with me."

He watched her sleek dark shadow disappear through the crowd. The captain's voice could be heard on the pool deck: "And now for my aria, the one promised by our cruise director. I hope you can stand it." Thunderous applause came from the crowd. "Thank you. Thank you," the captain said.

Christian headed for the elevator, sneaking away while Captain Stavros Manzione sang *Don Giovanni*. Although he admitted to himself that he was feeling a little nervous about what was to come tonight, he thanked the Greek gods for his good fortune. Before he passed through the glass doors, he was stopped by the familiar Southern accent.

"Hey y'all. Are you the pool boy? Can you possibly get me a towel? You are working up here, aren't you?"

It was that sardonic wit he enjoyed so much. He turned around to find Ally with a drink in her hand, Verena standing next to her with the usual cadre of teenage girls in tow. Ally moved toward him, a broad grin invading her face.

He played along. "Sorry Miss Collette, looks like we're all out of towels on this ship. I'd give you my jacket, but ..." He gestured that he had no jacket. "I seem to have misplaced it." He blushed, thinking about Nadia.

She smiled. "Christian, how about hanging out with us for awhile?"

"Sorry Ally," he soberly replied. "Honestly, I'm wiped out, off to bed. See you tomorrow."

"R-right. Well, y'all sleep tight."

She quickly waved and moved back to Verena's side. Please don't leave, she thought. Damn! Maybe I should let my guard down and give him a hint about my feelings before he's totally swept off his feet by Nadia. Why do I have such inane banter with the man I've fallen in love with? And where's that self-confidence that Daddy tried to hammer into me?

Evidently that doesn't apply to matters of the heart. Does Daddy even think of me anymore? I guess both men I care about have deserted me.

Back in his cabin, Christian nervously anticipated Nadia's arrival. Snatching up clothing from various spots on the floor and tidying up his bed, he wondered how he could sustain this exotic woman's interest in him. Rarely had he known how to say the right things to a girl, except for Ally, who probably hates him now, after his bad behavior in the club, and then him shining her on at the pool party. I'll apologize tomorrow. She'll understand.

He considered the potential dialogue he might have with Nadia before and after making love. I seem to have more compelling conversations in my head with myself than I do with people. It's always been that way, except with Ally and with his mother, Althea, who caringly drew out his innermost thoughts and ideas.

His mother would ask him: "Christian, tell me what you're thinking. I want to hear what's in your head."

Late at night, by the fire in their small cottage in Vouliagmeni, while his mother embroidered, Christian would feel at ease expressing his thoughts. He'd talk about how the universe was evolving, becoming more in tune with what's of highest importance to the human race, like friend-ship, love, caring for the earth. And he would talk about his plans for the future, how the world was out there waiting for him. He imagined all kinds of possibilities for cultures and races to come together and make posi-tive things happen. Christian believed in eternity, that things merged in the afterlife, that souls meant to be together stayed together forever. His mother's eyes would glow with love as she listened to him, eager to hear more, and proud that she gave birth to a son who had such far-reaching dreams. He'd switch gears and want to make her laugh before they both went to bed. So, while the fire flickered in their little living room, he'd tell her his joke of the day, usually something he read that day that tickled him, maybe a cartoon from the Athens newspaper, or something he found online in a travel blog. He longed to travel, see the world, experience people from diverse backgrounds.

Christian spent many hours of his young life hanging out and working at the Hotel Hyacinthe. His mother, Althea, was the swing-shift supervisor, overseeing the hotel maids. They were a variety of Greek women of all ages, from mid-teens to older women. Althea was a kind and considerate manager. Every maid, whether she was effective or not in her housekeeping duties, appreciated Althea for her kindness. She empathized with her staff. As a single parent, deserted by her young lover when she was pregnant at just seventeen years old, she understood the hardship, the everyday obstacles, experienced by young girls in these situations. Many of her employees were struggling in that very same scenario. And when they had a serious problem with money, they would come to her, more for her wise counsel than for financial assistance.

Althea would sometimes share these stories with her boss, Mr. Ezekius, the seasoned hotel manager, who occasionally contributed emergency funds to assist the employee in dealing with her personal plight. Althea was close friends with Mr. Ezekius, maybe at some point more than friends. Over the years, they grew together more as confidantes, exchanging their views on life. They would share a bottle of the local ouzo, the Greek national drink, sometimes sipping and talking into the early morning.

Mr. Ezekius took a liking to young Christian and gradually taught him the business of hotel hospitality, how to delight guests with the best service possible, ensuring their loyal return year after year. One day when Christian was six years old, Mr. Ezekius sat the boy on his lap.

"Do you know how fortunate you are to have such a wonderful mother," he said. "Son, you must see that she is quite a unique woman. Even your mother's name is special. Do you know what Althea means in Greek?"

Christian shook his head. "No, Mr. Ezekius."

"Althea means 'healer'—the perfect name for her. She has wonderful powers that touch everyone she meets. And, if a friend or a worker has a personal problem, she can heal them with her angelic spirit and natural wisdom. That's why I made her supervisor, not only because she helps this hotel flourish, but she's such an anchor to the many women who work long hard hours each day and yet are paid little. Yes, it's the nature of the hotel business, I'm afraid. Those in the bottom echelon barely make enough money to survive. Your dear mother is a beautiful soul, my son. She cares deeply about every maid who works under her supervision."

Christian listened intently to Mr. Ezekius, who hugged the boy and then dropped several coins into his hand.

"Buy your mother something nice."

Christian jumped off the man's knee and pushed open the heavy lobby door, running out to the cliff just outside the hotel where he could look down and see the ocean. He carefully selected and picked more than a dozen yellow and purple wildflowers, then ran back into the hotel straight to the hotel kitchen, where he grabbed some tin foil from the shelf. He carefully added some water and wrapped the bouquet of flowers as best as he could. He sped into the gift shop and asked Lannie, the salesgirl, if she had any small vases for sale.

"I need one for my mom to hold these flowers," he stammered, out of breath, one of his front teeth missing. "I have this much money," he said and held out the coins.

"Well, I do have this pretty blue one, and those lupines and mustard flowers would look amazing in it. I also have this nice slender pink vase. Which one do you favor?"

"I'll take the blue one," he responded with excitement. "She's wearing a blue uniform. This one will match her clothes."

Lannie laughed and helped the boy arrange the bright yellow and purple flowers in the wide-necked blue vase.

Christian ran upstairs to the fourth floor, searching for a hotel room where a maid's cart was parked in the hallway. A door was propped open. Althea was training a new young maid on the precise steps for making up the perfect bed. He pushed the cart out of the doorway and dashed into the room, managing to keep the vase full of water and the delicate flowers upright.

"Momma. Momma. Here, these are for you."

Althea dropped everything, smiling over at the new trainee, apologizing with her eyes for the interruption. She took the vase and set it down on the nightstand, gazing at the blossoms arranged with such care by her young boy. She showered him with little fish kisses everywhere on his face until he giggled and bit his lip, embarrassed in front of the pretty young maid. Then Althea began to tickle her son in his belly. He rolled back on the bed, laughing hard, losing all his inhibitions. Delighted, Althea sat him up on the bed.

"You are my little sweetheart. Where did you learn to be so charming?"

The young maid nodded in agreement, feeling fortunate to have this lovely woman as her new boss.

Althea passed away when Christian was just eighteen years old, having developed a serious case of pneumonia, then never recovering after three short weeks of illness. Her son stood at her burial site, Mr. Ezekius and several sobbing women in blue uniforms at his side. Only a week after his mother's passing, Christian was hired full-time on the swing shift at the hotel. In the daytime, before his shift started, he attended university classes, diligently studying hospitality management. Mr. Ezekius dedicated himself to coaching the young man on how to run a boutique hotel.

As Christian relaxed in bed on *The Prism of the Deep Blue Sea*, awaiting the arrival of the stunning Nadia, he took out a faded sepia photograph of his mother from the top drawer of the bedside table. He ran his fingers over the frame, across his mother's smiling face. He whispered, conscious that he'd left his cabin door slightly ajar for Nadia, bolstered open with a rock he picked up on the cliff just outside the Greek hotel where he had worked. I miss you so much Mama, but I am living my dream. You would be proud of me, he thought. Then he shut his eyes and could feel the touch of his mother's hand on his forehead. A devout Catholic like his mother, Christian believed in heaven and often imagined his mama circling the cruise ship, beyond the clouds, beyond the sun, beyond the moon, guiding him to reach new heights in his career.

Christian nodded off for a moment but awakened as soon as he heard the creak of the cabin door. Nadia lit the candle, placing it carefully down on the nightstand. She sat down on his bed and started to unbutton his shirt.

"I brought back your jacket, my friend. Please help me take this off, would you?" She guided his hand to the round gold buttons. He found her to be bare-skinned under his navy blue jacket. The bedside lamp illuminated her perfect skin as he slipped it off and threw it onto the floor. She sat up on the edge of the bed, the silhouette of her large perfect bare breasts before him. She got up, standing next to him. She was wearing a short black mini-skirt, which she seductively began to unzip.

"You will need to lend me one of your shirts to wear when I leave early in the morning. *Da*?" she whispered.

"I think that can be arranged. Anything you want, Nadia. Anything." He touched her skin and pulled her onto to the bed.

Chapter Nine

The Discovery

Dawn broke. The ship rocked gently on the open sea. The clouds had cleared. The sun splashed across the polished wooden decks. An attractive woman frantically roamed the ship, through the corridors, across the open-air venues, traversing each of the cruise liner's lounges and sitting areas. Searching, searching. But no sign of Amy. How could she have fallen asleep last night without waiting up for her daughter's late-night return to the cabin? How could her husband, Russell, have dozed off as well without first listening for Amy opening their cabin door? Did Amy possibly return to the cabin and then leave again before we awoke this morning? Where is Amy? I must inform Security, find the captain. Frantic Wendy Skyler, well-known British TV actress, was traumatized by her daughter's disappearance. She had downed two Ambien tablets last night, after another heated argument with her ever-complaining husband, and didn't discover her daughter was missing until the morning.

She gave up her fruitless effort to find her on her own and rushed down to the hotel reception desk, just off the ship's centrum area. Spotting a young uniformed man at the counter, she spilled out the words: "My daughter, my daughter, Amy Skyler, is missing. She never came back to our cabin last night. I can't find her anywhere. Please, please," she cried. "You're the hotel manager, right? You must help me."

"Of course. Don't worry. I'm here to help you. Let me alert our chief security officer."

Packo was crouched outside Dr. and Mrs. Caruthers' cabin. He was stationed there much of the night, hoping to catch someone trying to sneak into their stateroom while they were off at the sail-away festivities happening late into the night. Zero activity. Nobody suspicious all night long. Packo had relieved one of his security workers, Edward, around 10 p.m. the night before, after he found the twenty-year-old fast asleep, tucked away in an alcove, a few feet away from the Caruthers' cabin door. "Edward, you idiot," Packo had blurted out, as he kicked the Dutch security guard in his ass. "Get up and get out of here. And be in my office at 8 a.m. tomorrow for a demerit chat." The boy scrambled to his feet, bolted down the hallway, fumbling, almost losing his footing on the carpeted staircase, as he fled from his angry boss.

Packo shook his head, thinking about that inept excuse for a security guard, and glanced down at his watch. It was 6 a.m. This was a stupid endeavor, anyway. Why would the owner of the AK-47 even think that it would still be in the Caruthers' cabin at this point? The couple would have discovered it upon unpacking and presumably freaked out, calling Security without hesitation. Unless, of course, it was actually *them* who plotted to smuggle the automatic weapon on board. It was a ridiculous idea to stake out their room 24 hours a day. To what end? He grumbled and picked himself up from the plush royal blue carpet sprinkled with white airy bubbles that ran down each line of rooms on every deck on either side of the ship. My neck! Ach. I need some sleep before the captain's 10 o'clock weekly staff meeting this morning. But there will be nothing to report on regarding this washout surveillance. He could hear his middle-aged legs crack as he stood up.

To think that he had thought working on cruise ships would be a peaceful, low-key way to spend the rest of his career. Today it was ten years since he started his employment with Millennium Cruise Lines. He had successfully escaped his police officer job in Barcelona. Perceived as a natural leader, he was next in line as captain of the local force. But one night during a robbery at a convenience store he had killed a young teenager, a boy who lived only three streets away from him. The boy's name was Andre Salazar. When he saw the boy take the storekeeper by the arm and flash a knife in front of him, Packo pulled the trigger and watched the boy fall to the ground. After an investigation, the force took him back with open arms, his pending promotion still intact, no harm done. The investigating committee found the shooting to have been completely justified. But Packo's heart broke instantly when he saw the boy take his last breath and whisper, "I'm sorry. Tell *mi madre* that I love her." He couldn't bear to continue working on the police force and began to search for something in the security field but with a less stressful work environment where he could use his skills but live in peace. He had lost his ambition and even split up with his pretty fiancée, wanting a job outside Barcelona, maybe even outside the country. It turned out to be with Millennium Cruise Lines. Attending a job fair in the ferry building at the end of the Rambla the day after he turned in his resignation, he was successful in landing a job with Millennium. He was assigned to Security, as second in command on a ship named *The Aria of the Deep Blue Sea.* His new life proved peaceful and his relationship with the ship's captain was collegial and positive.

In just a couple of years, Packo was selected for a promotion to chief security officer and assigned to the newly christened *The Prism of the Deep Blue Sea.* He was both flattered and hopeful, anticipating a wonderful life on the brand-new ship. But meeting Captain Stavros Manzione was a shock to his system. He was gruff, demanding, and adversarial, and Packo felt continuously pressured by the new captain's leadership style. Manzione seemed to be in a steady war with every crewmember around him. As a result, battered and stressed, Packo gradually became a hardened man, though never regretting his decision to get away from Barcelona.

Now scrunched down in the hallway outside the Caruthers' cabin, Packo heard his c ell phone ring out several notes from "Livin' La Vida Loca." It was Christian's ring tone. Just yesterday when he found out that the twenty-nine-year-old Christian was to officially become the hotel manager by default, Packo selected this obnoxious Ricky Martin ring tone for him. He smiled to himself and quickly answered. *"Si?"*

"Packo, it's Christian. We have a problem with one of our guests. Stateroom 7240— Mrs. Wendy Skyler cannot locate her teenage daughter. The girl didn't come back to the family's cabin last night. We need urgent help from Security."

"What the hell? *Mierda!* These parents didn't know their own child was missing until this morning? How is that possible? Morons. The daughter is probably roaming around the ship with some no-good teenage boy right now."

Not wanting to alert the agitated mother with Packo's ill-tempered response, Christian faked it. "Okay, Officer Suarez, so you will come quickly. I'll ask Mrs. Skyler for a photograph of her young daughter, Amy. Excuse me, Mrs. Skyler, how old is your daughter?"

The troubled woman cupped her trembling hands over her head in exasperation and leaned her elbows on the Reception counter. "She's fifteen. Very pretty." Tears spilled down Mrs. Skyler's flushed cheeks. "Y-yes, I'll go get my camera. I have a photo of Amy that I took just yesterday." Wendy Skyler turned, her white running shoes squeaking on the diamond-patterned marble flooring. She quickly sprinted away.

Christian sternly whispered into the phone. "Packo, hey. The woman is panicking. It doesn't matter why she didn't wait up for her daughter— the daughter is missing. That's the problem here. For whatever reason, her child did not return to their stateroom. We need your help." Christian was surprised at himself, how strongly he felt, how confident he sounded.

Silence for a moment on the other end. Then a heavy sigh from Packo. *"Si. Si.* I will be there in five minutes to meet with the mother. You do the consoling, okay? I'll do the searching." Packo snapped his flip phone shut.

Something was disturbing Christian. He couldn't shake it from his mind. This morning a missing teenage girl and yesterday an AK-47 placed in a passenger's luggage. No. There couldn't be any connection but … He looked up and locked eyes with Nadia, who walked by the reception desk on her way to the restaurant to set tables before she went off to her daily morning Teen Scene duty. He offered a sheepish grin after their shared adventure last night. She kept walking, winked, and blew him a quick kiss.

Seeing her in the light of day reminded Christian of the heated passion they shared the night before in his small cabin. Nadia proved to be far from a novice when it came to making love. She knew how to take control, bring him slowly and exquisitely to the edge of climax with her mouth, and then beg him to enter her and come like a gladiator. She handled him with expertise. Once he was fully satisfied, Nadia led his hand to her still ravenous vagina, where he brought her to tears with his fingers. She responded well to his touch, to every slight wiggle of his fingers inside her. At first, she had moaned with pleasure and then she instructed him: "Be fierce, Christian. Make me come! Make me come!" Her sultry whisper sent his body quivering. When she yelled out in total abandonment at the pinnacle of orgasm, he noticed the light from the bedside candle brandish a subtle golden glow across her sculpted cheekbones, the delicate curve of her jawline.

He had read about the art of giving women repeated orgasms. Christian did not take sex lightly. Over the past few years, although he could count the number of his carnal experiences on one hand, maybe two, his desire to make it especially memorable for the girl was his number one focus. He managed to find the right spot to evoke a series of orgasms from Nadia. Her eyes opened wide, taken by surprise with his impressive lovemaking abilities.

He wanted to wow her and felt that he had succeeded, yet she seemed to have intermittent moments of emotional detachment during their sexual encounter. Part of Nadia remained untouchable, despite her obvious physical satisfaction. That mask she wore appeared to block any true union between them. It would take time and he accepted that challenge.

As he stood behind the hotel Reception counter the next morning, his body craved to rush down the promenade, grab Nadia, give her a long, unforgettable kiss, and then whisk her away back to his room for a few more hours of delicious lovemaking. But his brain snapped back to his duties when he heard Ally's Southern drawl.

"Y'all ready for another exhilarating day on the high seas? My. My. Someone is a sleepy Gus this morning." She started up her computer, entering her password and housing her purse on the shelf below. What she wanted to know was, had Christian gone to bed with Nadia the night before. She hoped that wasn't the case. "So, did you sleep well last night, Mr. Hotel Manager?" she demurely asked him.

"Sleep well? Uh." His eyes avoided hers. But he couldn't help the words that almost involuntarily slipped out of his mouth: "Yes, I did manage to find a little patch of heaven in my dreams last night." He caught himself and shifted his eyes back to his keyboard.

Ally got it, understanding everything. He didn't need to say another word. It was the way he responded. The glee of seeing him this morning and looking forward to their day together instantaneously vanished. She slipped into a colder, more businesslike persona. The sharp blade of reality twisted and turned inside her.

Ally stared straight ahead and noticed the petite silver-haired woman sitting on the sofa opposite Reception having her usual cup of morning tea. She put down her teacup on the table and looked over at Ally giving her a warm smile. The woman's teeth were gleaming white. Ally could see her blue eyes twinkling even from this distance.

Christian changed the subject: "By the way, are you aware that *you're* now the assistant hotel manager for this cruise, since I'm now the official hotel manager. I'm designating you formally with the captain in this email right now. Are you good with that? It will also mean a higher rate of pay for this cruise."

"Sure. Thank you," she responded back without emotion. "More money is always a blessing, and the experience won't do me any harm. Hope I can live up to your expectations." She booted up her computer, then located the weekly report she had been finalizing late yesterday, which was due to Christian this morning, known as the "Summary Guest Complaint Report." She pulled up the spreadsheet.

"Uh, listen, Ally, I'm sorry I left you last night in the discotheque but ..."

"But it was your one shot with Nadia. I know. It's okay, Christian. I was hanging with Verena and the girls, anyway. Don't worry about it. This wounded bird will live to fly another day." Ally brightened up. Well, at least he apologized for leaving me flat for the lust of his life. I better get used to it, she thought.

Ilze, a plump Dutch girl, their front desk colleague, stepped behind her workstation at the far end of the Reception counter, calling out a friendly, "Good morning."

Christian smiled back and waved at Ilze, then quickly turned to Ally. "Oh, you need to add one more guest complaint to that report before you print it. Mrs. Wendy Skyler, from Stateroom 7240, came by a few minutes ago. Her daughter, Amy Sklyer, is missing, didn't return to their cabin last night."

"What? That's terrible. Was Amy Skyler at the Teen Club event?"

Christian shrugged. "I think so, but I'm not sure."

Ally squinted and took on that faraway look she has when she's thinking hard about some problem that needs solving. Christian smiled to himself. I like it when she scrunches up her freckled nose with that quizzical expression. I can imagine her as a young girl on a Southern plantation, making that same face, wearing a broad-brimmed hat, and sitting under some giant oak tree reading an interesting book.

Ally stopped her data input and looked up at him. "Isn't she that tall slender girl with the long red hair? I'm sure that girl's name is Amy. She was with the Teen Scene in the discotheque, but she wasn't dancing. She was standing by the back wall alone watching everyone else. I was going to walk over and talk to her, but we were all dancing and having so much fun. Thinking about her now, she did seem kind of sad and lonely."

Christian raised his eyebrows. "Um. Wow. You really keep your eyes open. I don't know what she looks like, so I can't say. But Mrs. Sklyer is coming back here any minute with a photograph of her daughter. I've informed Packo, who seems to be in a foul mood today."

"I hope the girl's okay." Ally transitioned to another hot topic, but in a hushed tone. "So, what happened with that AK-47? Any news on that gun?"

He shook his head. "Nope, nothing new that I've been told. Maybe Packo will have more information this morning."

Ally typed in the data regarding Amy Skyler, adding it to the spreadsheet. "Anything else I should write on this report about the missing girl? Christian, can you look at this skeleton entry and offer more detail?" She turned her screen so he could read it.

He positioned his head just an inch or two from hers to view the spreadsheet. She could feel the warmth of his breath on her cheek. It increased her tension and elevated the wave of fear she had about completely losing this man to the Russian temptress. Her heart beat faster. She could hear it like bullets in her head. She had the urge to tenderly touch his hand as he moved the mouse over the mouse pad, fully focused on the Excel document. Somehow she needed to let him know that she was interested in more than a friendship. Her thoughts were interrupted just then by the gruff words from an angry and disheveled Packo Suarez.

"Did the woman bring the photo of her daughter? Where is she? I want to talk to her," he grumbled and slapped his notepad down on the Reception counter.

A nice-looking middle-aged man came up right behind Packo. "Can someone help me? I need to talk to Security."

Packo turned to the man. "Yes sir, that's me. I'm Packo Suarez, chief security officer. Flashing his badge, he clicked into his charm zone, offering a confident handshake to the man who appeared troubled.

"I'm Russell Skyler. My daughter, Amy, she's missing. I've looked everywhere. My wife is wandering around the ship looking for her. Amy never came back to our cabin last night. We can't find her. It's not like her. It's just not like her at all! Not at all." He spoke with a fast clip, hopelessly shaking his head. "She's a shy, responsible girl, doesn't stay out late. Ever! We made her go out last night to join in the teen club activities. She didn't want to go, but we wouldn't take no for an answer. My wife, she's … she's beside herself."

"Mr. Skyler," Christian calmly responded. "Yes, your wife was just here. She went back to your stateroom to retrieve a photo of your daughter to give to Officer Suarez. She should be back here in a few minutes."

"Yes," Packo added, "as soon as she returns, we can go into the office and talk. Then I 'll execute a thorough search. Do you want to start talking with me now, or shall we wait for your wife to return?"

"I-I guess I'll wait."

Ally's mind was racing as she listened to the disturbing dialogue.

"There's a comfortable sofa right over there in our centrum, if you like." Christian gestured, inviting Mr. Skyler to sit down on the plush crushed-velvet divan.

Russell nodded, hung his head, and slowly plodded over to the sofa. He was already exhausted and the day had just begun. His daughter was in limbo land, nowhere to be found. Amy's probably disgusted with us. All the arguing she's had to listen to over the past months, all the hostility. The child's probably worn out by her own parents. Did she run away? Run away on this cruise ship? When his wife had shaken him awake that morning, just before dawn, he was more than annoyed. He was peeved. He had been on the brink of throwing in the marriage towel, having had enough of this woman who seemed to care so little for him. All he and Wendy did was gripe at each other anyway, except for the huge chunks of time she spent away on location with her popular ITV soap opera, shooting episodes in faraway places instead of at the home studio in Twickenham. Wendy had literally been on the road for over twenty-seven weeks out of the last twelve months.

Now an unemployed architect, Russell was miserable and desperately homesick for Chicago, the hometown he hadn't seen for well over ten years. Restless and depressed, he was on edge and also developing a cocaine habit, taking several hits at least every other day when his daughter was at school and his wife was a thousand miles away. This cruise was a last-ditch effort to restore their marriage and save it from a bitter divorce.

It was sixteen years ago when Wendy and Russell first met in a bar in downtown Chicago. She was in the early stage of her television career, having snatched up a couple of national commercials in the U.K., but not much else in the way of acting. Wendy was on holiday for two weeks with her three English girlfriends. Her best friend's mother lived in Chicago and had plenty of room for them to stay as long as they liked. There she was, sitting on a leather stool in the hotel bar just a few feet away from Russell, gabbing, the special lilt of an upper-class English accent floating over to him. She was adorable, with her blonde-streaked, short bobbed hair and those translucent lilac eyes. What he also noticed most about her was her brilliant white teeth, unusual for a Brit, so perfectly aligned. Her smile was captivating and seemed to light up the room. He just had to invent an excuse to meet her. Interrupting his conversation with his two work colleagues, he pardoned himself and strolled past the raised bar table full of English women. Then he feigned tripping over the lovely woman's purse that was set down on the floor by her chair.

"Gracious. I'm so sorry. Are you okay?" she inquired, jumping down from the stool to check on him. Her girlfriends giggled, understanding exactly what was happening before them.

He looked up at the vivacious young woman and nodded. "Yes, silly me. I guess I'm not watching what I'm doing."

He sprang up from the parquet floor. That's when Wendy stepped back and stumbled. One of her shiny black high heels suddenly collapsed and broke off from her shoe. She sat up on the floor examining the damage.

"What a clumsy clown I am," she smiled. He helped her up, happy to touch her for even one fleeting moment. She picked up her broken shoe in disbelief, but, at the same time, gushed in amusement. "Oh, no bother. I'm not hurt, just a little mishap. Funny, isn't it? I mean … the two of us? We're hopeless." She couldn't stop giggling at the curious timing of the paired accidents that brought them so coincidentally together. "Well, it must be time for me to purchase some new pumps, and not from any trendy London boutique, I'm afraid." She giggled again and held up the evidence, then took off the other shoe to get her balance.

"By the way, I'm Wendy Singleton, originally from Dorset, England."

She fumbled and then held out her delicate hand to meet his. That was it. From that night on, the two were inseparable, engaged in six months, and married within a year, Russell making the immediate relocation from Chicago to London to be with his new wife.

Amy was born just fourteen months from their wedding day, and life was bliss for another two maybe even three years. Then Wendy's career heated up, and then it began to sizzle. It seemed to happen overnight. She became the most prized soap opera star in all of Great Britain. Everything changed. A full-time nanny was hired. Wendy was gone for days, then for weeks at a time. The paparazzi were close on their heels. It seemed like it was a 24/7 surveillance of the couple and their daughter. Russell grew to hate his life in London, longing to return to the *real* world—to his family in Chicago, to his former career as an architect in the most exciting city he knew. Over the past few weeks, he had been seriously considering a formal split with Wendy. That would result in not living with his daughter *or* it could mean taking his daughter back to the states with him. He had already spoken to his mother and sister about the possibility of his moving back to Chicago. But he hadn't mentioned it yet to Wendy, and Amy had no idea this was on his mind.

He felt the tap of someone touching his shoulder. Usually radiant, this morning Wendy looked haggard. "You didn't find her, did you?"

"No." He shook his head, looking dejected.

She sounded out of breath. "I've got a photo in this camera. I can email it straight from this thing. They can print it. Come with me."

Wendy didn't wait for her husband's response. She ran from the sofa back over to Christian and Packo at the Reception counter. Her legs were long and golden. A couple of strolling husbands turned around to catch a glimpse, without any idea that she was petrified with worry and fear. Packo eyed her approaching, at the same time taking in the woman's natural beauty. She wore no makeup. I think I've seen her somewhere before this trip, the security officer contemplated. Where would that have been?

Chapter Ten

Gorby's Nightmare

Gorby stumbled into the lighthouse. It was 4:30 in the morning. With a dusty brown flannel blanket under his arm, a newspaper-wrapped, greasy English fish-and-chips package in his other hand, he approached her. It was for the girl. He was still half drunk on Guinness, the heaviest beer known to mankind. He missed his cheap Russian vodka, but didn't seem to have any trouble sucking down seven or maybe eight pints of dark brown Guinness ale at the pub just a few miles from the abandoned lighthouse.

It was a typical coastal pub, full of old men and young boisterous fishermen throwing a game of darts in what first appeared to be a serious competition. Gorby observed these senseless men losing track of their scores several times during the match. They'd stop and drink a couple of rounds of pumped light ale after every five or so points of the game.

Gorby sat and watched as the men fell deeper into their drunkenness acting like a group of out-of-control kids. No stamina in these British poppets. No ability to hold their liquor, like us Russians, he thought. They drink piss while we drink hard vodka. When they started to chant obnoxious rugby songs, it turned his stomach.

Amy opened her eyes when she heard his work boots pound the cement floor. A smidge of moonlight dimly lit the arched entrance to the cold bare room.

In his drunken oblivion, he greeted Amy. "*Sooka! Sooka!* Food. I brought you some food. And it's English fare. La de da!" He got down on bended knees and stroked her hair. "Little *Sooka!* Chickadee. Are you sleeping?" Chuckling, he got up and danced around, pulling a small bottle out of his rank-smelling pea jacket. He took the plug out with his teeth and chugged a long sip, spilling most of it on the gray stone floor, some of it wetting her right ankle, which ached from the metal chain clamped around it.

He tossed the blanket down over her. "Here. You need to stay warm. *Da?* Okay, I'm a little late with the bedding. I admit it." He danced a few more steps and laughed to himself. "I'm not a very good host. Ah! I almost forgot the food. He dropped the fish and chips down onto the top of the blanket. She didn't trust him, but she was starved. She reached for the food and unrolled the grease-stained newspaper.

"Local delicacies, *Sooka!* You like it? You must be used to this grub since you're English, eh? For me, it's pussy food. I like my meat boiled and lots of Russian potatoes. I'm still a growing boy." He tripped over his own feet, laughed, and almost fell down.

She stared at him while she gained the courage to eat the chips. She tentatively reached for one. Although cold and soggy, the salt-and-vinegar-covered spuds tasted decent enough. She wasn't sure if she should touch the fish because she never could stand the smell.

"*Sooka.* What does that mean?" she mumbled, afraid to hear his response, as she took a second chip. Who knows when he'll give me food again, she thought. And maybe eating will help stave off a panic attack, a malady she has lived with for a few years now, and at fifteen years old, the frequency and severity seemed to be on the upswing.

Gorby slid down on the floor and pushed himself back to the wall just opposite Amy. He took another long sip from his whiskey bottle. "*Sooka?* It means 'prostitute' in Russian. *Da. Da.*" He raised the bottle as a toast. "We will be grooming you for your new profession. No worry. No worry," he said, waving the bottle in the air and then slapping one hand down on his leg in exclamation. His hand missed the leg and hit the stone floor hard. "Agh." His eyes closed and his head spun, and he almost lost consciousness.

In that delirious state, he had a flashback of the night he entered his sister's bedroom to make a startling discovery. He was seven years old and his eighth birthday was the next day. He was suddenly awakened by an ugly nightmare. A purple dragon was breathing waves of fire into his face, threatening to consume him. Little Gorby jumped out of bed, dragging his frayed blanket behind him, and made his way to Nadia's room. His older sister would comfort him in her bed until he fell back to sleep. At first, she was annoyed, but after his begging, she would agree, letting him slide in beside her. He rubbed his sleepy eyes as he opened the door to her room. But before he could leap into her bed, he saw his red-faced father sitting there, his arm reaching under Nadia's polka-dot flannel nightgown. Her eyes were closed, her body moving in rhythm to her father's arm movements. She moaned with what seemed like pleasure. Gorby's heart stopped. He didn't quite understand the whole scene, but it was enough for him to feel revulsion and even nausea. His sister turned her head, her eyes staring coldly in his direction. She didn't seem scared or unhappy, but it was like there was no sign of life in her face. Their father whirled around, then darted from the room, barely sober enough to make it past his young son, and headed downstairs for another drinking bout with his best friend, the vodka bottle. Gorby turned and on his way back to his bed he vomited in the hallway.

He almost vomited again right here in the dingy lighthouse as he looked across at the bedraggled young girl. *"Sooka.* It's a funny-sounding Russian word, isn't it?" Crawling across the chilled hard floor closer to Amy, he stopped and shook his index finger close to her face. *"Nyet,* pretty little girl, there is nothing for you to fear. You will have a good life, wear stylish clothes, your hair combed and decorated with colorful ribbons, adorned with expensive jewelry. You will be laid out each night looking elegant, waiting for your master to arrive to fuck you. You will always be ready and happy to see your lover, grateful that he cares for you. Captivity may frighten you at first, but you will get used to it, *Sooka.* You will be safe, that is, *if* you follow instructions and don't cause me any trouble. If not ..." He pulled out a switchblade from his back pocket. "If not ... well, I probably don't need to say more. Just don't become my nightmare. I hate nightmares," he shouted. She smelled his rank breath as he stroked her stringy red hair and chuckled to himself. "What about that fish, chicka-dee? You're not going to eat it?" He reached down and scooped up a large chunk of fish in his dirty hand. He took the fish, dragging the greasy newspaper, and moved back to the other wall.

Amy laid her head back down on the hard surface and silently sobbed, her tears falling one by one onto the stone floor, as Gorby gobbled down the rest of the deep-fried English cod, downing what was left of his whis-key. He soon fell asleep propped-up against the wall.

She started to shake. Her eyelids began to twitch. She felt a hot sweat overtake her and her forehead was dripping wet. It was happening. The terror. Her head thumped. Her vision was blurry, filled with spots of gray and black. She couldn't focus; she could barely make out the stubby man's form propped-up against the wall just opposite her. Her limbs were paralyzed. She couldn't move her arms or legs as hard as she tried. She wanted to die, disappear forever. Monsters leapt from each of the four stone walls around her. They closed in on her. Loud noises flooded her ears, screeches, sirens. An albatross clutched her in his talons and swung her from a tall mangled tree. She screamed out inside her head. Stop! Stop! I want my mum. Mum, help me. Please help me. For the next hour or so, she lay there in the clutches of a panic attack, without medication. She was this man's prisoner. She had to accept it. She would do what he says, give him what he wants. It didn't matter. Amy Skyler no longer existed. That girl was gone.

Chapter Eleven

The Captain's Orders

Stavros Manzione's staff meetings consistently begin at precisely 10 a.m. every Tuesday. Meeting attendees include, in addition to him, five crew-members: Chief Security Officer Packo Suarez, acting Hotel Manager Christian Stephanopolous, Cruise Director Carlos Mendano, Head Chef Theodore Marsalis, and Robbie Harbareth, chief engineer. The captain uses a "pressure cooker" management approach with his staff. He puts them on the spot, demands unrealistic results, and is always in command. Nobody is late when the captain calls a meeting. At these regularly scheduled staff meetings, each attendee presents an update on hotspots, accomplishments for the week, and foreseeable challenges over the next seven days.

Packo was up first with his update. Stavros abhors power-point slides and instead requires each officer to bring a succinct two-page report with enough hard copies for each team member. Packo walked through the usual headlines, then paused and put down the report. "Captain, I need to update you immediately on a confidential issue that has raised its ugly head this morning involving a passenger, probably better to take this offline."

"Is it urgent? Do we need to bring this meeting to a close for us to privately discuss it? You know our expected arrival in Gibraltar is at 1:30 this afternoon. A lot to do before then."

Packo nodded. "Yes, I'm sorry sir, but it may be a true crisis and need our immediate attention ... On the other hand, it may be a false alarm. It's difficult to say."

"Very well, Officer Suarez, let's cut this meeting short then." He looked over at the chief engineer. "Anything important to report, Officer Harbareth, as we get ready to cross the Atlantic for the first time this year?"

"No sir. We're on track for Gibraltar today, and I don't foresee any surprises on the Atlantic tomorrow in terms of either weather or engine issues. I'm down one team member today. Albert Funesse has taken ill. Looks like the flu. So, we are short one on the bridge going into Gibraltar, but shouldn't be a problem. I expect him back tomorrow for the start of our crossing."

"Now, you've got me curious, Officer Suarez. So, gentlemen, let's call it a day. Please leave your reports on the table for my review later this morning. I will summon you with any questions."

He furrowed his eyebrows and stared across the table at Carlos Mendano, the cruise director. "Mendano, you screwed up last week when your headliner didn't show up and you were caught off guard. Anything like that going on for this transatlantic crossing? Do I need to worry about you and your team?"

"N-no sir. I think I have it covered." Carlos didn't want to offer up his one trouble spot, his assistant cruise director, Lynette Dorado, who failed to show up this morning to teach her pool deck Zumba class because of a nasty hangover.

"All right then. Meeting adjourned. Suarez, we'll follow on now, just the two of us."

"Yes sir. And, I think we should have Officer Stephanopolous join in this discussion."

"Very well. So, when is our *real* hotel manager coming back? I hope she's here for the start of our next cruise. We want the quality of service to stay at its optimum level."

Christian received the slam and nodded his head, not daring to offer any comment or retort.

The other staff members filed out after dropping their reports on the table, dismissed like a bunch of schoolboys in trouble.

"Okay Packo. So, what the hell is going on? What's so urgent? Is it about the AK-47?"

"No sir. We have a missing teenager on our hands, sir. She didn't return to her family's stateroom last night. Her mother realized that she was gone around dawn this morning. The girl was at the Teen Scene activity last night but has now disappeared. I think maybe we should alert our passengers, have them be additional eyes and ears to locate the girl. There are two scenarios here, sir. Either the girl ran away from her parents and is hiding out somewhere on this ship or the girl was abducted by someone. It's hard to tell, but it may have been a criminal act."

"Are you insane, Suarez? I won't allow some pimply teenage rene-gade to wreak havoc on my ship. Got it? You've lost your mind if you think I'm going to have you notify our passengers of anything on this subject. Are we *clear* on who's in command here?" He shook his finger in anger. "Cruising stats are down this year. People find other ways to take luxury vacations. We need to be very careful about creating some kind of stir on board. We don't want to create any fear. You're acting like a moron in sug-gesting that we alert our passengers."

Packo was tired out, his body still aching from last night's hall duty outside the Caruthers' cabin. His fury took control once he heard the captain refer to him as a "moron." He whipped the photograph out of his starched white shirt pocket and dropped into the chair next to the cap-tain. Packo shoved the photograph in Manzione's face. "Does this look like a pimply teenager to you? Damn it. Does it? No, she's fifteen years old, and she's beautiful. Amy Skyler. Her mother is a well-known British actress, Wendy Skyler. We need to take this seriously, Captain. An ab-duction! Yes, this could be an abduction on our ship."

The captain examined the photograph. The girl was pretty. His daugh-ter would have been fifteen years old this year, if she would have lived. He was suddenly moved. What would they have named her? Where would she be now? My lost little girl. Tears welled up in his eyes. He struggled to camouflage his emotions.

Christian was worried. Manzione will likely come unglued at Packo's disrespectful words. The captain moved to his desk, took out a tissue from his top drawer, pretending to wipe the sweat from his forehead, but instead looked away and dabbed his eyes. "It's so fucking humid today," he said. "What's the story with the parents? Is it likely that she's just a runaway? Let me be clear here. We are not announcing any possible foul play."

Packo composed himself and thought, I'm lucky the captain didn't kneejerk and throw me out of the office altogether. He softened his voice. "I-I'm so sorry, Captain. Please forgive my behavior. I'm just concerned about this girl. Both the mother and father are beside themselves. Yes, there is some tension behind the scenes. The parents have been arguing and the girl was most likely upset, maybe feeling desperate to get away from them. She could be hiding out in some teenage boy's stateroom or with some other girl she may have befriended last night."

Still fairly controlled, the captain inquired, "What are your thoughts on this, Mr. Stephanopolous?"

He still can't seem to refer to me as a true officer, Christian thought, just as personal guilt began to invade his thoughts. If Amy Skyler were at the Teen Scene activity last night, he should have somehow protected her, been more aware of her actions, and where she wandered off to after the discotheque. He didn't even notice the red-haired girl. All he could focus on last night was Nadia. But Ally was paying attention. She knew who Amy Skyler was, even noticed her hair color as well as the girl's withdrawn manner at the club. Ally, she doesn't miss a thing.

Christian looked up at the captain, and with a convincing spark of confidence and clarity, he responded, "Sir, I think Officer Suarez has the right approach for this scenario. He's already got half a dozen security crewmembers out there with Amy Skyler's photo in hand searching for some sign of the girl. If there's no sighting of her by lunchtime, then I think we need to reconsider informing all of our crewmembers to start searching along with Security. And for those not working today, let's assign them to help with our investigation. It may be a tiny clue that leads us to the missing girl." Christian looked for some reaction in the captain's face, but he got none. Damn, did I say too much? He quickly cleared his throat. "At least, that's what Officer Suarez's plan is at this stage, and he's taking the appropriate course of action as far as I can see."

Packo glared over at the Greek. At first he was annoyed since what Christian had described was not at all his current plan of action. In fact, he had no plan at this point and his security force had not yet begun an official search for the teenage girl. He had been stalling, wanting to keep it low key until he fully informed the captain. At the same time, Packo felt grateful for Christian's attempt to cover him in front of the captain.

"I do have one thing to add to Packo's plan," Christian continued. "We need to have a distinct description of what Amy Skyler was wearing last night and anything she might have been carrying with her. That way, if a personal item is found, we tag it to her. Anything tagged will certainly give us a clue about where she might be now."

"I have the complete list of all that," Packo responded. "I'll make sure my security team gets it, too."

Christian took a bold but necessary leap in the conversation. "Captain, we can't ignore the white elephant sitting here with us this morning. There is a remote possibility that the fifteen-year-old cannot be found because she is no longer on the ship. She may have gone overboard, by her own volition or because of some violent act against her."

The words stung Manzione's ears. "No, we would have received some report from the bridge or Engineering if that happened."

Packo squirmed, thinking it best to keep his mouth shut, but he couldn't help himself. "Captain, our sensors are not that effective, like all other cruise ships. We know this. The technology to indicate 'man overboard' is just not there yet, being still relatively unsophisticated."

Stavros winced, but knew this to be true. "I'm not convinced anyone has gone overboard on my ship, on my watch. Your plan is the right one for the moment. Decent work, Suarez. But don't let me catch you being snide with me ever again. Get out of here now, both of you. Go implement this action plan of yours. *Pronto! Pronto!* Packo, you should be out there looking for her along with your team. Got it?" His eyes gripped the security officer's. "Stephanopolous, you should go back to work and keep your ear to the ground with the passengers. I want you both back here in my office at 1 o'clock. I'll be on the bridge until then."

"Yes sir," they obediently responded, a touch to their caps with a salute to the captain.

"Again, sir, I'd like to apologize for my—"

"Bag it, Suarez. *Basta!* Enough on that subject."

They both moved to leave.

Manzione stopped them. "Wait. Officer Stephanopolous, that was nice work just now. Impressive articulation of your colleague's plan."

The captain sat down at his desk just as the two men closed the door behind them. Stavros couldn't wait for them to leave. Quivering with raw emotion, he held his throbbing head in his hands. All he could think about was his daughter, the child he never knew. The Amy Skyler affair released his buried grief, memories of the tragedy resurfacing.

Stavros joined the Navy on his eighteenth birthday, becoming part of the Marina Militare. He was married at nineteen in Roma, his birthplace. She was a stunning Italian girl, named Polonia, who had moved to Roma from a small village called Orvieto. Just four months after the small ceremony, Stavros was sent away on his second naval mission, deployed out to the Baltic Sea for the standard run of seventy-five days. Everything was secret. He could tell Polonia nothing about the ship's targeted destination or their intended military tasks. His barely eighteen-year-old wife had a job at the Casa di Cura Hospital on Via Nomentana working as a nursing assistant on the swing shift from 4:00 in the afternoon until midnight. She adored her work, especially the close contact with patients, who beamed whenever she'd enter their rooms. With her long eyelashes, wavy black hair, and snow-white complexion, she was a welcome vision of youth against the backdrop of the usual middle-aged, haggard nurses who worked the unpopular swing shift. Polonia felt needed when engaged in service to the infirm.

One hot September night, Polonia was leaving the hospital at the end of her shift. It was exactly two months to the day since Stavros had been called to sea duty. She started the short stroll to their third-floor walkup. It was bad luck when two young men in their early twenties spotted the shapely Polonia. She didn't hear them, her headphones plugged in her ears. She was happily listening to one of Giuseppe Verdi's famous operas, *La Traviata.* It was her favorite. Stavros, her multi-talented new husband, sang opera. She quickly became a fan, appreciating the drama and the vivid storylines. She would listen to opera during every moment of spare time, whether walking to or from work, baking cookies at home for the neighborhood children, or even when bathing alone in their chipped porcelain bathtub after a long night at the hospital. The music somehow seemed to link her with her husband at sea. As she stepped down the Roma street, taking her usual shortcut, she hummed the opera and imagined her next reunion with Stavros, pulling out the ribbon holding back her hair, letting the long curls fall loosely around her shoulders. What a beautiful evening, she thought.

The drunken thugs came from behind her without any warning, one covering her mouth with his sweaty hand and shoving her into a small alleyway behind a large garbage dumpster. She could smell the rank odor of the trash from La Strata restaurant, remnants of unfinished garlic linguine and anchovy appetizers. Her headphones now twisted around her neck, she could hear the squeak of a mouse rummaging through the remains in the large metal rubbish bin. One of the men ripped open her white uniform, the tiny buttons popping off and sprinkling onto the ground. The taller man let go of her mouth, turned her around, and took her by the neck, pushing her up against the brick wall, face first. She could read the crude graffiti for just an instant, illuminated by the back light of the restaurant. Her forehead hit the hard stone with a thud. She felt something gooey and warm trickle down her face and then dribble down her neck. Blood ... my blood. She tried to scream, but nothing came out.

"Shut up. *Sta zitta. Sta zitta,*" he whispered in his raspy spine-tingling voice. He lifted the skirt of her uniform from the back, pulled down her panties, then drilled into her, releasing himself within just a few seconds.

She felt the sticky venom spurting out inside her. She gasped, the pain acute. "*Basta. Basta,*" she said, barely able to mumble the words. He pushed her forehead into the wall a second time. Polonia had no idea that the pair didn't let her fall to the ground until the second one emptied himself inside her. She was already unconscious when the shorter man drew a knife and plunged it three times into her back, finishing the job. She fell over dead.

Stavros was due home in just another fourteen days to be with his lovely wife for at least a month. Lying in his cot, the ship rocking gently in the waves, he thumbed through a magazine featuring the life story of a famous Italian opera singer, now turned sea captain. He mused to himself. He looked up from his magazine, as the ship's priest approached his bed, transmitting bad news in his solemn expression. The man of God's eyes were bloodshot, as if having cried, his cheeks flushed.

"My son, I have grave news. Your wife, I'm afraid she's gone." The words sliced into his heart. He lost track of the man before him, the line of bunk beds turned into a blur. He was suffocating. When the saddened priest tried to place his hand on Stavros' shoulder, he pushed him away with force. "My son, please, please let us pray together," the priest said.

Stavros wanted none of it. He pushed the man again. Taking the stairs two at a time, he burst through the metal cabin door that opened to the top deck and breathed in the cold salty air. The sea was serene, a sheet of never-ending glass. It was late at night, the full moon seeming to ironically bid him a good evening. He wanted to jump, bury himself forever in the dark waters. Staring out across the black horizon, his eyes filled with angry tears. The adrenalin of mental chaos was the only thing preventing him from thrusting his body overboard. Minutes turned into hours. He suffered, maniacally grieving his young dead wife. It's my fault, leaving her alone in a dangerous city like Roma. I will avenge her murder, he repeated to himself as he clutched the boat's railing, his rage consuming him.

For more than an hour, his friend Aldo watched the heartbroken man from under the metal stairwell, before making his way out on deck to stand by the side of his grief-stricken friend. "Stavros, I heard about Polonia. I am so sorry for you. She was the sweetest thing in the world. I remember you introducing us last summer." Stavros turned to him and raised his fist to punch him in the mouth, then suddenly realized that what he needed from his friend was some comfort. When Aldo produced a bottle of brandy from his pea jacket, Stavros accepted the drink.

The shock of Polonia's rape and murder was overwhelming. He was further stunned when he returned to Roma to learn that Polonia was in fact four months pregnant with a little girl. The autopsy uncovered her condition. His blood ran cold. He named the baby Mia, the daughter who would never be. She danced in his dreams, blew out the candles on her birthday cake, learned how to ride a bicycle, even hugged him before she fell off to sleep, her fuzzy yellow duck in her arms, her hair as black as Polonia's, falling in waves across her pillow. His mind would play tricks on him, thinking they were both there with him in the one-bedroom flat, the ghosts of his dead wife and unborn daughter. Stavros remained in a drunken miasma for the next twelve months. During this time, basically all he did was read the works of various philosophers and listen to Italian opera on his old phonograph, a prized antique he and Polonia had picked up at a flea market.

The two killers were never apprehended, although for several months the *policia* searched high and low for the bastards. Stavros hung out near the crime scene night after night, hoping to catch the suspects. He honestly didn't know what to look for. He'd get drunk after these stakeouts and wander home, losing his way several times before he'd make it back to his flat.

After seven months of sorrow, he circled back to his second love, the Navy. Once back in military life, he buried himself, becoming obsessed with achieving success on all his sea missions, standing out as a talented young leader. He solved complex navigational problems, making his mark saving a military ship in distress on the Baltic Sea. Soon he became the leader of a crew of fifty men who obediently followed his every order. Stavros grew to enjoy the power, the ability to give directions and have people unconditionally obey him. Things were under his complete control—the control he didn't have when his wife was being attacked, raped, and murdered.

His career progressed at rocket speed, first a promotion to assistant captain and then to full captain of a mega military vessel. In the privacy of his cabin, he'd sing to his dead wife and to his little daughter, Mia. He didn't marry again, but instead women became his weakness, whether wedded or single. He liked the feel of their skin, their red lips, and he could fool himself into thinking it was Polonia in his arms every time. He'd find women to be undeniably attracted to him wherever he went. It was his uniform, his sculpted Italian features, and his level of personal command and confidence. He took full advantage of these qualities, bedding women from all walks of life, but never becoming emotionally attached. He began to think of women as objects to be obtained, not relationships to be built. He craved acquiring one female possession after the other.

Now, sitting at his grand baroque wooden desk on *The Prism of the Deep Blue Sea,* he was falling apart. The disappearance of Amy Skyler brought forgotten emotions rushing to the surface, the painful feelings that he had suppressed for the past fifteen years. He lost everything when he lost his wife and now with the disappearance of Amy he was reliving it all over again.

Chapter Twelve

Wash Your Worries Away

Nadia took out the blackest eyeliner she could find in her cosmetic bag—the type that pops her large brown eyes. She applied the sticky mixture dark and heavy above and under each eye. She wanted to look her best in her spandex black tights and her cut-out white fitted top. She was ready for the early-morning crewmembers yoga class, held in the gray-carpeted staff lounge on Deck 2. Visualizing stretching her long body into a Down Dog position, she would be the perfect piece of ass to make a German lesbian's mouth water. And that's just what she was planning to do in today's yoga class.

She felt Verena's gaze upon her as she performed each move like a trained yogini. Verena stood behind her. She didn't want to stare at her colleague's incomparable form, but she was losing the battle. As the session ended and the rest of the group filed out quickly, headed to the locker room, Nadia stopped her.

"Verena, wait." Her objective was for the two of them to lag behind the other girls by about 20 minutes. That should do it, guarantee them some privacy when they start removing their clothes in the crew locker room. "Verena, can you stay for awhile and show me the two new positions I missed last week? I didn't do them correctly today. I could use your help."

"Uh, what?" Verena was puzzled. Typically Nadia barely paid her any attention outside of their time together at the Teen Club. "Oh, *ja,* those two new positions." Verena smiled broadly. "Well, honestly, you seemed to get them down perfectly, but if you want I can show you again."

"Yes. Splendid. Thank you. I'll watch you and follow. You're not going ashore today in Gibraltar, are you?"

"No. No. I have plenty of time for yoga right now. I'm working later this morning anyway. Some of the teens are staying on board, and I have an activity planned with them." Verena attempted to lengthen her short stocky German body as far as she could, sucking in her stomach, demonstrating the tricky yoga position. "This is called the Lord of the Dance pose."

Nadia chuckled inside. It's a bloody arabesque, my ballet specialty, the Russian mused to herself. "Thank you, Verena. You do it well. Let me try that." Nadia took her time, pretending to have problems getting it right. "Adjust my pose, so I do it correctly. Please."

Verena was delighted, pulling her left leg a little higher in the air and helping her arch her core, then lowering her right arm now extended out in front of her. "Pull your leg out as straight as you can. *Ja. ja.* That's it!"

Nadia slowed down their pace, trying this pose, and then the second one several times. She gazed into the walled mirror as she did each movement, also watching Verena track every stretch of her ballerina body with her round green eyes. Verena noticed Nadia's scent. Mmm, she smells like a fragrant flower that springs up through the ground, a beautiful sight on the edge of the Danube.

After several minutes, Nadia rolled up her yoga mat. "Thank you, Verena. I am indebted to you."

The crew's female changing room was all clear as they both found their lockers, just opposite each other's, sharing a bench area. Verena appeared nervous but wanted to continue the connection with this stunning woman.

"Nadia, did you hear what happened last night? A young girl is missing. Amy Skyler. Remember the red-haired teen from last night? You were talking to her in the discotheque. She's the one who's disappeared. Didn't make it back to her parents' stateroom last night. I heard the story at breakfast this morning from one of the security guys. The speculation is that maybe this Amy girl wanted to get away from her parents. Evidently, she was upset with them."

"Hmm, really?"

"So, what did you talk with her about? What did she say to you? Nadia, I don't think you noticed me, but I actually walked by when you were talking to her. I thought I heard you say something about meeting her later? Honestly, I really didn't hear much of your conversation. You know, whatever you discussed might help give Security some important clues about what happened to her. She is a quiet girl, so she didn't talk to that many teens in the group and not much with me either."

Nadia felt cornered. She needed to distract Verena, and she had a plan mapped out to do just that. "That red-haired girl? Ah yes, I was talking to her, but for only a brief moment. I'm afraid that I can't recall much of what she said to me, though she did seem to be in a depressed mood. *Nyet,* I had no plan of meeting her later. You must have misheard me. I-I'm sure that she'll turn up," Nadia said.

As Verena retrieved her towel and flip-flops from her locker, Nadia smiled and inquired, "So, are you going to shower now?"

"*Ja.* Of course." Verena fidgeted with the back of her bra, trying to get the clasp unhooked, nervous in the company of this beauty, and in such an intimate place as the crew's locker room.

Nadia watched her. "Let me help you, Verena. Turn around."

The German almost gasped as she looked up and saw Nadia's naked body standing there before her. She fumbled, barely managing a response, trying hard not to stare. "Yes, thank you. Ach, this is such a tricky bra. I need a real sports bra."

She turned back to her locker, biting her lip and then felt Nadia's fingers on her back. Nadia released the pronged clasp, snapping it open and letting Verena's white bra fall to the floor, then pressing her bare breasts up against the girl from behind, reaching her long arms around to fondle Verena's nipples ever so gently, circling them with her index fingers, then giving them a slight pinch before dropping her hands. Nadia picked up her towel from the metal bench. A fully dressed coworker walked brusquely past them but didn't glance in their direction. Nadia looked over at Verena, who was dizzy with surprise, her mouth almost gaped open.

"Have a pleasant shower, my friend." Nadia said, as she wrapped her white fluffy towel around her slender form. She moved in closer to Verena. "You never know who might join you," she whispered in her ear.

Instantly aroused by her words, Verena wrapped her towel around her waist, retrieved her shampoo and soap, then walked timidly toward the shower area, scouting for any lurking coworkers who may have been listening or watching. Her mind spun, her body was excited. She hung her towel on the metal hook inside the shower stall and turned to pull on the faucet. The warm water soaked her skin. She heard someone behind her as the plastic curtain was pulled back. Nadia hooked her towel over Verena's and once again moved her hands to Verena's breasts as the *Fraulein* turned and looked up into her dark brown eyes.

Nadia slid down onto her knees, keeping eye contact with the dazzled Verena. No words were exchanged, only the sound of the rushing water. She spread her friend's legs and stretched up, placing her tongue inside the stocky girl. Verena floated away, voyaging to some other reality as Nadia performed her dance of licks, frenzied and then slow, slow and then frenzied. The German longed to keep that sublime connection with her unexpected new lover's eyes, but she couldn't help but close her own and take the ride to paradise with the Russian goddess.

Da. She is mine, Nadia mused. She is mine, and will never betray me, never give me away. We have a bond. I am sure of it. I will need to have a talk with her about not saying a word about Amy and me talking last night.

I could love this woman, Verena thought, as she reached a mad climax. I could love this woman.

Chapter Thirteen

Tension Mounts at Gibraltar

At 2 o'clock in the afternoon, over 1,700 tourists aboard *The Prism of the Deep Blue Sea* clamored to get off the ship and descend on Gibraltar. The gangway was packed. Carlos Mendano, cruise director, and Verena Keppler, director of the Teen Scene club, stood side by side, interacting with the passengers as they left the ship. Each departing passenger pressed their magnetic plastic cruise card up to the electronic recognition machine, waiting for the magical *bing* sound, signaling that it was clear for them to disembark.

Every few minutes, the jovial Carlos yelled out, "Be back on the ship by 6:30 tonight folks. We don't want to leave you behind. Your ship sails at 7 p.m. sharp. And remember to take a minivan ride up to the top of the rock above this great city of Gibraltar. You will be delighted with the crazy monkeys up there who will jump on your shoulders and play with your hats and your sunglasses. Keep your eye on your belongings."

People laughed and waved *adios* to Carlos. As many stepped off the gangway onto the dock, they took a minute to have their photo quickly taken with two humans clothed in monkey costumes standing behind a white life preserver stamped with the location, Gibraltar.

A young couple and their two children walked up to the cruise director. "Carlos, may we ask you a question?" The man had an English accent and wore a green-and-white striped shirt and gaudy plaid Bermuda shorts. "We hear it's possible to catch a short ferry ride over to Tangier. Is that true? I'd love to touch my feet on African soil if that's possible. Is the dock for Tangier close by?"

Carlos looked concerned. "Oh, trust me sir, I don't recommend it. You would be risking not making it back to the ship on time."

The man narrowed his eyes. "Oh, then right mate, we won't be doing that. Come on kids. Let's catch a minivan to the top of the rock and see the monkeys." The two young children screamed with joy. His wife sighed with relief.

Verena glanced up at Carlos, giggling. "Tourists. They're funny, *ja?*" she said under her breath.

On board, the morning was filled with tension, at least for Christian and Packo. Word had circulated among some of the crew. A teenage female passenger was missing. The trusted security staff, specifically Henri and Edward, was the careless culprit and to whom the protests to come would be aimed. Packo was not aware of his security team's inability to keep a confidence. At this point, a handful of crewmembers performed their duties knowing that a girl named Amy Skyler has vanished. Tomorrow, as the ship begins crossing the Atlantic, all 3,000 passengers onboard would know about the missing girl.

At 1 o'clock in the afternoon, the three officers reassembled at the captain's conference room table. Docked in Gibraltar until the early evening, most of the passengers were in the midst of their half-day excursions or frenzied shopping in the crowded town of shysters and street vendors who fervently push fake designer-brand watches and handbags. The captain sat across from Packo and Christian, distracted, fidgeting with his miniature model of *The Prism of the Deep Blue Sea*, turning it upside down, rubbing its smooth, robin's-egg's-blue-colored hull.

Packo was the first to speak. "Captain, although we searched the ship a number of times, my security team turned up nothing related to Amy Skyler." Waiting for an avalanche of disparaging remarks from his boss, he thought after my bumbling words this morning, I'm sure to get a shit storm of rage. Yet the captain sat there, solemn, looking down at his shaking hands, tossing the miniature ship from left to right and back again.

Stavros studied Kierkegaard after Polonia was killed, burying himself in book after book with a bottle of bourbon as his trusty partner. Soren Kierkegaard emerged to become his favorite author, a sage philosopher speaking out to him from the pages of yellowed leather-bound books. Often he'd sit in his lonely Roma flat lost in a half-drunken stupor, reciting quotes from Kierkegaard's insightful writings. Stavros would memorize iconic Kierkegaard phrases and quotes. Night after night, he'd recite passages as he looked at himself in the wall mirror opposite his bed, the pretty ghost-like faces of his deceased wife and daughter looking back at him.

What would the adept philosopher say about this "missing girl" scenario? Looming over the captain's head was his own guilt. How could this calamity happen right under his nose, a passenger missing now for more than half a day? "Anxiety is the dizziness of freedom," he recalled Kierkegaard's crisp but brilliant quotation. I must get control of myself instead of wallowing in sorrow and uncertainty.

He placed the tiny boat replica down on the tabletop and spoke with measure. "Officer Stephanopolous, have you heard anything about this situation in your interactions with passengers this morning? Anything unusual or suspicious?"

Christian learned nothing. It wasn't in his best interest to divulge that he had mentioned the missing girl to Ally, his close colleague.

The captain continued, "Let's identify every crewmember who spoke to Amy Skyler in her first hours on the ship. You need to interview each one of them. Also, we need to have an 'All Hands' crew meeting in the theater. Let's do that at 3 p.m. with half the crew and then at 4 p.m. with the second half. That will be well before we sail at 7 o'clock. At these meetings, I will request that the entire crew become our confidential data gatherers." He impatiently looked over at Packo. "Can you organize and tell the others about this 'required' meeting? Can you do that immediately?"

"Yes sir, I can do that. Anything else? Should we alert the passengers or have the Coast Guard start a search?" He cleared his throat. "I mean, supporting Officer Stephanopolous' comment earlier this morning, I agree ..."

"No Officer Suarez. Not at this time. I need to work on my messages for these crew meetings. Dismissed, both of you. Packo, be on stage in the theater ready to go by my side at 2:30 and have everything set up. Make sure there are no technical problems. Clear?"

"Sir, before I go, I'd like to apologize for my poor behavior this morning. I-I..."

"Save it, *per favore*. Get out of here, both of you."

Chapter Fourteen

In Their Stateroom

Wendy and Russell Skyler huddled together on the contemporary blue and gray diamond printed sofa that sat adjacent to the open sliding glass door of their stateroom. Wendy held the photograph of their missing daughter in her quivering hand. She sobbed as Russell consoled her with his weak embrace.

"It's my fault," she cried out. "I should have stayed awake. How could I have been so irresponsible? My little girl, my pixie." She used to call Amy her pixie, but that was years ago, in happier times. Wendy stared at the smiling face of her daughter in the photograph. She could see behind the teenager's smile the sadness, the anger, the anxiety. A knife twisted in her chest as she thought back to last night. Her daughter missing. "I've been a poor excuse for a mother, haven't I?" she said to her husband.

"Wendy, it's okay. She's probably hanging out with another teenager right now. She'll let us know where she is, and why she did this. But it will be on her own terms, when she's ready, most likely within the next few hours. She could see that we were constantly at each other's throats. She probably got fed up. We need to be patient."

"Patient? How can we just sit here and wait? I can't do that," she yelled and moved outside to the grand suite's balcony that swept around the right front corner of the ship. It was a special suite, one fit for a celebrity the likes of Wendy Skyler. "I'm through being patient. I want my daughter back!" The ocean seemed endless as she looked to the left while to the right she saw the bustling city of Gibraltar just below the giant rock. Tears blurred her vision, the lights and colors blending together. Something in the air here was irritating her. Gibraltar felt dirty.

"Come back Wendy," he called to her from the sofa. "Come back inside."

"What about you?" She screamed and pointed her finger in his face. "Don't you have any guilt? Don't you regret being a bad father?"

He couldn't believe his ears. She was accusing *him*.

"Me?" he fumed. "I'm not the one who's never home, off in some godforsaken location filming some meaningless episode of some sordid soap opera. I'm not the one who doesn't give a shit about her family. Are you kidding me?" He shook his head, leaning his elbows on the lustrous wooden balcony railing, staring out to the right. The evening street lamps now lit up the center of Gibraltar. He turned to her. "You're such a bitch, Wendy. Blaming it on me now. You were correct in the first place when you said it was all your fault."

"I hate you Russell. I should never have married you!"

He threw his head back and responded to her with sarcasm. "Yeah, that's a joke. You hate *me*. How do you think I feel? What about you and Finn Galloway, the heartthrob of English daytime TV melodrama? Oh I'm sorry, he's doing film too, isn't he? One lousy vampire movie to his credit, isn't that right?"

"You know it's over between us. Why bring it up? I haven't been with him for over a month now."

Russell fell into the balcony deck chair. "Because ..." He stopped, hesitated, then continued, "Because my sweet innocent little girl knew about you and Finn. That's probably why she disappeared last night, why she ran away. She couldn't bear to spend another moment anywhere near you."

"That's crazy."

"Crazy? I don't think so, Wendy. Amy heard you on the phone with that narcissistic asshole. That was just three nights ago. I overheard you, too."

"No. No," she mumbled as she collapsed like a ragdoll into the other deck chair.

"Yes. Sorry, but *no* is not an option here," he shouted. "I found our daughter outside the bathroom door listening to your sexual banter. Don't you know that sounds echo throughout the house from our proper little English powder room? Every word is twice as loud as anywhere else in the god-damn flat. A design flaw from the Brits, I guess. Our little Amy heard every memory of your last bout of fucking … your saccharine misgivings about leaving him for three weeks undoubtedly gripped your daughter's heart like a vise, squeezing any love and respect she had left for you right out of her."

"Oh my God," Wendy muttered, startled.

Russell couldn't stop himself, his anger reaching new heights. "Yeah, I watched her face as I stood there at the top of the stairs … watched your daughter painfully listening to you while you practically fucked your lover on the phone, again!"

He scooted his chair closer to his wife, placing his face just inches from hers, then mimicked her upper-class English accent: "Finn. Oh Finn. I can't wait to see you again. Feel your arms around me. I need you Finn. I want to be with you."

Wendy was shocked and timidly reacted. "She … she heard me say all those things?"

"Me, I wanted to puke, Wendy. I wanted to break down the bathroom door and throttle you, but instead I tiptoed back downstairs. I didn't want our only child to know that I, too, heard your every sickening syllable."

Wendy began to sob like a frightened little girl. "You're right. It's all my fault that she's gone."

Russell instantly regretted his tantrum, the release of his pent-up emotions, and at such a bad time. But Wendy stepped on a land mine when she started to blame him for Amy's disappearance. The verbal lacerations just inflicted were nothing compared to what he had daydreamed about doing to his wife for several weeks now. As he sat there, his rage having been released, he felt his wife's heart breaking, the deep sadness and pain in the eyes of the woman he'd loved for over fifteen years.

He took her hands and gently lifted her from the deck chair and spoke in a soft hushed tone. "Wendy. Wendy, we're both to blame. *Both* of us." He held her close. She savored his embrace, astounded that he would choose to ever touch her again.

She looked up into his damp eyes, then gazed out at the darkened ocean. The stars twinkled, the moon shone brightly. "Russell, what if … what if Amy's not on the ship? What if she's been taken by someone, or worse? Her medication, it's not here. I looked. That's one good thing, one paltry little blessing on our side. If she has an anxiety attack, if something terrible is happening to her, at least she has the Paxil. At least she has the one thing that can help her through a crisis."

Chapter Fifteen

Confidentiality

The first group of crewmembers filed into the theater as the technical team finished setting up the microphone on the cruise ship's mega stage.

Gabriel, the lead technician, addressed the captain: "Pardon me, Captain, sir, but can you test out the microphone to ensure it's working properly for you?"

The captain frowned. He wasn't interested in playing the guinea pig in front of hundreds of his crew.

Packo rushed over to Gabriel. "Let me do this, Gabe." He spoke into the microphone. "Testing. Testing."

Gabe nodded and left the stage. Packo stood there with the captain covering the mic with one hand, for fear something might be picked up accidentally by the hundreds of crew already seated in the theater. A healthy-sized cadre, representing every corner of the world, Packo assessed. All of them between nineteen and thirty-two years old, except for the senior officers, who were generally a little older. Mostly kids running this ship. Packo glanced at his watch. It was 3:02 p.m. He tapped its face, signaling the captain that it was past their targeted 3 o'clock start time.

The captain looked up from his notes, peering over the black frames of his glasses with disdain. "I'm aware of the time, Suarez. Give me another minute to breathe, will you?"

He grunted with added dissatisfaction. The idea of one of his officers rushing him felt reflexively objectionable. Christian approached, sitting just below the stage, in the first row center.

"Good man Stephanopolous, you made it," the captain muttered. "I may need you. I want to point out who you are as a key contact."

"Yes sir," Christian nodded.

Ally rushed in and sat down next to Christian, her best faux "good little crewmember" mask plastered on her face. Ilze and a couple of the other front desk junior staff filed in next to her. She couldn't help but resort to her playful nature, stepping on Christian's shoe within 15 seconds of sitting down.

The captain, once again, peered over the top of his glasses, checking out the cute blonde crewmember in the front row, and then got back to his notes. What else do I want to say in this meeting? His brain was mush, thinking about his deceased wife and little girl and at the same time about this situation with the missing Amy Skyler.

Manzione gestured to Packo, and with another burning glance at his chief security officer, said, "I'm ready. Let's do it."

Packo spoke into the microphone. "Settle down. Let me have everyone's attention. Our captain is ready to begin."

A hush fell over the apprehensive crew, many wondering if there was some big announcement coming, possibly a change on the horizon affecting them personally. It was unusual to have such a meeting this afternoon when they already had the monthly "All Hands" meeting just a week ago.

The captain clasped the microphone. "First, let me begin with saying that what I'm about to tell you is to stay completely confidential." He scanned the theater with his unforgiving eyes. "Anyone leaking this information to passengers will be terminated i mmediately. Do I have your attention now? I swear this to be true, as your captain," he shouted, his words echoing across the theater.

His dead wife's eyes flashed before him. He was feeling worn out, stressed. This disturbing image only caused him to become rigid, more authoritative in tone. He worried that he would expose the cracks in his armor.

He looked down at a fidgety Asian girl who sat in the second row. She seemed to be looking at something that her friend next to her was showing her. They both shook with laughter. He pointed at the skinny Asian girl.

"You! I need your undivided attention. Get up. Yes, you! Go to the back of the theater. Stand back there and listen." The girl was startled, mortified. "I'm serious," he shouted. "Get up. Go!"

The embarrassed young girl squeezed past her colleagues and scurried to the rear of the room. Stavros was pleased with the complete attention he now had from every crew underling in the spacious gilt-decorated auditorium.

Verena sat quietly in the third row of the theater next to Carlos. She thought back to her glorious shower with Nadia. Where is her lover right now? They had arranged for Nadia to stop by her cabin at around 4:00. Now at 3:05 Verena was beyond excited even as she took in the severity of the captain's disciplinary words with that hapless crewmember.

At the back corner of the balcony, Nadia leaned against a mahogany post and as inconspicuously as possible listened with great interest to Stavros Manzione. He's a weak, pompous macho man, she thought. Everything I hate.

As the captain talked about the missing girl, he circled back to the stiff consequences that would result for anyone who breaks confidentiality. "You need to all be our eyes and ears for anything you may have seen."

In each aisle, a crewmember stood with a stack of Xeroxed black-and-white photos of Amy Skyler with information in bold type below the girl's face. "The flyers are now being passed out to you," the captain continued. "Look at this photograph very carefully, then stuff the paper in your pocket. Carry it with you. Don't leave it anywhere to be found by passengers. Eat it before you leave it on a table or a chair. Take it out and look at it when you have a private moment. We need to find this girl and gather any clues as to where she may be. I'm sure she's somewhere on the ship.

"You all know Officer Suarez, our chief of security." He pointed to Packo, who stood only three feet away scanning the audience. "He is your contact for anything you find—pager number, Officer Suarez?"

Packo moved to the captain and spoke into the microphone: "Pager 26420. Yes, I will be available—"

The captain grabbed the microphone, interrupting Packo. "Officer Suarez will be available 24 hours a day. The pager number is also printed on the flyer. We cannot sleep until we find this girl. You can't either, none of you! We hope to get results within the next few hours, hopefully even before we leave Gibraltar.

"Mr. Stephanopolous, please stand up."

Christian obediently rose and turned to face the crowd. Ally was jolted, regretting her earlier frivolity.

"This is our new hotel manager, Christian Stephanopolous," the captain said. "He is also a key contact for you. His pager appears on the flyer you all should be holding in your hand right now. You can call on your stateroom phone. Go to either of these two officers with any information on this missing girl, even if you think it's trivial. She's most likely a runaway and hiding out with another teen passenger. There will indeed be a reward if you locate Amy Skyler," he added, without having thought of what it might be. "Time for you to leave as the next—"

Before the captain could finish his sentence, a man in a white uniform sitting in the middle of the theater shouted out, raising his hand, "Sir. Sir." The captain rolled his eyes, at first annoyed at the brazen interruption. He instantly reminded himself that he was asking for help from these people, and acknowledged the man. "Yes? Do you have a question? What's your name?" He pointed in the direction of the hand in the air.

The twenty-year-old Indian crewmember from New Delhi stood up, feeling embarrassed but eager to offer important information. "Um, sir, I am Baldeep Singh, a waiter. I was waiting tables in the buffet today and I poured coffee for a middle-aged couple from Canada. It was about 10 o'clock in the morning. The man asked me about this missing girl."

The meeting attendees gasped. There was chatter everywhere in the theater.

Captain Manzione stood there in shock. "What?" he bellowed. "Quiet, all of you. What are you saying, Mr. Singh? Continue!"

"Yes sir. The couple didn't seem to know the missing girl's name, but they heard a male crewmember talking about it to a female crewmember early in the morning. They were conversing just outside the couple's stateroom as they were leaving for a walk just after dawn. The Canadian woman asked me if I knew anything about this disturbing incident and whether or not the poor girl had been found yet."

"Well, what did you say, Mr. Singh? How did you respond to this couple?"

"I-I ... Well, sir, I told them it must be some kind of rumor. This kind of chatter is probably a made-up story. I-I didn't know what else to say, sir. I wanted to set their minds at ease."

The captain swallowed hard, trying to gather his thoughts, and then firmly addressed the group, his voice too loud for the sound system, producing an electronic screeching sound, which continued until he moderated his volume. "I'm telling all of you, if you have leaked this and I find out, you will not only be fired, but I will make sure you never work again on any cruise ship in the world. Do you understand me?"

He jabbed his index finger in the air as he spoke. The crewmembers nodded, many intimidated hearing his threats.

"Mr. Singh, thank you. We will follow up on this news. Please say nothing else if this couple approaches you and asks about this girl again."

Baldeep nodded and sat back down almost sorry he spoke up in the first place. He could feel the sharp daggers shooting across the room from the captain's eyes.

"Mr. Singh, I appreciate what you just did. But before you leave this theater, you will need to come and talk with Officer Suarez. He has a few more questions for you. We will be in further communication with you. A warning to all of you: Don't gossip about this missing teen, especially in earshot of our passengers. Now, all of you, go back to your jobs! Meeting adjourned."

The captain stepped away from the standup microphone, feeling agitated, his stomach doing flip-flops, the churning almost painful. Packo turned off the switch on the microphone. He could see that the captain had turned as pale as his starched white shirt. People rustled out of the theater, grateful to be getting out of harm's way.

Manzione paced the stage, saying under his breath, "Suarez, find out where the breach came from. It must be from one or more of your fucking security staff. And locate that couple from Canada, set them straight. Let them know that it was just a rumor! Work with Stephanopolous to identify them. But first talk with Singh, that waiter. Coach him closely on precisely how to handle it if that couple comes back to him. I don't trust him."

Christian remained seated, waiting for the second group of crew-members to file in. Ally and her front desk colleagues got up to leave. Before she moved away, she placed her hand on Christian's shoulder and looked down into his eyes.

"I'll be looking for clues about the girl. I promise. You know how smart I am," she winked, trying to lighten up the moment.

He acknowledged her effort. "Thanks girlfriend. I'll see you in an hour at the front desk. Oh, wait a minute. You're off tonight. Well, see you in the morning then."

She grinned. Did he just call her girlfriend?

Christian walked out into the aisle, hoping to appear completely approachable in case any crewmember from the departing group might want to come and talk to him about Amy Skyler. He wondered if he should go up on the stage with the captain and Packo. Instead he decided to stay down below by the first row of seats as the crew filed out from the first meeting and more crewmembers entered for the second.

The captain's fury increased as he paced the stage, making some additional scribbles on his notepad, getting ready for the next set of crew-members now noisily crowding the theater. The Indian man's announcement had jolted him. He shook inside and as a result appeared even more hardened on the outside. Baldeep Singh was off to the side with Packo in an animated but hushed discussion, the security officer jotting down notes. Finally, they were ready to get started with the second group.

Stavros Manzione lectured the crewmembers using an even more demeaning tone than earlier. Like a curmudgeon headmaster, he whipped his words across the auditorium, making eye contact with each individual. He was like a hammer, banging on every nail, with purposeful and direct pressure. Manzione left no doubt with regard to his expectations. He asked the same rhetorical question at least four times during the next hour: "Am I being perfectly clear?" And each time he asked, he waited to see nods from the audience. His desire was to put the fear of God into them, ensuring that they did their best to find the girl, but also keep their mouths clenched up tightly with the passengers.

Chapter 16

Country-Western Night Romance

Between her shift as restaurant hostess and her assistance at the Teen Scene discotheque activity, Nadia romanced Verena in her cabin, as the sun set over Gibraltar. The women entwined themselves for almost an hour.

Nadia sat up on the bed, sliding on her sling-back shoes.

"Wait, don't go," Verena said. "Please. There is more than an hour before the Teen Scene activity begins. I want to give you pleasure like you have given me."

"The pleasure has been all mine, my love. I must say *do svidaniya* for now. There's only an hour before we leave Gibraltar. I need to return to my cabin and change into my country-western costume. You need to do the same, *da?* Passengers are already returning, getting ready for a big shindig tonight. Ah, the cruising life! It's rush, rush, rush for us crew when the passengers get to relax and enjoy. Unfair, *nyet?*"

Her tone now became serious as she said, "Verena, before I leave, I need to talk with you about something very important."

Oh no. The letdown is coming. Verena anticipated a broken heart around the bend. It was too good to be true. She's already finished with me, she thought. "Yes, okay, let's talk," Verena replied as she looked down at the twisted blanket around her naked body. She must face it. She gazed up into her sultry lover's eyes.

Nadia placed her hands on Verena's thick shoulders, exerting just an iota of pressure, to get her attention, but at the same time transmitting a promise of tenderness to come. "That very brief conversation I had with that red-haired girl last night. You know, with that Amy Skyler you mentioned earlier today in the locker room."

Verena nodded in silence, but was unable to keep her puzzled expression from being detected. She thought back to the captain's meeting about the missing girl.

"Please Verena, don't divulge that to anyone. Nobody! I don't want to get in trouble or be in the limelight in any way on this cruise ship. Please, I am begging you. It's important, very serious. Can you understand that? Can you give me your word?"

Nadia's hands slid down Verena's arms, then gently stroked them with her long manicured nails. Verena closed her eyes, still listening, but feeling chills from her touch.

"I know it may not seem to make sense to you, but I have some problems from the immigration side. I need to stay low profile, especially with the ship's senior officers and with the captain." She brushed her fingers across Verena's forehead, pushing back a few wild strands of hair that had cascaded over her face.

Danke Gott. Nadia's not breaking up with me. Thank you, *Gott.* Pleasantly relieved, Verena said, "Yes, yes, no problem Nadia. I will say nothing about this to anyone. I promise. Not a soul will know that you talked to that girl." She crossed her heart with her right hand.

Nadia placed a tender kiss on Verena's lips. "Thank you, my love. I must leave now. I will see you at the discotheque, then." She looked down into her eyes. "Ah, what a romance we already have brewing. You see that twinkle in my eye? *Da?* It's because I am falling in love with you, my sweet *Fraulein.* I just can't help it."

Nadia turned, grabbed her purse, and dashed out, closing the cabin door behind her. Verena sat up and watched her quick yet graceful exit. She lay back down on her pillow, thoughts of Nadia dancing in her head. She stretched and savored her sudden good fortune at love.

It had been over a year since Verena had her last sexual encounter. It was with Anya, a Polish girl, five years older than Verena. Anya was a server in the buffet, working long hours. Sturdy stock, plain appearance, but fun-loving, much like Verena herself. Anya had noticed the German staring a little too long at her during the monthly "All Hands" crew meeting. She was seated only two chairs away from Verena, a chubby, ruddy-cheeked cook named Otto stuffed between them. Anya was boyish looking, with short brown hair and heavy dark eyebrows, but she had a glimmer in her eyes when she smiled. Anya always seemed happy, having a compelling combination of warmth and confidence about her. This attracted Verena, who quickly became friends with the Polish girl. They'd stand in the halls or on the staircase between their duties, chatting about different events and funny stories of life on the giant ship.

One night Anya took a chance and knocked on Verena's cabin door. She held a bottle in her hand. "Good evening. I knew you had the night off, and, well … I thought I'd stop by and see if you wanted some wine. It comes from Poland, my home country. I snuck it on board. Want to share this with me?" Anya was a little cautious about testing the waters with young Verena, but it was the only way to find out if she was interested in more than a work relationship. Once the two glasses of wine were poured, Anya gently kissed her on the neck. Although Verena was surprised, she turned to face her, closing her eyes to indicate her readiness for something more. Anya took the lead from there, a little awkwardly coaxing her new acquaintance over to the bed, then making love to her with her somewhat less than tender touch. But it was satisfactory for both of them. Twice a week, for the next four months, they would find time for each other, a comfortable union, which went on until Anya's mother became ill with life-threatening lung cancer. She immediately quit her job and left *The Prism of the Deep Blue Sea* behind. Since returning to Poland, she hadn't connected with Verena again, at least not yet. Verena was lonely and missed those cozy nights with Anya. She buried herself in her work, becoming a more creative and engaging Teen Scene director. Although she was outgoing at times, she was still a shy lesbian and avoided having the spotlight on herself. She wanted the teens to like her as a person and not be focused on her sexuality. Who knew what it might conjure up in the minds of at least some of the parents?

With Nadia, it was a dream come true. Verena could be herself, at ease with her sexual preference. The Russian was such a beauty, a master at lovemaking, a seductive Romeo in woman's clothing. With Nadia gone for almost 10 minutes, Verena was still reeling in disbelief. She felt like the luckiest girl in the world.

Just down the hallway in a cramped crew cabin on Deck 3, Ally got ready for "Western Night." As she dressed, she hummed "She'll Be Coming 'Round The Mountain."

Checking herself in the full-length, chipped, antique mirror she picked up in a flea market in Venice, Italy, she sang out, "When she comes, when she comes. She'll be comin' round the mountain when she comes." The mirror had been a bargain that she couldn't resist. She had clumsily mounted it on the armoire closet door in her cabin, which made it difficult for the door to lie flush when shut. Ally traded off perfect quality for a little damaged antique opulence. The faded gold-leaf wooden frame of the mirror reminded her of the affluent Southern plantation life she left behind eighteen months ago.

With one last look in the mirror, she saw a vision of herself dressed up as a cowgirl. She had two long blonde pigtails and a flurry of added brown freckles sprinkled across her nose. She was wearing a mini jean fitted skirt, a plaid cowgirl shirt clad with shiny metal snaps allowing her breasts to tastefully peek out just a little, and a perfectly faded jean jacket. A cotton print red kerchief was knotted around her neck, and the final touch, popping the whole look, was her very own cowgirl boots, which had been transported all the way from Georgia. Hmm, I look good! Her blue eyes shone. Tonight she felt taller than her 5 feet, 3 inches, wearing her ankle-high cowgirl boots and her new mini skirt. Her legs were tanned, highlighting the muscles in her healthy calves and shapely thighs, well proportioned to her petite 105-pound frame.

"Time to get outta here," she nodded to herself in the mirror, placing the broad-brimmed cowgirl hat on her head, the leather string tie dangling under her chin. "Now that looks decent," she declared. She grabbed her cell phone, zipped it into her jean jacket pocket, fully equipped to take plenty of fun-filled photos. She clipped her pager in her skirt pocket, ensuring that she could be reached by Christian or other staff members if there was any emergency or if she came across any clues about Amy Skyler's disappearance.

She picked up her lasso and left the cabin, headed for the Texas two-step dance class she taught with Carlos Mendano, the ship's flamboyant cruise director. Whenever they taught a dance class together, they were infectious, fully entertaining the delighted passengers, who were all keen to learn the western dance. Ally and Carlos came off as experts as they demonstrated the sometimes complicated sidestep moves, although the truth was that both learned the series of line dances in one afternoon from the talented Bailey Baxter, one of the Prism Theater's lead production dancers.

Flying down the hallway, ready to join in some fun, Ally was content despite her still bruised heart from the night before. Amy Skyler's disappearance also flashed across her mind. She looked down the corridor and saw Christian standing there.

"Well, park my horse on your doorstep! Where in the hell is your cowboy get-up?" she asked.

Christian turned from his cabin door after he shut it and ensured it was locked. When he saw her, he stopped in his tracks. She looked adorable ... like some young teenage girl.

"Wow. Is that *the notorious* Ally Oakley I see before me?" He hurried up to her, meeting her at the hub of elevators.

"To be sure, y'all! *The* one and only." She curtsied. "So, honestly Mr. Hotel Manager, where are you hiding your western wear?"

He moved closer, looked down at her, and tapped her turned-up freckled nose. "Sorry, I won't be playing 'cowboy' tonight. I'll be working until late."

Her eyes were a vivid crystal blue with tiny spots of gold and green at their centers. For the next few seconds, he couldn't seem to look away from them. Ally caught him staring. She felt hopeful. I think he's got a sparkle in his eye for me, tonight. Crap, maybe I'm just hallucinating. But this could be an opportunity for me to encourage him. She smiled.

"I look good, don't I? I see you admiring me," she teased. She stepped back and tipped her left foot up like she was about to do the cowboy two-step. "Do you like my genuine leather cowgirl boots? They came straight from a Southern plantation to the Straits of Gibraltar. These are what must be mesmerizing you, Wild Bill. Am I right about that?"

"More than you think, cowgirl. More than you think!" He nodded and exaggerated the gesture of checking her out. "You look even better than you did at Western Night' on the last cruise."

She responded by twirling her lasso liked a skilled horsewoman.

"Whoo Hoo," he said, thoroughly impressed at her dexterity combined with gracefulness. "I can smell what you're cooking, ma'am."

He looked up at the elevator's electronic display, changing the subject. "Geez, when are they going to fix these elevators? Damn things operate at a snail's pace."

He shuffled his feet, realizing that he could be late for the start of his next shift, not ideal behavior for a type-A hotel manager. Thrilled by his flattering words, although maybe in complete jest, Ally searched to say something, anything.

"So, no sign of Amy Skyler yet?"

His face paled. "No. Nothing."

"Christian, I'll keep my ears and eyes wide open tonight. Some teen might drop a hint without intending to. It's good that the captain had those meetings with the crew today." She touched his arm. "I wish I could do more to help find her. But what?" She lowered her voice just in case anyone was in earshot. "I know the captain doesn't want the passengers overly concerned, but they might be able to actually assist in the search. You know what they say: You can't skin a chicken without some help catching it first."

He burst out laughing. "What? Ally girl, you sure have some outrageous Southern expressions, don't you?" What a quirky sense of humor, he thought, as the elevator door opened.

"Yeah I do, thanks. I'll use that one on my date tonight."

They entered the empty elevator. "So ... so, you have a date? I didn't know you were seeing someone." He pushed the Deck 5 button and Deck 10 for Ally. The door jerked and then closed. They both raised their eyebrows regarding the elevator. "A date, huh?"

She was thrilled to see his interest in this topic. "Yeah, well it's ... it's new. He's the bartender up on the pool deck. I think you've probably seen him. His name is Jake, from Sydney, Australia. He's very funny." The elevator jiggled, hesitating before closing its doors again. "Yep, we're having an early drink, maybe a bite to eat, then I'm teaching the two-step with Carlos, and then the Teen Scene party, where Jake will most likely join me later. It'll be a crazy night, but don't you worry, I'll be at Reception ready to rumble at 7 in the morning, looking forward to the first of several days at sea, which could translate into solving a lot of passenger issues."

"Well, have a great time. You look ... you look peachy, Ally. Georgia peachy." They both smiled. "He's a lucky guy, your date."

"What are you saying, Christian?" Damn. Should she stretch this conversation out and fish for what he is thinking?

"Oh, nothing. Sometimes it's good to keep things below the surface. Not everything has to be written on our sleeve. Good night Ally Oakley." He pinched her nose and exited the elevator.

Ally wondered about his parting words. Was there a message there about how he felt about her? A group of costumed passengers entered the elevator, each wearing cowboy boots and cowboy hats, and one with a fake handlebar mustache. I think I made him a little jealous, she thought, as the elevator door slid shut. His remarks were cryptic to say the least. He's probably got a late-nighter with Nadia himself. She frowned, as the elevator seemed to chug up to Deck 10. When the door opened, Ally saw tall, good-looking, tanned Jake waiting to greet her.

As Christian approached the reception desk to start his evening shift, he thought about Ally. Flashes of jealousy filled his mind. What's wrong with me? I can't fathom why I'm having this response to Ally. I put that idea to bed a long time ago. He shook his head with confusion as he positioned himself behind the counter. Looking up, he saw Nadia. She didn't see him. She flew by, not even glancing in his direction. Her hair appeared disheveled, which was highly unusual for her when she was in the public eye. Christian also noticed that she seemed rattled. His mind sailed back to Ally, surprising himself. It's good to see her happy and dating another crewmember. But that sun-streaked Aussie? I think she's got three times the brains of that guy. Good-looking, yes, but not worthy of her. Right. Now, get off it, Stephanopolous. It's not your business, he reprimanded himself. I guess Nadia wasn't impressed enough with him to even glance over at the front desk. Face it, she's just not emotionally connected to me. The question is, am I feeling connected to her? His thoughts were interrupted by an agitated man who slammed two cruise cards down on the counter.

"Dr. Caruthers, what can I do for you?" Christian said.

"These don't work. Are you trying to ruin our vacation even more? Neither of these cards opens the door to our suite. They were operating just fine this morning. Look at me, I'm dripping wet from a quick dunk in the pool, not prepared to be locked out of our room."

Mrs. Caruthers came up behind him, the German shepherd service dog obediently by her side. The dog paused, stretching out his body, looking already worn out from the family vacation. She grimaced and then let Christian have it.

"Are you people kidding? First, we get accused of having an automatic weapon and now this! It's embarrassing." She was noticeably distraught as if some major catastrophe just occurred. She barked, "And don't think we didn't see you last night up on the pool deck making out with that girl like two sex-crazed teenagers at a drive-in movie? We walked right by that lounge chair where you were practically .... um ... um ... well, screw—"

Her husband clutched her arm, interrupting her. "Shush, Sissy. That's enough. None of our business." He lowered his voice and looked over at Christian. "We just need new cruise cards, that's all." The dog sat, staring up at them as if wanting to ask a question.

Christian reissued their cruise cards and ordered a bottle of Mumm's for their room as soon as they plodded away, Sigmund the dog having left wet track marks on the mosaic tiled floor. He quivered slightly with embarrassment, hearing someone describe his behavior as adolescent. It was so out of character for him to act like that among the passengers.

An elderly woman approached Reception. She smelled like flowers. It was the lady that Ally had pointed out the other night, the woman who waits for the string quartet to play each evening. He couldn't help but notice how bright the woman's blue eyes were as she looked up at him.

"Pardon me, son, but may I make a comment to you about this ship? Something I've noticed," she said with a glint in her eyes.

Damn, he thought, it looks like even this sweet old woman finally has a complaint. "Of course. Is there some problem I can help you with? I've noticed that you've been cruising with us for quite some time. I hope you're still enjoying our beautiful ship."

"Well, actually, I wanted to give you some personal feedback. I've been watching you for over three weeks now, almost every night. My dear, you have such a lovely way about you, always helping people, solving their problems. I can see how rude some of them seem to be when they approach your Reception counter. Ooh, they can be quite nasty, can't they?" The woman's voice was melodic and seemed to sound much younger than her likely eighty-five plus years.

"Well, we're here to offer the best service we can." He leaned over to her and whispered, "Honestly, when I was a young boy, it was my dream to work on a grand ship like this one and travel the world meeting people just like you. And I like helping people, even the most difficult ones."

The petite woman beamed and reached up to touch his hand. "Son, you are such a gem. That's why I stayed on this ship now for your past three consecutive cruises. My plan is to continue to take advantage of your exquisite hospitality for at least another two cruises after this one. By the way, dear, you two make a very nice couple."

Christian was suddenly thrown off by her comment. Did she see him with Nadia? Hopefully it wasn't last night up on the pool deck. Maybe she noticed them on the elevator when they came out of the discotheque on their way to the pool party?

"Um, yes, well she's statuesque," he nodded. "A stunning woman, I'm a lucky man." He felt awkward and could feel the heat of his usually olive skin now most likely turning crimson.

The woman narrowed her eyes but then laughed. "Oh my dear, I wouldn't describe that cute little blonde girl as 'statuesque.' She's adorable, but a little thing, so lovely, and I can see that she has great affection for you. I've watched you two together. Good chemistry between you, I'd say." She winked.

Christian felt nervous, having almost said Nadia's name when the woman must have been referring to Ally. He nodded and smiled, not wanting to add more fuel to the fire.

The woman tapped his forearm with her dainty freckled hand. "Well, I'm feeling a bit tired, dear. I must return to my stateroom for my nap. An elderly woman's weakness, I'm afraid. Nice to talk to you, and keep up the good work." She waved, walked a few steps away, stopped, and turned around to look at Christian. "So that you can put a name to this wrinkled old face, it's Flora." She limped away, her sparkly blue cane helping her move brusquely past the centrum area and down the promenade of shops.

Christian pondered the woman's words about Ally. The truth was that at one point he had considered Ally as potentially more than a good friend. It was early on, during their first cruise together. They were sitting in the staff lounge, enjoying each other's company during a lighthearted game of checkers. He had almost kissed her that night. It was when she dropped a red checker just after she kinged him for the fourth time. She was on her way to winning their weekly checker game. As she lifted her head up from the floor, her twinkling blue eyes just inches from his face, he had the immediate urge to kiss her. But instead, he froze, reminding himself that this pretty girl reported directly to him. Ethically, it was the wrong thing to do, date one of his subordinates. He had promised himself that he'd never stoop to such unprofessional behavior. It could only go wrong in the end. So he stopped himself and recommitted himself to enjoying Ally's friendship, but nothing more. After hearing the sweet woman's remarks about Ally tonight, he couldn't help but smile. It was funny how this little elderly stranger put them together as more than just coworker and boss.

On the top deck, Ally, Verena, and the teens spent over an hour with Carlos singing an array of popular cowboy tunes. Cold drinks and barbecued chicken and hamburgers and hot dogs, with all the trimmings, were set up by the poolside for Teen Scene club members to enjoy. As the ship pulled out into the Atlantic at 9:00 in the evening, "Western Night" activities were well underway.

As Carlos finished his last song, Verena yelled out, "That was really fun. You guys are amazing singers. Let's give Carlos a big hand for his music."

Several teens stood up and cheered; some of the boys raised their fists in the air and howled, "Carlos. Carlos." More clapping, teen girls flashing photos.

"Okay everyone, it's time to party up on the pool deck," Verena managed to shout above the roar of the teens. "Let's go! Follow me, and don't forget to clean up your trash before you leave." She started to lead the way to the elevators, as the teens scrambled, picking up their paper plates. "Remember," Verena continued, "we recycle on *The Prism of the Deep Blue Sea,* so plastic cups in the blue bin. *Ja?* Thank you."

Chapter Seventeen

Sail Away from Gibraltar

Jake was a 6' 3" dream. He was an Australian Bondi Beach surfer with blond sun-streaked hair and a lean yet muscular body. That night he was wearing tight faded jeans and brown leather cowboy boots.

"Is that a badge on your vest, cowboy? Are you by chance the new sheriff in town?" Ally said, looking up at the Australian hunk, flirtatiously.

He nodded, beaming at her.

"Well, twirl my lasso, I didn't realize that I had a date with a lawman. Hmm, not sure if I'm quite ready for this."

He pulled her to him. "I'm ready for you little lady," he said with a fake John Wayne twang. His Aussie accent stuck out and stole the scene.

Ally grinned. I wish I had the chemistry with this hunk. But it's still early in their relationship, she tried to convince herself. They had a quick soda and a charbroiled burger from the poolside barbecue station.

Carlos caught her eye as she sat on a tall stool joking with Jake. He sauntered over in his noisy cowboy chaps and spurs.

"Well little darlin', are you all set to two-step with your ever-loving cruise director? The band is almost set up for the 'Western Night' sail-away party. Yes ma'am, you sure are lookin' fine tonight!" Carlos glanced over at Jake. "And you too!" He feigned fanning himself to fight the intense sexual heat being generated by the suntanned hunky Australian.

Ally giggled. "Well, Mr. Mendano, I must admit, you've got a much better Western twang than this Aussie boy here. You remember my friend Jake, don't you?"

Carlos nodded. "Hee haw," he said, wishing the Aussie was checking him out as much as he was going over every inch of Ally's body. "Such gorgeous heteros! You really get on my nerves," he joked.

Ally smiled and took a final sip of her coke. She took Carlos's hand. "Time for us to shake a boot. See you later, Jake." She pecked the tall cowboy on the cheek. "But whoa, you're going to join in our line dance lesson, aren't you?"

"I wouldn't miss it for the world. Once you start up the music, I'll be lining up with the crowd, but I'll stay in the back row for obvious reasons." Jake motioned with his hand above his head, to emphasize his height. "I'm what they call vertically gifted."

"You spoke too soon, mate. Look behind you." She playfully jabbed him in the arm. "See that guy over there? I think he's a Ruskie, but I don't know his name. He works in the laundry room I think. He must be what maybe 6 feet 5 inches? At least that! Compared to him, well, you're a shrimp. You just can't top that," she said, smiling.

Jake tipped his cowboy hat. "Whoo whee. You've got a point." He removed his hat and slapped his knee. Sitting atop the stool, he pulled her to him and kissed her lightly on her freckled nose, connecting with her sky blue eyes. "I'd like to get to know you better, Ally. You look adorable, tonight."

Carlos took the hint and cleared his throat. "Hmm hmm. Things are heating up around here. Time for me to exit stage left, Ally. The crowd is certainly gathering. Let's get this party started. I'm going up there to talk to the band and make sure they know the sequence of tunes I expect from them. *Ay caramba,* they should be playing already." He pursed his lips, shook his head, and rushed away.

Leo picked up a load of dirty towels and transferred them to the rolling laundry cart. Fucking towels, I hate this job, he thought. They have me coming up to the pool deck now when I'm trying to stay away from the god-damn guests. Head down, he looked at his cell phone to check whether Nadia had texted him yet with the when and where of the identified teen target for tonight.

Jake took Ally's hand. "After the dancing, I'll see you. Okay, little lady?"

"Well, y-yes but not until much later. You remember I will be working with Verena with the Teen Scene club for a few hours. But I'll meet you here on the pool deck by the bar let's say at 11 o'clock? We can have a drink and maybe dance a little."

He tried to control his disappointment since he had completely forgotten about Ally's commitment tonight with the teen club. *I want to shower this sweet girl with kisses, have tonight be ultra-romantic. At least, I'll have some time to figure that out,* he thought.

Up on stage, Carlos broke in on the microphone. *"Buenos noches,* ladies and gentlemen. I am Carlos Mendano, your cruise director. How do you like my outfit?"

The crowd went crazy—whistles and shouts from everywhere. The band began with a fiddle preamble.

"So, are y'all ready to learn the Electric Slide?"

Over a hundred western-clad cowboys and cowgirls yelled, "Yes!"

"Let me hear you!"

"Yes," the crowd screamed.

"Gotta go, cowboy," Ally said, pecking Jake one more time on the cheek, yelling so he could hear her above the cheering crowd.

She skipped away to join Carlos on the raised wooden platform. *Nice guy,* she thought, as she left the good-looking Aussie. *Unfortunately, I prefer the chiseled jaw of the Greek I'm in love with. If only I had the guts to give him a hint.* She considered how she might manage to politely excuse herself from Jake before midnight. *I like him, but don't want to lead him on about me. I wish I had more chemistry with him. Damn! It would take my mind off Christian.*

As she danced by Carlos's side, in perfect unison, she had a good time, losing herself in the Texas line dance music. Guests learned quickly and felt confident within about 15 minutes into the session. Ally spotted Jake at the back, the tall, rugged-looking surfer. She also watched how the women dancing around him had taken notice of him, smiling up at him and flirting between dances, while Carlos shouted out instructions. *If only*

I felt as taken with Jake as they do. The lesson ended with a grand finale as Carlos requested that participants put all they learned so far into the final dance.

They ended the one-hour country-western dance session with the Bayou City Twisters, Ally's favorite. The men in the crowd, mostly those who were already full of too much beer, occasionally gave her a whistle.

Carlos called out specific instructions, switching back and forth from his natural Spanish accent to an exaggerated Texas twang. "Touch right heel forward. Step right together. Touch left heel forward, step left together. Right heel forward, right toe back. You got it, folks!" He was in his element, having fun with the crowd.

Just as the dance came to an end, the ship's deep horn blasted out—one long blast alerting the surrounding ships and passengers that the ship was about to move. Then Captain Manzione took the mic.

"Good evening. This is your captain, Stavros Manzione. We are about to leave port. Thank you for all being back on board before our targeted sail-away time. Please wave goodbye to Gibraltar and to that large rock sitting atop this special city. You may not be able to make out the black rock very well in the dark, but trust me your appreciation to the hill monkeys will be heard. Enjoy your evening on board and the country- western-themed activities we have planned. Don't forget the parade in the promenade at 11:00 tonight. Over and out."

As the ship's horn blasted a final time, Ally stole away to meet Verena at the Teen Scene, according to plan. *Damn, I should have at least waved goodbye to Jake. What's wrong with me? Some kind of date I am.* As she exited the elevator on Deck 12, she spotted Verena, who was surrounded by two dozen or more teens clad in an assortment of cowboy hats, denim vests, jean jackets, and leather boots.

Verena yelled out, "Hey there Ally. Good timing. We're just about to go up to Deck 15 and have a country-western sing-a-long."

Carlos snuck up behind Ally as she reached Verena. He played his guitar and sang, "Oh, she'll be comin' round the mountain when she comes. She'll be comin' round the mountain when she comes."

Ally laughed. "Hey, I was just singing that tune in my room." She glee-fully joined in with Carlos. "Comin' round the mountain, comin' round the mountain, comin' round the mountain when she comes. Whoo Whoo!"

Some of the teens got in the spirit and started singing the next verse at the top of their lungs. Several girls rushed up to Ally, wanting to show off their get-ups and praise her about her western dancing demo up on the pool deck. Frieda, Marta, Sally, and Cloris compared cowgirl boots and then snapped photos as they made their way to the elevator on their way to Deck 15. Carlos followed in tow, playing his guitar and singing "Sweet Georgia Brown," smiling hello to the various passengers they en-countered along the way. The group of teens had grown to over forty now.

Carlos found an unoccupied chair on the deck. He plopped down, his guitar in hand. Verena and Ally encouraged the teens to join them. At first, some of the teens appeared shy, hesitant to sing. But gradually most of them got into the spirit of the themed evening. Several teens started practicing the line dances they just learned.

A shy girl named Leticia sat off to the side, watching the others. She had blonde pigtails and wore a plaid shirt, a short jean skirt, boots, a denim vest, and a wide-brimmed tan cowgirl hat. She fidgeted with the lasso in her hand. Leticia glanced at the crowd and eyed Ally. Wow, she thought, I wish I had her personality. Look at that crewmember. Everyone likes her. I guess I kind of look like her tonight in my cowgirl outfit, even down to the pigtails and lasso. But I'm so different. I just wish I could be like her, she thought.

Nadia stood off to the side, scouting out the teens from a distance. She noticed the blonde, pigtailed girl sitting alone on the perimeter of the deck. She was the other one I spotted last night. Leticia. She was shy, slender, reserved, and stunning to look at. A French accent, too. Nice! She looks about fifteen, maybe sixteen, years old. Da, she is perfect! Those long, naturally blonde locks and her slim figure will make us a lot of money. I must get her alone and make some arrangement for her to meet me privately later tonight. These girls are so easy to fool.

Chapter Eighteen

The Deep Blue Sea

As Ally rose from her deck chair, a dark-haired teenage girl approached her. "Um, excuse me, Ally. I'm Jasmine." The girl looked dejected. "I, um, I need your advice, if that's okay. Can we talk privately? It's a girl thing," she said hesitantly, as she hung her head, showing a hint of embarrassment.

"Well, sure," Ally gently responded. "Shall we stay up here where it's quiet? I think everyone else is headed to the pool deck. We could just move over to the far end where the mini golf course is located. Nobody's out there and we can talk—just you and me."

"Yes, okay. Thanks." The girl looked grateful.

They walked in silence in the gentle wind of the evening. Nobody was around. When they got to the edge of the mini golf course, not a passenger or crewmember was in sight. Ally led Jasmine to the wooden railing so they could look down at the ship's wake, which was lit up. They could see the white froth of the water being emitted from the engine and hear a slight rumbling sound coming from many decks below them.

"Dang, that wake looks beautiful from up here, doesn't it?" Ally gave Jasmine a friendly hug around the shoulders. The girl nodded and smiled. "So, what's going on with you? How can I help?"

"First, I need to tell you that I know you."

Ally was puzzled. "You know me?"

"Yes, I'm from Savannah, Georgia, just like you. I've seen you in our local newspaper. It was sometime over a year ago. I remember because I cut out your photo from the paper. Well, actually, I kept the picture and the article. You were standing with your dad. Isn't he Randolph Colette, the 'Cotton King'?"

"Why, y-yes." It felt strange to have someone pinpoint her as the Cotton's King's daughter way out here on the other side of the world.

"I thought it was so cool that you joined your father in donating $50,000 to the Savannah Women's Shelter. I was in that shelter with my mother, who had escaped from a domestic violence scene with my dad, I'm sorry to say. She managed to leave him before he killed her. Now she's just married a nice rich guy and we're on this cruise. It's their honeymoon. Incredible, isn't it?" She paused to catch her breath after talking so fast. "But Ally, I never forgot you and your wonderful father. You guys kind of saved our lives." Jasmine grabbed Ally and gave her a grateful hug.

"Is that why you wanted to talk to me tonight, to say thank you?"

"Well that was part of it. But, actually, I wanted to get your advice about a boy. Conrad. You know him? He's on this cruise and in the Teen Scene club. He was wearing that black cowboy hat tonight. You were sitting right by him. He's got wavy dark hair, large green eyes, and well, kind of a permanent five o'clock shadow. Totally sexy. You know the guy I'm describing?"

"Ah, Conrad. Yes, I noticed him. He's the cream of the crop. Very handsome."

"Yes, I think so, too. Actually, I wanted your opinion on something important." Jasmine suddenly held her stomach.

"What's wrong? Are you okay Jasmine?"

"Y-yes. Oh my God, I think I just got my period. I need to run to the restroom to take care of this."

"Of course. There's one close by, just inside, through those sliding glass doors. I'll wait right here for you. No worries."

Jasmine forced a smile, visibly in some physical distress, and dashed off. She shouted out her apologies. "I'm really sorry. I want your opinion on Conrad. Something happened this afternoon with him and I'm not sure what to do about it. I'll be right back."

"Yes, yes, go. I'll be here. Waiting."

Alone, Ally looked out to sea and then down below at the gushing wake of the ship. Her pigtails were flying in the wind. Ooh, that breeze seems to be picking up. She held her short jean skirt down so the wind didn't catch it and picked up her lasso from the deck chair just beside her, concerned that it might be whisked overboard. She saw him out of the corner of her eye, the unusually tall Russian crewmember who works in the laundry room. He was rolling a large laundry cart across the top deck. I hope Jasmine is okay, she thought. She's a bit lovesick I guess. I'd recognize those feelings anywhere, her mind suddenly flashing on Christian.

Leo came up behind Ally. Seeing the girl with blonde pigtails and a lasso in hand, about 5 feet 3 inches, he thought, that's her. That's Leticia, my target. She's a cute little thing. Before Ally could turn around, he took out the needle and jabbed her in the upper arm. The scene swam before her. She felt arms wrap around her, drag her, then pick her up. He's throwing me into some soft encasement, she thought, as he stuffed her into an extra-large black duffel bag, which sat inside the laundry cart, behind a curtain. Ally was scrunched up in a ball. She couldn't scream. Her mouth was numb, her body felt limp, like she was partially paralyzed. She looked into his cold eyes just before he zipped up the bag. What is he doing to me? What is he doing? Staring at the dark cloth around her, her eyes clouded over. Her brain swirled. Her chin was awkwardly pinned to her chest, making it hard for her to breathe. Her brain whirled round and round in circles, spiraling down into a dark tunnel. Spinning, spinning. Gray, black, white, black, gray. Then nothing.

Satisfied with having captured the girl, he closed the curtain and wheeled the cart quickly inside, through the automatic glass doors, into the designated staff work elevator, pressing the button down to Deck 2. He looked around as he exited. It was late, not a lot of activity on Deck 2. He found the remote locker area normally used by the day shift bridge crew. He lifted the weighted-down duffel bag and stuffed it into the deep and narrow cubby hole, then locked the locker door, twirling the lock so it couldn't be reopened without the right five-digit code numbers.

In less than hour, at close to midnight, he hoisted the duffel bag from the locker, unzipping it to see if she was still unconscious. She moved, just a little. He picked up the pink foam log he nabbed this morning from the water aerobics area. He looked at the girl's face one more time. Her eyes were trying to open. Good, she's regaining consciousness, precisely as planned. He grinned as he pulled the duffel bag from the locker, placing the lock firmly in the deep pocket of his trousers. He stared into her face. Cute nose. Nice freckles. Lovely. Very natural, he thought. Another fifteen-year-old beauty. Nadia, she has a good eye. She could be older actually. He took a closer look. Whatever. She was still a stunner whether she looked fifteen or eighteen. He placed the long foam roller inside the zipped bag, leaving the zipper completely unzipped, the foam roller sitting just inside the bag on top of the girl's body.

He then dragged the duffel bag to the wooden railing and looked down. Only a couple of decks and she'll hit the water. He could see the wake of the ship as the engines pumped along. With both hands, using his well-developed upper body, he hoisted up the duffel bag and dropped it overboard. Ach, that's heavy. A body is always awkward and cumbersome, even if it's a petite teenager. Hard work. I better get paid well for this. Time to call Nadia and give her my update.

Cold and wet, Ally was petrified. I can't get out of this thing. Oh God. I'm in the ocean. Whatever the hell thing I am in, it's plunging deeper and deeper. Fuzzy, but conscious, Ally quickly pieced together her predicament. Holy crap. She felt the foam roller above her and intuitively pushed it upward with all her might, until it popped out of the unzipped heavy cloth bag. Using all of her physical strength, she kept pushing up, determined to release herself from this compartment. She fell, then repeated the process three more times, pushing up and out harder and harder. Her upper body broke out of the bag, but one of her boots got caught on something. Damn it. What the hell? She pressed down her left boot and tried to unhook what appeared to be the strap of the cloth bag from her right boot. She finally freed herself, kicking the bag away from her. She kept kicking, as she held onto the foam roller in the black freezing water.

I'm going up. I'm going up. Her mind raced as she held on tightly and concentrated on one thing, kicking up, all the time wishing she could lose the boots, but it was impossible to do. The weight of everything she was wearing seemed to be dragging her back down. But she was determined. Air, I need air. An object rose out of her jean skirt pocket. She watched her pager fall down, down to the depths of the sea. She realized how much salty water she had swallowed. Push, kick, she told herself. Frantically dog-paddling, she could detect the s urface of the water above her.

Snapshots of her childhood flashed before her mind's eye. She could see her father tucking her in bed. The scene shifted to him placing some cotton seeds in her small hand, while she sat wearing her white-trimmed sun hat in the hot field. Her father kissed her forehead and whispered, "You are the Princess of Cotton … the Princess of Cotton." His voice echoed in her head. She came back to her current circumstances. God. Oh my God. I'm going to do this. She continued to kick her legs. An image of her mother trickled into her conscientiousness. Her inebriated mother sat by the poolside of their house, a daiquiri in hand, a sour expression on her face. "Goodbye my child. Goodbye. Don't fight it, Allison Rebecca. I'm alive but have been dead for a long time. Don't fight it." "No Mama, No. I don't want to die. I don't want to die."

Her face broke the water's surface. She spit out a mouthful of salty water. She gagged. She spit again, then gagged a second time. She tried to catch her breath and started to swim toward the ship's fading lights. She held onto the buoyant foam roller, watching *The Prism of The Deep Blue Sea* putter indifferently away. The sky was clear. The sea around her was calm, but ice cold. She squinted, vaguely making out what looked like the city lights of Gibraltar, but land still seemed very far away. Geez, I felt like Houdini getting out of that bag. She tried to yell out, but it was hard to speak and there was nobody to hear her. Her brain hung in a fog. She recalled the sharp stab into her arm. The sting. An injection of some drug that knocked me out. She couldn't tell how long she'd been in the water. She was confused and in shock, her thinking jumbled.

Out of the black came a light beaming brightly on the water. She could hear a voice from afar. Is it my imagination? No, no it's real. She wanted to survive, to see Christian again, confess her feelings for him—full disclosure. A boat. Thank God, it's a man in a small boat.

"Girl. Hey girl! Look over here. Are you there?"

She could hear his thickly accented voice. It was someone searching for her. She turned. "Yes, yes, over here. Over here!" She waved one hand furiously. "I'm here, in front of you, to your right."

While Karl was busy rescuing the cowgirl with the blonde pigtails, Leo made a call to his sister.

"Da?"

"It's Leo. I nabbed the girl. She's already overboard in the water."

Nadia paused in disbelief, not comprehending what her brother was saying. "What do you mean, Leo? I'm standing here on the pool deck and staring at the girl at this very moment. I've made all the arrangements. She will be there on the top deck in 10 minutes, so you can grab her, drug her, stuff her in the cubby, and then tumble the bag into the ocean, as planned. I've arranged for her to meet me on the top deck expecting a private talk with me."

"Are you fucking kidding me, Nadia? I've already thrown the girl overboard."

"Nyet, Leo. Who did you grab? What girl did you throw over?"

"The cowgirl. Cute. Long blonde hair in pigtails. A lasso in her hand. About 5 feet 3 inches tall. Tan-colored cowgirl hat, short jean skirt, jean vest. What do you mean, who did I take? I did exactly what you told me. Picked her up by the mini golf course on the top deck."

Incensed, Nadia exploded, "You cretin! You were too early. You weren't scheduled to grab her for another 15 minutes. Fuck. What did you do, Leo?"

"I-I'm not sure. I took a different girl, I guess."

"Well, who was it? I have no idea what girl you took. Was she French?"

"French? Who the hell knows. I didn't listen to her talk, I jabbed her from behind with the needle, just like we planned. Karl was out there ready in his boat. I'm sure that he's picked her up by now. She'll have to do, Nadia. She's a beauty, in any case. Does it really matter if it's a different girl than the one you targeted?"

Disgusted with her brother, she disconnected. Which girl is he talking about? Her selected target, Leticia, was sitting right there. I better tell her to forget about our one-on- one meeting tonight.

The man speeded up in his motorboat. That must be the girl bobbing up and down, but I think it's too early. He looked down to check his backlit waterproof wristwatch. She wasn't supposed to be in the water for another hour. He came up close to the girl, reached out his arm, and yelled, "Come on girl, try to grasp my arm. Wait, first grab this life preserver." He threw it into the water. It landed less than a foot from her body.

This man must be from the Spanish Coast Guard, she thought, but with the beam shining on the water, she noticed that there were no letters printed on the side of the boat. And the white life preserver now in the water had no lettering on it either. Maybe it was printed on the side below the waterline. It was odd.

She reached out for the life preserver. "I got it. Thanks," she shouted. The boy who introduced Nadia to prostitution back in Russia some years ago, now twenty-nine years old, stood there pulling the desperate blonde closer to his chartered boat. She released her grip on the foam roller she had been hugging desperately up to this moment, and watched it float away. The water was cold, but it felt like black silk around her—serene.

She thought back to what had happened so far tonight, the sequence of mind-blowing circumstances—a Russian laundry worker drugging her, stuffing her into some kind of duffel bag, and then dumping her into the Atlantic Ocean. Unbelievable! But thank God she was being picked up and it seemed like it was happening very quickly after being tossed overboard. Like magic, good luck was now knocking on her door. As she was pulled closer to the small craft, the man's face became more visible. He was in his mid to late twenties and appeared to be Scandinavian, maybe even Russian. Russian? Oh God. She wanted to turn and swim away, but where to? Where could she go? She'd never make it to land even though she could see the dim lights off the coast of Spain. Both of them, Russians. They must be linked, the crew laundry worker and this man rescuing her. Shit. Shit. Nothing else for me to do now but play dumb. Play dumb Ally Collette.

He grabbed her hand, sensing some hesitance from the girl. "Come on, take my hand, and hold on tight. I'm going to swing you up here on deck."

She obeyed, now fully recognizing his accent to be Russian. When she landed on the slick deck, she was thrown facedown. Her soaked clothes felt heavy; her cowgirl boots, full of water, still covered her feet. She could feel her cell phone, still zipped into the pocket of her jean vest, pressing into her flesh. Why is the man pushing down on me? Her face was smashed sideways, her right cheek flush with the metal deck.

"Ach," he bellowed. "My back. You're going to kill me. Those clothes you have on are too heavy. Maybe I need to remove them. *Nyet.* I'm in too much of a hurry."

My intuition was right on, she thought. Bad men, both of them, the tall Russian on board the ship and now this one. No doubt in my mind. God damn it.

He pulled her right hand behind her back and then grabbed her left wrist, tying the two together with a rope. He whispered in her ear: "Little Leticia, you are a pretty one. And for us, that's excellent news." He shoved his face down near her cheek, pushing down on her back and straightening her pigtails, while her cheek was still pressed to the hard metal floor. He touched her hair. "Nice pigtails, little one."

She wriggled. "Let me go, you pig. You don't want to deal with me. I can run circles around you!" Her intention was to show strength. That's what she learned from her father. Never show weakness especially when you don't have the advantage. You can pretend certain things to throw off your attacker, but never show submission. "You asshole, release me and just drop me off on the coast. I'll find my way. I don't need your help." I'll just keep talking, throw him off, she thought.

"Hmm, fifteen years old." He sat up, letting her squirm, which only served to tighten the ropes around her wrists pulled behind her. "You seem mature for your age and much more feisty than I expected." He thought those dumb ass back street Russians found me a pretty teenager who acts twice her age and doesn't stop talking—the exact opposite in terms of typical personality to be targeted for sex trafficking. Oh well. He rolled her over and playfully pulled her pigtails. "You are a little cowgirl tonight. *Da?*"

She reflexively lifted her body and kicked him as hard as she could, right in the balls. He tumbled down on the hard metal deck. He reached for the other rope from his belt loop. Ally squirmed, trying to get up on her feet. The boat rocked and she fell down, her boots slipping and sliding on the slippery deck.

He grabbed her left leg, pulling her toward him. "Agh. Gotcha." He scrambled to his knees and reached for her right leg, yanking both her limbs together and tying the rope tight around her ankles. "Agh. There! Scream your head off, you little cunt. American, huh? I thought you were supposed to be French. Leticia, the French girl, I was told. " He looked puzzled.

Shit, I just blew my cover, Ally realized. Wait, this guy is dumb enough. She started to speak in short French phrases: *"Je parle francais. Je pense que vous etes un imbecile. Laissez moi! Laissez moi!.* I've been living in America, Savannah, Georgia, for seven years now, so my *Francais* is rusty. What's it to you? *Pourquoi?"* Pourquoi?"

She kicked her bound feet, trying to get out of the tight ropes. She knew she couldn't do it, but wanted to show that she's steamed about it. At least I still have my cell phone. The goon has no idea. It must be waterlogged, for sure. But I heard somewhere that if you stick it in a bowl of rice or something like that it can dry it out and make it usable. I just need to keep these clothes on, no matter what. He disappeared for a moment, then drug out something behind him from the other side of the deck. He picked her up like a bundle of hay and lowered her into a wooden crate. She wriggled, causing her to be dumped into it with a jolt. Startled and scared, she laid there, her back now aching, mentally off balance, and staring up at the brute.

"Ohh, I'm sorry, my pretty. You should have kept still." He chuckled. "I hope that didn't hurt too much. After all, I need to keep you in one piece. After we fix you up with a scrub and a bath, some new clothes, and some pretty ribbons and baubles, you'll look as lovely as ever. You'll be perfect for our wealthy clients. *Da.* Too bad I can't take you back to Russia. I'd have a picnic selling your ass to my sex-starved comrades."

"Please, please, let's just talk. You see, I don't hold grudges. Let's make a d—"

She didn't get a chance to finish her plea. He unknotted the soaking wet red kerchief from her neck, wadded it up, then stuffed it in her mouth, before she could say another word. "That's enough, cowgirl. No more chit-chat. You certainly are a pretty little thing, but much too talkative. I hope the other girl we got has the sense to keep her mouth shut." He threw a blanket on top of her and slammed the wooden lid shut.

Did he say the other girl? There's another girl. Can it be Amy Skyler? She wanted to ask the man, but it was no use. The more she fidgeted, the worse she felt. Her boots seemed hardened, rigid, the sharp-edged leather digging into her skin, and the left one, in particular, felt like it was cutting into the middle of her left calf. A dripping-wet pigtail was wrapped across her face, unnerving her. The neckerchief in her mouth had produced a disgusting salty taste. She tried to push it out with her tongue. Her attempts were useless, only wedging it further down. She stopped moving and lay there thinking about what the man said. They were going to clean me up and then dress me up, probably dress her up too. Then what?

Jasmine stood at the ship's railing on the top deck by the mini golf course. What happened to Ally? She's disappeared. I thought maybe she went off somewhere for a few minutes, but she hasn't come back. She pulled her sweater around her shoulders. It was getting windy. Maybe Ally's at the pool party waiting for me to show up. I took a long time in the restroom. God, I hate having my period.

On the pool deck, Verena entertained the teens, who were laughing and singing along to the band's country-western tunes. Many were dancing and shouting hee-haw.

A shy French girl named Leticia stood off to the side. She watched the crowd but felt uncomfortable in the party scene. Her blonde pigtails flopped back and forth in the wind. Her wide-brimmed cowgirl hat almost blew off her head. She caught it and tightened the clasp under her chin. She thought about leaving, retiring to her family's stateroom and maybe curling up with a Guy de Maupassant novel. Leticia enjoyed reading the classics, in French as well as in English. She was happy to call it an early night.

Chapter Nineteen

The Gate to Hell

Nadia sat on the bed in her cabin, feeling the stress, unable to sleep most of the endless night. The clock read 6:20. Almost time to get up anyway. She couldn't seem to breathe, the walls of her cabin closing in on her. What girl did the idiot grab? She looked across the room and stared out to sea through the small round porthole. The sun was shining. Rays of light crawled in and traversed the walls of the modest space as the ship rocked. Not too far above sea level on Deck 3, she could see and hear the waves slapping into the side of the ship. Her body quivered.

She engaged in the sex trafficking business for the money, but it was more than that. She had a physical reaction when a deal was done, when a transaction was completed. A jolt of exhilaration traveled through her body. She felt like a scientist, a genius, an artist. She was the creator of the master plan, and when everything fell into place, she felt elated. She was the one who selected the girls and gave directions on how, when, and where to snatch each one of them. Leo, Gorby, and even Karl were like her assistants, her underlings, blindly following her orders to achieve their end.

She was the one who came up with the cruise ship idea in the first place. Sure, Karl had a brainstorm when he recruited Nadia and her two brothers, but Nadia was the one who excelled at planning and implementing their brilliant schemes. Karl's niche was more in the area of communicating with the potential buyers, with those wealthy and twisted gentlemen from remote parts of the world, and arranging the exchange of money and young women. And even then he was using a Japanese middleman to make his transactions.

After things went so wrong last night, Nadia felt forlorn. Images of her father reaching under her nightgown and having his way with her tormented her. Feeling like that lost little girl again, she was frightened and longed to escape her current reality. In her mind, she invented scenarios where she was somewhere else, maybe in America or better yet in France, working in a Parisian boutique, possibly doing a little modeling on the side for extra money. Twice a week, she'd study ballet again, perhaps become an extra at the French Opera House.

She turned her head and looked into the mirror, the same rectangular wall mirror provided to each non-officer crewmember onboard the ship. She sat cross-legged on her bed, leaning against her pillow, and stared at the reflection in the mirror, her slender torso, her long black hair cascading over her shoulders, her large dark eyes, which, this morning, though alluring, were bloodshot and puffy. She couldn't help but admire her own raw beauty. No one could deny her that attribute, she thought.

Why did I take this path to destruction? Sex trafficking, surely a gate to hell.

She sobbed, crying out, "Mama. My poor mama." I left her alone and now my sister will marry and leave her to rot with that bastard of a husband, my fucking, no-good father. I should have killed him instead of running away with my two feeble brothers.

Get yourself together, she told herself as she rose from her bed. It was time to shower and get ready to meet up with Verena, the homely little German, for the usual morning gig with the Teen Scene. I need to keep her under my spell, she thought. Maybe I can glean from her which girl is missing. We know it's not the targeted Leticia, the intended little blonde French girl. "*Skata,*" she shouted. Picking up her nightgown from the floor, she tossed it at her reflection in the mirror, then grabbed a tissue and dabbed her moist eyes. I'm such a fool! A failure.

Chapter Twenty

No Scruples

Karl hid out in the boat until 4:00 in the morning and then motored up to the small Spanish dock just 10 miles down the coast from Gibraltar. It was a deserted, crumbling dock. No services available. Nobody around. He jumped out and tied up the small boat, ran down the path, and found his rented black truck parked behind an abandoned dump-site full of rusted boat parts, old furniture, and piles of trash. Seabirds swooped in and picked at the large open plastic bags, but swiftly took flight again into the air, disgruntled and still hungry. Slim pickings here boys. God, this place is worse than my pathetic village in Russia, he thought.

Headlights turned off, he drove the vehicle closer to the dilapidated dock, as close to his boat as he could get, and retrieved a beat-up metal dolly from the bed of the truck. He had strong arms and managed to slide the wooden crate from the boat down the short ramp and onto the dolly, turning it carefully on its side. He could hear her body sliding upon the turn. Then he heard her thumping, kicking her feet. It didn't matter, not a soul about in this godforsaken place. The truck was equipped with a hydraulic lift, which he used to raise the crate to the truck bed. He jumped in, opened the crate, and gazed at the girl, who looked a mess. Her hair seemed to have dried in two thick clumped-up pigtails. Her eyes were open and were the deepest blue he had ever seen. Black eye makeup was smeared under each eye. The stink of her damp clothes almost made him heave. He noticed her short jean skirt, became slightly titillated, and laughed.

"Oh, I would like to fuck you, little darling, but I need to show some restraint. I'm a married man." He jumped down out of the truck and yelled back to her. "Oops, almost forgot my stuff. That would be so disappointing for you."

He rushed back to the boat and grabbed a brown leather bag from the dark cabin, threw the boat's ignition keys down on the cabin floor, snapped up his pea coat from the built-in sofa, looking around for anything else belonging to him, and bolted, heading back to the truck. The crate was open, the lid lying down by its side. Ally tried to yell out, which was useless with the red bandana still shoved in her mouth. He could hear her muffled cries. He considered that maybe he should give her some water and then changed his mind, thinking that she'd scream her head off if he removed the kerchief from her mouth. He'd rather be cautious.

He opened the leather bag and took out a small oblong cloth pouch that held a hypodermic needle. He reached for it, carefully spilling some liquid from its pointed end. Ally watched in terror as he lunged inside the wooden crate, the needle in hand, her eyes open wide. How can this situation get any worse? She struggled, wishing she could magically break out of these ropes. The sting of the needle. She was falling, falling into a deep, dark trench. Before she lost consciousness, she could feel her father's presence. She saw him in her mind's eye reaching out his arm and soothing her. "My poor Ally, my poor little princess. Let me help you, precious. Let me help you."

Karl smiled as he watched her lose consciousness within less than 5 seconds, enjoying complete control of this frisky yet now helpless girl. She'll be out for several hours, he thought, long enough to get to the Marbella airstrip and load this crate onto the chartered jet headed for Fairoaks Airport near London. The pilot will be waiting for him.

Everywhere Karl's been in Spain, he's used a German alias, having craftily stolen a German passport under the name Henrik Schmidt. There will be no trace of Karl in Spain or for that matter anywhere in Europe. The man's passport picture actually resembles Karl, and anyway, the man is dead. Having read the newspaper back in Moscow, he came across news about a German man from Munich, only two years older than Karl, who, traveling alone, had suddenly gripped his heart while on a walking tour, falling dead on the pavement not far from the Kremlin. Upon reading the obituary, Karl noted the name of the local Russian funeral home handling the man's small memorial service. He read in the obituary that no family or traveling companions had come forward in Moscow and no German family members could be located. Breaking into the funeral home's morgue late at night, Karl found the German's personal belongings tucked inside a wooden box that sat in an unlocked desk drawer. The box included a German passport, three major credit cards, 7,500 rubles, and 375 euros. He took everything from the small box except a set of car keys evidently provided by a local Moscow car rental company. He started to flee out the window, but suddenly stopped in his tracks, turning back for the car keys, realizing that the rental car was most likely parked somewhere near the dead man's hotel. Of course, he could use the car. It was perfect. Noting the car's license plate number on the key fob, Karl located the vehicle and then drove it away, parking it just four blocks from his apartment building in Moscow, where he lived with his young family. Two days later, he used the stolen rental car to get to the airport, hopping the first flight to the south of Spain, disguised as Henrik Schmidt, German national.

Once in Marbella, he rented a black Ford truck and drove it to Gibraltar, where he proceeded to lease a small motorboat with a powerful engine. He congratulated himself on his ingenuity, as he drove the truck in the early morning light, loaded up with the nailed-shut wooden crate, headed for the Marbella airstrip. He had been careful to drill several air holes in the large box. Of course, the girl needed to breathe. Based on his calculations, he figured he'd arrive at the runway at Fairoaks within less than four hours, where he'd meet up with Gorby for the sex slave trade. Gorby would have the first girl who was grabbed from *The Prism of the Deep Blue Sea*. Karl felt a sense of pride as he sped down the narrow coastal highway, wishing he could share his clever achievements with someone. But his wife knew nothing of his criminal career, and he wanted to keep it that way, especially with the new baby just born two months ago.

He wished that Nadia was close by and they could drink to their accomplishments achieved over the past few days. He still had feelings for the tall, slender Russian, whose career he had launched, shaping her to become a great success, with a promising future. He would like that open, raw intimacy that he couldn't seem to get with his wife. He and Nadia were well matched, both smart, cagey, inventive, and hungry to make big money whether legally or not. Neither had any scruples. They could spill their guts to each other without inhibition and occasionally screw their brains out without any guilt or promise of something deeper between them. He acknowledged that Nadia was now a jaded criminal, with no interest in romance. With his wife, he had simplicity and peace, an oasis away from his shady world of sex trafficking and prostitution.

Chapter Twenty-One

Covering the Bases

Verena awakened, having slept barely an hour. Her pillows were off the bed and she was sprawled out, her head flat on the mattress. Twisting and turning all night, she had tried to get her intense feelings for Nadia out of her head. She had missed Nadia last night. Every crewmember had been fully absorbed in the country-western activities happening around the ship. Nadia ran the upscale restaurant's big western cuisine extravaganza. Verena had come by and watched Nadia from the designer handbag shop just opposite the restaurant, observing her new lover performing her usual work duties, following with her eyes as Nadia escorted a couple to their table and then greeted another family that was getting ready to dine.

The gorgeous Russian was dressed in saloon girl attire. Her colorful red, green, and black plaid taffeta skirt, hemmed at the knees, flounced over thick petticoats. Her breasts spilled out from the white frothy fabric of her blouse. Around her neck was a black velvet ribbon, a large green gem dangling at her cleavage. As she moved, the skirt swung around, her petticoats making a scratchy sound. In her long raven black hair, she wore two tall red feathers, attached to a black-sequined elastic headband. On her legs she wore black tights and on her feet black patent-leather high heels. She was an arresting vision to behold.

Verena's mouth almost fell open as she secretly gazed at the stunning woman. When Nadia led the next group to their table, Verena quickly fled the scene. She didn't want to risk being caught as a voyeur.

Now, with the bright sunlight beaming in and falling across her bed, Verena wondered about her behavior, her obsession with the Russian beauty. Am I too consumed with Nadia? Hell, I don't care. She reached down on the carpet, grabbing the pillows she had thrown down earlier. I'm in love with her. She hugged a pillow, as if it were her lover.

I want to give Nadia something. Yes, a gift to show her how excited I am about the possibility of us becoming more seriously involved. Verena turned her head and eyed the photo of her white fluffy Cheshire cat in the small jeweled pewter picture frame on the nightstand. Her cat Seigfried, also known affectionately as Siggy, now lived at home in Munich with her brother, Martin. Verena reached for the framed photo and grinned at the snow-white cat sporting a miniature cowboy hat, his furry head pitched to one side as if pleading for treats and wishing his owner would quickly remove the silly hat. She laughed out loud, recalling Siggy's saucy feline personality, so perfectly represented in this photograph. It would make Nadia smile and give her more of a window on Verena's sense of humor. The fancy frame was decorated with tiny Swarovski blue crystals. The sun caught the edges and patterns of colorful light flashed on the wall. Verena sprung up from the bed. I need to wrap it and put it in a pretty bag with a personal note. I can leave it by her door this morning. She'll see it when she leaves to go to breakfast.

She hastily showered and dressed, wrapped the gift, and wrote a message on a card. She didn't sign the card just in case someone else picked up the bag outside Nadia's door. She quickly walked down the Deck 3 corridor, rushing past dozens of crewmember cabin doors. Arriving at Cabin 3129, she placed the gift bag down on the floor propped up against the door. As she bent down, the door unexpectedly opened. Nadia was at first startled to see the girl kneeling on the carpet.

"Verena," she said tersely. The German girl jumped up, the gift bag in hand. "Oh Verena," she sung out, immediately changing her tone. "My love, are you checking up on me?" She giggled. Verena was without words. "Please, come in for a minute. You need a proper good morning," she purred. Once inside, Verena was led to Nadia's bed. "Sit back and let me see you in the morning light. You look so pretty today." The wrapped gift fell out of the small bag onto the bed.

Verena blushed. "Oh Nadia, I apologize. I didn't mean to disturb you. I just wanted to leave this—"

Nadia placed two fingers on the girl's lips. "Shh my *Fraulein*. No need to explain yourself. I was just teasing you about checking up on me. I'm happy to see you." She placed a long kiss on Verena's mouth and ran her fingers through her cropped pageboy. "You are so sweet. Now, what is this? Something for me?" She picked up the small package, took out the little card, and read it aloud. "To the most beautiful Russian. You make my heart sing! Love, Siggy." Nadia laughed. "Siggy? Who is that? May I open the gift?"

"*Ja,* please."

Nadia ripped off the paper and removed the crystal-framed photograph. She fell back next to Verena on the small bed and raised the framed photo in the air above them. "How darling. Is this your cat?"

"*Ja.* It's Siggy, my cat from home. I wanted to give you this little frame and well, I thought Siggy's funny expression would amuse you."

"*Da. Da.*" The sun caught some of the frame's crystals. The two women giggled. *"Spacebo. Spacebo."* Thanking Verena, Nadia held the framed photo to her chest, pressing it close to her heart, then glanced down at her watch. "Oh, Verena, I must go." She rose from the bed, brushed down her clothes, and pulled Verena up, leading her briskly to the cabin door. Inside, Verena was jumping over the moon. It wasn't just an isolated one-night stand.

"Your gift is precious to me," Nadia proclaimed, tenderly brushing Verena's cheek with the back of her hand. It will remind me of you when I'm not in your sweet company." She placed a long soft kiss on her lips. "Come, we must go. Verena, I may be a little late with the teens this morning. I have something important to take care of and need a little more time. Would that be okay?"

"*Ja,* sure, not a problem, Nadia. I have a sports activity planned for the boys already. I'll just include the girls until you arrive for their cosmetics session."

"Thank you. Oh Verena, you won't forget our little secret, right? Say nothing to anyone about me talking with Amy Skyler. *Da?*"

"*Ja. Ja.* You can trust me."

Nadia shut the door, happy to rid herself of Verena. She took a quick glance in the mirror, adjusting her clothes so she looked immaculate once again. Stupid girl. But I like the little gift. She picked up the picture frame, admiring it.

Suddenly she was reminded of home, the day before her father began sexually fondling his young daughter. It was a Sunday. Nadia's mama had the day off and planned to take her daughter to the playground, leaving the two younger boys with their father. They sat on a park bench, bundled up in heavy coats, the wind whipping across their faces, the air cold, the winter's first snow about to fall, mother and daughter sharing a bar of chocolate, while feeding stale breadcrumbs to the pigeons. She was just an innocent eight-year-old enjoying an afternoon with her hardworking mama.

Nadia returned her focus to the present, dashing from her cabin, headed for the hotel front desk on Deck 5. She wanted to see Christian for just a few moments, maybe sneak a kiss and root around for any clue as to what girl was grabbed last night. Damn, it's already after 7:30. I want to catch him before he's surrounded by hotel guests and that annoying girl, Ally, with her syrupy Southern accent.

Chapter Twenty-Two

Questions and More Questions

Christian stared down at his screen. No passengers complaining at the reception desk yet. It was 7:37, and no sign of Ally, now more than 35 minutes late to work. At 7:20, he had buzzed her cabin phone, but there had been no answer. At 7:30, he had paged her, but no response. Now it was 7:38. She must be in bed with that guy, that sun-baked surfer-looking dude from Australia. Could she have gone to bed with him? Christian shuffled items around his desk and then scanned his email a second time. His instinctive response to Ally not showing up for work was a disturbing sense of unrest and agitation. He noticed the time again. It was 7:41. Now I'm starting to worry about her. It's just not like Ally to be late for work. The desk bell rang, startling him out of his thoughts.

"Excuse me, Mr. Stephanopolous, would you like to join me for a cup of coffee? My treat." Her black hair was pulled back from her face in a long ponytail. Her eyes jumped out at him as she flashed her coquettish smile. "I've missed you, Christian." Nadia looked down on the counter, her long fingers reaching out to circle the tip of the desk bell. "You know what I'm saying?"

"N-Nadia. You look terrific. Um. I-I'd like to take a break, but my colleague, Ally, is late this morning. Only two of us on shift until 9:00. Honestly, I don't know what's happened to her. She's never late to work."

Nadia lost her flirtatious mood, as her brain fixated on Ally not show-ing up. "Well, she probably overslept," she said, as her head started to pound, strange images flashing through her mind. "My darling, there are *no* passengers lining up here. They must be sleeping after last night's partying. Can we just steal a moment away together?" She looked behind him and pointed to the door to the hotel manager's office, now Christian's office. "How about we go into your new office. Hmm? Just for a few minutes, *da*?"

"I'd like to, Nadia. I mean I'd love to actually, but ..."

She kept moving, her finger still going back and forth over the shiny gold metal bell. She reached up and touched his cheek. "I'm starving for you, my love. Have you been missing me, too?" she said.

He fumbled nervously. "Okay, I can take just a couple of minutes. I've been thinking about you, too."

She circled around the counter as he opened the office door, taking one last look around to see if any passengers were approaching the Reception area. Nobody. When the door closed behind them, she threw her arms around his neck.

"So, how did your evening go last night?" he asked, looking into her eyes.

"Rather boring without you," she said dejectedly. "How about your evening? Anything interesting happen? Did they find that missing girl, Amy Skyler?"

"No signs of her. But I haven't seen Packo, our chief security officer, around yet this morning. No Packo and no Ally." He shrugged his shoulders.

The sound of Ally's name sent shivers up and down Nadia's spine, distracting her from the seduction at hand. She dropped her arms.

"I wanted to steal a kiss, but it looks like you have your hands full. I'm feeling a bit like a nuisance. I better go." Her eyes looked down at the floor as she moved to the door.

He came up to her, pulling her over to the office desk, as he leaned up against it, his arms hugging her waist. "Of course, I missed you. You don't know how long I've waited for the other night to happen between us. Nadia, you're my dream girl, my fantasy. From the first day I saw you,

I wanted to touch you. But, at the moment, I'm concerned about Ally, my good friend and colleague. I need to get out there and try to find her, make sure she's all right."

She sprinkled him with soft kisses, landing on his left ear. "Good to hear all that, my love. I understand. Do you want me to phone Verena and tell her I'll be late to the teen club? I could stay with you for a while, help you out here at Reception?" She kissed his left ear again.

"Um, well ..."

The door burst open. Packo was stunned to see Christian with his arms around this gorgeous creature.

"Excuse me." He cleared his throat. "I mean ..."

Nadia was startled, glaring up at the man who just entered. Packo felt the chill.

Christian stiffened. "Hey Packo. Um, just give us a minute. Would you? I-I ..."

"*Si. Si.* No *problemo.* I will wait out here."

Before he left, she flashed her best smile at the overweight security officer, having recognized him. Nadia was feeling flustered. She didn't want to have Packo discover them like this. She didn't want to attract attention from any of the senior officers.

Stupid Russian, she said to herself, thinking of Leo. "I-I better go, Christian." She wanted to get away, think about the circumstances surrounding her. Why was Ally missing? Her brain was jumbled, her thoughts colliding. Vivid snapshots flickered through her mind: Ally in her blonde pigtails last night. Click. Ally wearing her short jean cowgirl skirt. Click. Ally holding a cowboy lasso in her hand. Click. Ally being shoved by Leo into an oversized duffel bag. Oh shit. I must get away. Hide. But instead she smiled and looked at Christian with her large dark eyes.

"*Da. Da.* Let's connect later. Christian, are you free tonight?" She slid the palm of her hand down the front of his jacket, attempting to show no noticeable quiver in her movements or any hesitation in her voice. She needed him to remain loyal to her. She had to stay connected to him to keep abreast of the latest developments, but right now she had to leave or she would collapse from high anxiety.

"I'm scheduled to finish work at 8:00 tonight," he offered. "Maybe after your restaurant shift, we can meet. Would that work? I want to spend time with you."

She'd won the battle. "Sure. How about we meet in your cabin at about 10 o'clock? I would love to see you but out of this formal attire. I can bring my candle along again for a romantic evening."

He could already envision her in the flickering light. "See you then, Nadia." He opened the office door for her. Packo looked over at them, rolling his eyes, then watched the fetching woman glide around the Reception counter and swing her hips elegantly down the promenade.

"Wow. Now that's a very fine piece of ass, *amigo.* Probably the sweetest one on this whole fucking ship. What's her name? I've seen her around. How could I miss that?"

"Her name is Nadia. Yes, she's very special. She hostesses at the Crystal Dining Experience."

"Man oh man, she is something. So, you are here alone this morning? It's unusual, no?"

"Hang on, Packo. Sorry, but I need to check something again." Christian punched in Ally's cabin number on the phone set, trying to contact her for the third time this morning. The phone buzzed several times. No answer. The computer screen told him it was 8:15. Ally was over an hour late at this point. "Packo, you didn't see Ally come by while I was in there with Nadia, did you?"

"No. I guess your cute little partner didn't show up today. Is that what's got your pants in a twist? Poor guy. Two women on your mind? Ah, my poor troubled friend." Packo jabbed him in the shoulder. "I have new respect for you. New respect! To be honest, *amigo,* I always pictured you with Ally, not so much with Nadia. You seem simpatico together. Please, no offense intended."

Christian smiled. "Hmm, I admit that there is an undeniable chemistry between myself and Ally, but not a romance." He looked into

Packo's eyes. "I'm worried sick. This is so out of character for her. Whenever she's sick or, hell, even when she's 10 minutes late, I get a phone call to let me know, and that scenario is rare. She's basically a maniac for being on time." He paced the Reception area. Packo leaned against the office door and followed him with his eyes, realizing the Greek's feelings for Ally were well beyond platonic even if the man himself didn't consciously realize it. Christian's concern escalated. "Just where the bloody hell is she?"

"What does your gut tell you, my friend? What do you think happened to Ally?"

Christian's eyes began to tear up. He stared at his computer screen and shook his head. "A hole is being drilled in my gut at the moment by some chilling thoughts. Maybe she's with that guy, Jake. Do you know him? He's a bartender at the pool bar. Australian. Tall guy. Bleached-blond hair. Looks like a surfer. Personally, I think he's a simpleton."

Packo laughed. He shoved Christian away from his computer. "So, you don't have romantic feelings for her? *Si,* I can see that! Let me look him up. I have access to the employee database. Turn around, please. You might be the new hotel manager, but employee information is still hands-off to you. I'll find this Aussie on the system."

A disgruntled passenger approached the counter. The grimace on the man's face gave him away. Christian attended to the guest while Packo tapped in his secure password and scanned the database for any employee with Jake as the first name. Christian had a brief conversation with the guest, who appeared to be in a hurry, and handed the man two re-keyed cruise cards.

"Packo, we really need to get these cruise cards right in the first place. They're getting demagnitized too often. Guests are disgusted with the damn things not working." He threw the passenger's old cruise cards in the waste bin behind him. "Damn it, what's happened to Ally? It's 8:35. She's now one hour and 35 minutes late. "

"Bingo. I found him in the database. I'm going to his cabin. Stay here."

"But Packo, I want to ..."

Ilze rushed in behind the reception desk and stood beside Christian. "Good morning, Christian." She nodded at Packo. "I'm just dropping off my purse and getting a quick coffee with Tanya from the casino. I'll be back at 9:00. Where's Ally?"

"Ilze, please, can you cancel your coffee and start working now? I'm not sure where Ally is. She's late. I need to go check on her."

"Sure, I'll text Tanya that I can't meet her," Ilze responded. "It's not a problem."

He turned to Packo. "I'm coming with you to talk to that guy."

Packo shrugged. "Fine with me. Let's go. But I do the talking."

Christian turned off his computer and looked over at Ilze. "Be back soon. Thanks Ilze." He rushed to catch up with Packo, who was already halfway down the promenade.

Upon opening the door, Jake was bewildered. I must be in trouble, he thought. Shit, the head of security.

Packo entered the cabin, immediately pulling open the door to the compact bathroom to see if anyone was behind it, then scoured the small space looking for any evidence of Ally having been there. He didn't make eye contact with Jake, but kept moving. Christian followed, closing Jake's cabin door behind him.

"W-what are you looking for? Is there some problem?" Jake nervously inquired.

"Are you edgy, boy? You seem to have the jitters. I'm Packo Suarez. You know me, chief security officer, and this is our hotel manager, Christian Stephanopolous. Sit down, please. I have some questions for you."

He stood there staring at Packo. "But why? At least you can ..."

"Sit down!"

He obeyed and sat on the bed but persisted with another question. "Am I in some kind of trouble?"

"Well, I'm not exactly sure."

Packo looked down at Jake's desk, which he saw was covered with surfer magazines, paperwork, an open pack of cigarettes, a book of matches, a laptop, and an assortment of clothing, including underwear

and grungy socks. A surfboard was propped up against the wardrobe attached by a few hefty elastic bicycle ties, hinging the board to the closet
door. A wetsuit hung on the hook by the shower, towels all over the floor.
Packo winced and slammed the bathroom door shut, his facial expression suggesting disgust with the clutter.

"You certainly have a lot of stuff in this tiny cabin. There's no mystery
as to your favorite hobbies, *amigo*." He bent down close to Jake's unshaven tanned face and asked, "So, where were you last night? Did you
spend any time with Ally Collette?"

"Um, y-yes I did. Why? Something happen to her?"

"I'm asking the questions. Your job is to answer them. Maybe later I
will entertain a question from you. *Comprendes*?"

Jake closed his mouth, which was now shaped in the perfect "o". He
squirmed, seated on his bed, shirtless, his muscles bulging.

"Well, yeah, I saw Ally last night before she led the line dance session with Carlos. We had some dinner together. I was supposed to
meet her later on the pool deck at 10 o'clock, but she didn't show up.
I rang her up in her cabin at about 10:30, but no answer. I-I guess she
just blew me off. " Jake spoke with a lazy Australian slur. "She probably went off with some other guy. You know how pretty girls can be.
Know what I mean?"

Christian couldn't keep from erupting. He wanted to punch this cocky
Adonis in the mouth. He pushed Packo away from Jake and took the
Aussie by the arm, pulling him up from the bed.

"So, you were with her and then she didn't show up? Are you sure,
Jake? Tell us what really happened. You must have seen her later. She-
she's not in her cabin, and she didn't show up for work this morning." He
pushed him full force up against the surfboard. "Ally's not with some other
guy. She's not like that. She's a decent girl."

Packo jumped in, peeling Christian from the boy, thinking, Wow, this
Greek kid's got some balls, going after this guy who must be at least 4
inches taller than him, and with some impressive muscles. "Come on.
Calm down, Christian," he urged.

The Aussie was stunned by the hotel manager's aggression. "Look. Look, I like this girl. She's fun and I-I'm just glad you're not accusing me of something else. What can I do? That's all the information I know."

Packo moved closer to Jake. "What you can do, my friend, is say nothing about this to anyone." He pointed his bulky index finger in his face. "You understand? We need to investigate Ally's disappearance, and I don't want to hear any gossip from any crew about this. Got it, mate?"

"Y-yes. I got it. Very clearly."

"Look Jake, I-I'm sorry I blew up. I have strong feelings about Ally. She's, well, she's my good friend and I-I—"

Packo interrupted. "He's in love with the girl," he said, placing his fingers to his lips, and whispering, his sarcasm slipping out. "But it's our little secret, between us guys. *Si?*"

Christian could think of nothing to say. He followed Packo out of Jake's cabin into the hallway vestibule. Packo swung his arm around Christian's shoulders, pulling him close as they walked down the narrow corridor.

"We will find her. Let's go to her cabin. I have a master key. Cabin 3158, *si?*"

"Yes. Thanks Packo. Thanks."

When they got to Cabin 3158, Packo stopped. "Have you been inside before?"

"No. Never. We always spend time in the staff lounge or go ashore when we hang out together."

Christian was almost afraid to step through the door, but his curiosity tiptoed through him like an excited child. He wanted to feel her around him, any way he could get it. The stateroom was empty. Same floor plan as Jake's. Everything was tidy, the bed made properly with two lacey pink pillows propped up to the wall. An opulent, antique, gold-leafed framed mirror hung awkwardly on the closet door. A Georgia Tech bumper sticker was plastered across the top of the mirror. He could see Ally's clothes peeking out, all hung perfectly on plastic hangers. All blouses hung together, all skirts in another section, a couple of uniforms at the far end. "A neat freak," Packo said, smiling at Christian. A snapshot of Ally and an older man was taped to the bottom of the wall mirror, both of them wearing wide-brimmed straw hats, standing in a field.

Christian sat down on the chair in front of her desk and hung his head in his hands. He felt like crying. He was even more worried than earlier. He looked up. "You're right, Packo. I'm in love with her. I've been such a moron. Hooking up with Nadia and not realizing what's most important to me."

"A moron? No, no. That Nadia creature is a magnificent female specimen. How could you resist a woman like that? And anyway, you weren't ready for love, until now."

Christian's eyes welled up with tears of sorrow, tears of regret. He walked over to her desk and pulled a tissue from a red-velvet-covered box. When he looked down at her laptop, he accidentally tapped the keyboard and was instantly faced with a screen shot of Ally and himself staring back at him.

He burst out, "Oh my God." Half laughing and half crying, he exclaimed, "It's us." Ally was smiling in the photograph. Christian's eyebrows were raised; he was laughing, his hand up in the air, attempting to block the photograph from being taken. They were standing together in the staff lounge by the ping-pong table, just after Ally won the tournament, and he lost the 10 euros, the bill Ally held up in full view as she snapped the selfie. It was an absurd action shot, the impromptu variety that Ally loved to take.

Packo stared at the computer screen. "That's you two falling in love, isn't it?"

"Yes, it might have happened right at that moment. I just didn't recognize it." Christian scanned the small cabin with his tearful eyes. "Packo, I-I don't see her cowgirl outfit anywhere. Do you? That means she didn't come back here last night."

"Quite the sleuth, aren't you?" Packo looked around, pulling the closet door open, thumbing through the items of clothing. "Good eye. No cowgirl clothes in sight. It doesn't look good. I think we better get to the captain on this."

Chapter Twenty-Three

Sexy Girls for Big Money

The small Citation jet made a smooth landing on the Fairoaks runway, the commuter airport just off the M25 motorway, 35 minutes from central London. Conrad, the pilot, assisted Karl in sliding the wooden crate down the airplane's ramp and onto the tarmac. A black flat-bed truck met Karl 30 feet from the airplane. Karl passed an envelope to the corpulent bearded pilot as the dark gray sky exploded in a downpour of heavy rain. The pilot climbed the stairs, jumped back in the plane, and started up his engine.

"Hurry. Load the crate," Karl yelled out to the Asian truck driver.

The airport was for light aircraft, housing two resident training schools and the London Transport Flying Club, and was also utilized as a maintenance airfield. It was quiet, not much activity on an early Sunday morning.

Karl lit a rolled-up cigarette as he sat down in the front passenger seat without uttering a word. He was catching a cold and his head ached.

"You want the Kawasaki hangar, is that right?" the driver asked.

"*Da*. Yes. That's the one."

Karl's eyes darted from side to side, slightly frazzled, a variety of aches sweeping through his body. His left ear was bothering him, not yet cleared from the fast airplane descent. It took just over 10 minutes to get to the remotely located hangar, which appeared to be under construction, scaffolding around both sides of the structure. The steel exterior's metal siding was rusted in many places and much of the blue paint was peeled away.

The hangar door slid open, revealing a distinct contrast in scenery. Two unusually large Japanese men stood at either side of the door. No planes were inside the enormous hangar. A large metal cage was set at the back right corner of the space. What looked like two black leather hair salon chairs sat in the center of the cage. A Caucasian girl sat in one of the chairs. At the front of the hangar, just off to the right, two expensive black leather couches were set adjacent to each other, a rectangular, black, bamboo coffee table and a set of four chrome leather-cushioned folding chairs arranged around the couches. A bar and three tall metallic stools were situated at the front left side of the hangar, just opposite the leather couches. A rectangular, oriental-style, designer rug was spread under the furniture. The scene resembled a sleek contemporary living room in a high-rise apartment building in downtown Tokyo. Two elegant, lacquered, Japanese, black and white shoji room dividers were positioned around the perimeter of the living-room space.

Gorby, the Russian, stood near the cage, drinking from a bottle half full of vodka. The two Japanese men, resembling massive Sumo wrestlers, clad in black overalls, jumped down from the tall bar stools. They quickly moved to retrieve the wooden crate from the flat-bed truck, water sliding down their shaved heads, as they carried the load into the hangar and placed it down in the area between the living-room space and the cage. Karl's eyes widened at the scene before him as the hangar door closed behind him with a jolt. He could hear the truck driving away.

A well-dressed, slender Japanese man with a martini glass in his hand sat at the bar. He stubbed out his cigarette in an ashtray and hopped down from his stool, heading straight for the wooden crate that just arrived.

Some muted human sounds came from the cage at the back of the hangar. Karl glanced to the back. He saw a red-haired girl sitting in one of the two leather beauty parlor chairs. The girl was bound to the chair, each wrist in metal handcuffs attached to an armrest.

Amy Skyler awakened from her drug-induced nightmare with the noise of the hangar door banging shut. "Mummy, Mummy," she mumbled.

She opened her heavy eyes and for the first time caught a glimpse of the new environment around her. Her throat felt sore and her body cold. She looked down at her manacled wrists. Is this somehow the first step to me becoming a prostitute? Are they planning to rape me in this cage? It didn't matter to her that she was unable to run, imprisoned like some animal. Hazy thoughts trailed through her drugged mind. I'll stay alive for as long as they let me. I can't fight them. I can't.

What the hell is that girl saying back there? Karl wondered, annoyed. Is she going to be cooperative through the trading process? He spotted Gorby, who was standing at the back of the hangar, peering into the locked cage where the red-haired girl sat in one of the salon chairs. "Hey Gorby, is she behaving for you?" Karl questioned.

"*Da.* She's docile, seems to be in and out of her own private world. She's not a threat. She should behave without too much drugging."

The Japanese man in an impeccably cut pinstripe suit stared down at the wooden crate for a moment, then walked over to greet Karl. "Good to see you again, Karl." He held out his hand, offering a handshake.

Karl eagerly took the Asian's hand, applying a degree of pressure, letting the man know, without words, who was strongest. The Asian man registered the tight squeeze but chose to show no reaction.

"*Da.* Good to see you too, Takahashi," the Russian smirked, knowing the Asian felt the power in his grip.

"Is this the other girl, then?" Takahashi pointed to the rain-stained crate.

"*Da.*"

"Open it up. Let's see what she looks like," Takahashi commanded. "We need to hustle, gentlemen. Less than two hours to get these girls ready for sale. My women are waiting, ready to start the transition. The buyers will be arriving on schedule, one Japanese and the other from Saudi Arabia. They expect high quality from you Russians. They were very much impressed with the last batch of girls you supplied to them from South America."

"*Da,* this one in the crate is a beauty but high-spirited."

Takahashi shot Karl a piercing glance. "You have drugs to quiet her down if needed, yes?"

Karl nodded. Gorby walked over to the crate, curious to see the new girl.

Takahashi continued, "The one we have already in the cage has long red hair. And the other one in the crate, what color is her hair?"

"Blonde. Blue eyes"

"Good. That sounds perfect for our clients. Dark eyes and dark hair are unacceptable to them. This time they want fair-haired meat."

Ally could hear men speaking just outside the box she was enclosed in although their voices were garbled. Her head felt groggy. She opened her eyes to the black surrounding her, a sliver of light seeping through one corner of the crate. Her limbs were not responding, but she could gradually sense some hint of life returning to her body. She felt a cramp in her neck, and she had a pronounced ache in her right shoulder. Someone was prying open the crate with a tool. Her mouth felt dry, like she'd been chewing on a cotton ball. I wish I were in those cotton fields right now instead of here, she mused. Now she could hear the Russian's voice clearly.

"Take a look, Takahashi. The bluest eyes you've ever seen, I guarantee. And what Arabian prince wouldn't want to fuck that body."

Takahashi's satisfied grin dissolved. "No need for crude language, Karl. You may prefer that crude style in Russia, but in the East we have more decorum." He set his martini glass down on the coffee table, sat down on the couch, and lit another slim cigarette, placed in his silver-plated cigarette holder. He detested the unrefined demeanor of the Russians.

Gorby sat on the opposite end of the couch, making eye contact with Karl. The youngest of the Russian brothers grinned, a silver tooth peeking out of the upper right side of his mouth. He was enjoying the tension between the two opposing cultures. He liked to see Karl squirm a little, finally show some vulnerability, something rare to behold from his usually self-assured comrade and leader.

Karl threw the wooden crate's lid down on the stone floor, seeking to unnerve Takahashi with the loud crashing sound, but again, there was no physical reaction from the Asian.

Takahashi peered inside the box and found two blue eyes looking up at him. He curiously wondered about the Old West costume the girl was wearing, but he appreciated the short jean skirt, which served to show off her shapely tanned legs. A few buttons dangled from threads on her fitted jean vest, her breasts heaving out of the shirt underneath that appeared to be ripped and missing some of its buttons. Her hair was matted and hanging in two clumps of stringy blonde pigtails. He hoped that her ankles were slender under those cowgirl boots. Despite her dirty clothing and disheveled appearance, she was quite a beauty, he noted.

Takahashi took a drag on his cigarette and said, "You have outdone yourself, Karl. This one is a diamond, I agree, but perhaps somewhat older than fifteen or sixteen, the age requested. But I think she'll work just fine. Let's see what she looks like out of the box."

Gorby sprang up from the sofa, rubbing his palms together as he approached the crate. He peered into the box, bent down to scoop Ally out, and lifted her up in his muscular arms. He carried her over to the cage, jiggling keys in one hand as he clenched Ally tightly in his arms. She felt disoriented and had little energy to fight him.

He yelled out to the other men, "She feels good, Karl. Can I play with her a little before we make the trade?" Gorby was a weak man, his bravado unable to conceal his low self-esteem.

Takahashi twisted his face in dissatisfaction. This clash of cultures unnerved him. He looked over at Karl. "Tell your Russian colleague to resist the urge to shoot off his mouth. I don't want him touching her. He could transmit some sexual disease. I will tolerate no more crass behavior from him."

The pricey vodka had gone to Gorby's head. He erupted with thunderous laughter, satisfied to have agitated Takahashi. "It's a joke, my friend," he yelled out. "Just some humor to lighten things up. I won't touch her." Still chuckling, he pushed the cage door open and dropped Ally down on the other salon chair. She felt pain in every part of her body, her right shoulder most of all.

Karl looked down at the designer rug and took a long drag on his rolled-up cigarette, silently grateful for Gorby's deliberate insult to the pompous Takahashi. Gorby noticed the red-haired girl staring over at the blonde, who now appeared to be more clear-headed. He pulled out a set of handcuffs from his jacket pocket and clasped each of Ally's wrists to the chair's armrests, the red-haired girl sitting a foot away in the other salon chair. He left the cage, locked it, and sauntered back to the living-room setting. Picking up his bottle of vodka from the coffee table, he took a long swig, then settled down on the sofa next to Karl. He looked over at Takahashi and scratched his crotch.

Takahashi watched Gorby with disgust. "Enough! It's time to dress and bathe these girls." He glanced over at the two Japanese Sumos in black overalls standing to one side of the hangar. Clapping his hands twice, Takahashi jerked his head back and forth, signaling them to get to work.

The two men slid the hangar door open to the sound of the pouring rain. A white van was parked just outside. Two petite Japanese women also clad in dark overalls jumped out of the front seat. One opened the back of the van, and together they pulled a large leather trunk down a short ramp from the vehicle. Dragging it into the dimly lit hangar, they set it at the back near the cage. The tiny women rushed back out to the van, their clothes quickly becoming soaked by the rain. They carried in a metal tub, hauling it back to just outside the cage, one of them then pulling a long hose out from inside the tub. The Russians stared as if observing a well-choreographed Asian dance production. One of the women quickly hooked up the hose to a water faucet on the back wall and then turned on the faucet. They were unusually graceful yet quick with their tiny feet.

Takahashi paced back and forth, waiting for the women to begin the girls' transformation. He looked over at Karl. "Tell your partner to open the cage so my staff can get started," he gruffly ordered.

Karl nodded at Gorby, who wanted instead to plant a fist in Takahashi's chiseled yellow face.

One woman began to fill the tub with water as the other poured in some pink liquid, creating a frothy bath full of bubbles. From the leather trunk, they took out a variety of cleaning supplies—soaps, washcloths, towels, sprays, shampoo, hairbrushes, lotions—placing each item on a plastic mat not far from the tub. Once everything was laid out, without words between them, the Asian women walked into the cage, stopped, and stood on either side of the chair where the red-haired Amy Skyler sat petrified.

Gorby unlocked the handcuffs and yanked Amy out of the chair. "Stand up. Time for your bath, little princess," he gruffly announced.

Amy's legs almost crumpled beneath her. The tiny women took the girl from his large arms, lifting her off the floor, their combined strength surprising to the Russian. One of the women attempted to comfort her, smiling at Amy, as they had her stand in front of the tub. She seemed bewildered and frightened. Amy was several inches taller than both of the petite women. One woman held a large towel up in front of Amy, as the other woman unbuttoned the girl's dirty clothes, and without expression, undressed her. Amy offered up no resistance. Her arms hung limply at her sides. She looked over at Ally, who still sat inside the cage, now fully alert and struggling with her handcuffs. Ally's anger was beginning to surge. She could see the big, slimy Russian brute peering over the towel at Amy's body, licking his lips, enjoying the sight before him.

Ally screamed out, "You idiots. Turn around, all of you. Have some decency!"

Takahashi snapped his fingers. "The blonde is right. Every man here needs to sit down and face the front of the hangar. And don't turn around until I get the word from Heiko. I'll let you know when it's okay."

The two Russians reluctantly moved to the sofa, both snickering, The Japanese Sumos scurried back to their bar stools, adjusting the seats to face the hangar's sliding door. Gorby grabbed his vodka bottle from the coffee table. Karl took a knife from his pocket and started picking at his fingernails.

Ally took in the whole scene. Damn. I need to get free. She looked out at Amy, who sat in the tub, one woman holding her upright, the other washing her hair. Amy doesn't look good, Ally thought. How could women, Japanese or otherwise, be okay with what's going on here? How can they dare to enable such indignity to women? Obviously brainwashed. Ally's mind clicked into focus. Oh God, they're fixing us up for some sort of trade, some kind of sale. They're sex traffickers, she suddenly realized. Oh my God.

She felt like she could explode with rage. She pushed herself back into the leather chair, her limbs tensing up. Another sharp pain shot through her right shoulder. Tumbling around in that crate must have injured her shoulder.

A hopeful thought hit her. My cell phone. Shit. It's zipped in the breast pocket of my vest. Her mind whirled, as she considered her options. She pressed her chest forward to the right, extending her upper body, the vest's zipper almost touching her right hand, which she could wriggle, despite being handcuffed. Her manacled hand couldn't quite grasp the zipper tab. Damn it. She sat up straighter and made another attempt to plunge herself forward, stretching out as far as she could, moving her bottom up the back of the chair, allowing her to expand her torso. Her shoulder pain worsened. She tried to ignore it. She could almost touch the dangle of the metal zipper tab on her vest. Thrusting her chest one more time, she caught onto it and zipped the pocket open, then pulled the phone out. Don't drop it, she told herself. What now? She managed to slip the cell phone between her thighs onto the chair's cushion and quickly sat on it. She raised her lower body up slightly from the chair, straining her leg muscles, and with her bottom again, guided the phone to the back of the seat, stretching out her legs and pushing it carefully into the seam between the seat cushion and the back of the chair. She could still feel the edge of the phone. Maneuvering her hips a few more times, she was satisfied that the phone was almost concealed behind the seat cushion. I don't know how the hell this is going to help us, but it's a first step, she thought.

One of the Japanese women glanced over at her and pointed. Crap, Ally thought. The woman saw what I did. The two women shuffled back into the cage, escorting a cleaned-up Amy Skyler back to her designated salon chair. Amy now wore a fluffy pink terrycloth bathrobe. Ally was relieved. I guess they didn't notice my cell phone shenanigans. Amy looked pale, but her face was angelic, nevertheless. Ally's heart broke. This girl was so young, and so visibly traumatized. The Japanese women sprinted back to the metal tub, running the faucet and adding more pink bubbles. Amy gazed out in the distance, her expression almost catatonic, disconnected from the scene around her.

She recalled a moment when she was maybe five or six years old, sitting in a wooden swing, a sunny day at Twickenham Park, her mummy pushing her higher and higher in the air. Frightened little Amy began to panic.

Her father stood in front of her. "Amy, you're flying, you're soaring!" He smiled, but then noticed his daughter's frazzled expression. "Honey, are you okay?"

"I'm scared Daddy," she whimpered. "Will you catch me if I fall?"

He nodded and held out his arms. "Of course, I'll catch you. You're fine, pumpkin. I'm spotting for you. Don't worry."

She tried to smile, feeling a sense of safety. She felt calm for a few brief seconds.

"Okay, Daddy. I love you. I love you." But the terror, her fear of heights, revisited, overtaking her. "No. No, I don't like it. Stop! Make Mummy stop! Please Daddy. Get me down."

The knot in her stomach tightened. Her mother paid no attention, continuing to push the wooden swing higher and higher, laughing with delight, even after hearing her child's plea to stop.

"Amy. Amy," Ally whispered. "Hang in there. I'm going to figure out our escape."

Startled out of her reverie, Amy focused her eyes on Ally's dirt-smudged face.

"Amy, I'm Ally Collette from the ship. Do you remember me?"

Amy nodded.

"Listen, we're going to get out of this. I promise. I think we're in some kind of airplane hangar." She glanced up at the metal wall on the right side of the cage and saw a hand-scribbled cardboard sign that read: "Loo, outside around back right corner. FO 35." "Loo? Amy, I think we might be in England. Loo, isn't that your word for 'bathroom'?"

Amy looked bewildered, but nodded her head. "Yes, we call it the loo. I want my daddy," Amy begged.

Tears welled up in Ally's eyes. "Oh Amy, I know. This is bad, but please trust me. You're not hurt physically, are you? They didn't touch you, did they?"

Amy's blue-green eyes stared into Ally's. She shook her head. "N-no, not yet," she mumbled in response.

"Good. I'll try to keep it that way. I'll think of something." She looked up again at the cardboard sign. "FO 35. I wonder what that means."

Amy shook her head.

The Japanese women rushed in without any suspicion of Ally harboring her cell phone. They signaled that they needed Gorby to un-cuff the other girl and re-cuff the red-haired one.

The smaller woman yelled out, "Takashasi-san."

The impeccably dressed Japanese man turned to the back of the hangar. He looked at Karl, not wanting to talk directly to Gorby. "Tell your comrade to get the keys and get to work. The other girl needs a bath."

Gorby rose and pushed past Takahashi, barely missing his slender frame. Ally looked over at Amy and winked, intending to offer her some confidence. Just as Gorby un-cuffed Ally, she kicked him hard in his chest. It was her only chance before she was off the chair to press her lower back one more time down into the leather seat and shove the edge of the cell phone into the space between the cushions.

"You little cunt," he shouted. "Get the drugs Karl. This one is a bitch."

Karl rolled his eyes. Nadia, what the fuck was she thinking, selecting this one out of all the teenage girls on that ship? He moved to the cage and snapped out his switchblade, holding it close to Ally's bewildered face.

"You want the drugs, my little dumpling? If you're not nice, I will need to quiet you before the buyers arrive. Or, shall I hurt this one instead?" He grabbed at Amy's robe, looked into her eyes, and held the blade at her cheek. He turned his head and locked eyes with Ally. "Which would you prefer?"

Ally realized that he didn't really want to mar their faces or their bodies if indeed she and Amy would be up for sale, but on the other hand, she didn't fully understand these thugs. They seemed unpredictable. Karl could see the confidence and intelligence in Ally's eyes. A sly one, he thought. He moved close to Ally, flashing the blade.

"You know we need to keep you looking good. *Da.* You're a smart little treasure. But we can present you in 'zombie' condition, although we may get a few pounds less for your ass. It's not my preference, but we can't spend any more time on your nonsense.

"Gorby," he shouted out, "bring me the drugs and the needle. Come—"

"N-no, okay, I'll cooperate," Ally interrupted. She sat back in the chair, obediently folding her clamped hands in her lap. "No drugs. I'll be quiet, no more fighting you."

"Good! Forget it, Gorby," he yelled. "It seems that I got the bitch's attention." He turned back to Ally. "Just one more hint of resistance from you, Blondie, and you *and* your chickadee girlfriend will be injected without any hesitation. *Da?*" He flipped his switchblade shut and shoved it back into his jacket pocket, bent down, and with his fingers pinched both of Ally's cheeks very hard. "We want you to look your prettiest." He chuckled. Ally was startled by his rough behavior, her face stinging from the pinches. "*Da.* You needed some color in those dimpled cheeks. We don't want you too pale for our clients."

Takahashi stood outside the cage, listening to the dialogue. He snapped his fingers, calling "Heiko."

The two Japanese women gently escorted Ally, each taking one hand and moving her to the metal tub just outside the cage. Takahashi signaled for all the men to resume their seated positions facing the front of the hangar. He ambled past Gorby, who started to watch with wide eyes as the women undressed Ally. He raised his hand at the back of Gorby's head, snapping his fingers twice by his right ear. Gorby spun around. It was Takahashi's turn to snicker at startling the depraved Russian.

Chapter Twenty-Four

Protest aboard The Prism

Dr. Mathew Caruthers and his wife, Sissy, rounded up their family for the evening entertainment at the Prism Theater. The theater, holding hundreds of seats, was at least two-thirds full that night, everyone gathered full of anticipation for the inaugural show, planned to begin at 7:00 p.m. Sitting in first row center were seventeen people, all part of the Caruthers' family, traveling together from Mink Creek, Idaho. Thirteen adults and four children formed the group. Several of them hid flyers under their seats. Before the show began, they all rose from their seats and separated across the theater, vigorously handing out flyers to passengers, who reacted as soon as they read the information. Many gasped in shock at what was written. Others nodded and responded with "Yes, we heard something about this."

The flyer read as follows:

A YOUNG TEENAGE GIRL IS MISSING FROM THIS SHIP!

AMY SKYLER HAS VANISHED!!

THE CAPTAIN AND CREW ARE DOING NOTHING TO FIND HER! WE, THE SHIP'S PASSENGERS, HAVE NOT BEEN FORMALLY INFORMED. CAPTAIN STAVROS MANZIONE IS PURPOSELY HIDING THIS INFORMATION FROM US! WE FIND THIS TOTALLY UNACCEPTABLE. WE MUST FIGHT BACK, AND HOLD HIM ACCOUNTABLE AS CAPTAIN. WHAT ELSE IS HE HIDING FROM US?

TONIGHT, WE MUST UNITE AS A TEAM OF CONCERNED PASSENGERS AND BE VOCAL! WE MUST DEMAND ALL THE INFORMATION AND A CLEAR PLAN OF ACTION!

The lights in the theater dimmed. The cruise director, Carlos Mendano, stood behind the curtain, while the band played several bars of background music, his standard introduction before he goes on stage. Red and blue lights flashed as he danced to center stage, then into the microphone, he sang "I'm Too Sexy." Carlos adored this entrance routine, and made the most of it. His intent was to set the mood for nothing but smiles and laughter and good cheer. "I'm too sexy for my love, too sexy for my love. Too sex-y," Carlos crooned, dipping and swaying, his arms out as if he was a showgirl in high heels. He glided across the stage to the beat of the music, laughing and pointing to the kids in their seats, as they screamed at his array of huge colorful feathers, resembling those of an oversized peacock, his plume boldly swooping out from his red-sequined costume.

As Carlos looked out at the audience as the music faded out, he realized that something was not quite right that night. The kids were laughing and screaming with enthusiasm, the usual reaction he gets with this opening number, but most of the adults looked disgruntled, some of them even angry. What the hell is going on here? he wondered. Yet he persevered, determined to entertain the audience and bring forth the usual reaction from the crowd.

"Am I too sexy for my clothes or what?" he said into the microphone. He paused and did one last twirl. "I just can't decide if I'm a Las Vegas showgirl or a cruise ship host." He giggled and shimmied as if performing a number from *La Cage Aux Folles*. "Good evening, ladies and gentlemen." He deepened his voice for a gravelly effect. "I am Carlos Mendano, your very sexy cruise director. Are you all ready for some fun?"

He didn't get much excitement in return from the crowd. Only one child's voice yelled out, "Go Carlos." Nevertheless, he plowed forward with the rest of his introductory patter. "Welcome to the Prism Theater! Before presenting our fabulous Prism of the Deep Blue Sea cast of talented dancers and singers, I'd like to first turn the stage over to our illustrious leader, who not only commands this great vessel, but as many of you know, can also belt out an aria equal to that of Pavarotti. Here he is folks, our very own Captain Stavros Manzione!"

Carlos kicked off the applause, expecting the audience to follow. But hardly anyone clapped. People mumbled to each other and then stared at the man walking out to the microphone. The captain wore a fitted black tuxedo, a red bow tie, and black patent-leather wingtips. His chest puffed out like a rooster, as he prepared to publicly welcome the guests to his ship, his kingdom on the sea.

Matt and Sissy Caruthers wasted no time. They charged up onto the stage along with several other members of their extended family, Sigmund, the service dog, at Sissy's side. A dozen or so additional passengers followed them. Five members of the Caruthers' family held large hand-painted signs attached to sticks. One sign read, "Save Amy Skyler! Find her now!" Two other signs both read, "The captain can't be trusted! He hides information!" A fourth featured a caricature of Captain Manzione singing out an aria with a word balloon that read, "I'm a liar! I know nothing about Amy Skyler!" A fifth sign read, "Security sucks on The Prism!" The protestors stood in a line, shaking their signs in the air, moving them up and down. The people on stage were in an uproar, gesturing to the audience to join their protest.

Dr. Mathew Caruthers grabbed the microphone from the captain as Manzione backed up, almost tripping over one of the sign holders. A security guard in the back of the auditorium paged Packo with a brief message: "Get to the Prism Theater quickly."

Caruthers spoke into the microphone: "We know about Amy Skyler. We know that she's missing from this ship. A fifteen-year-old girl was out two nights ago, having a good time with other teenagers, but she never returned to her stateroom. She is still nowhere to be found on this cruise ship! Amy Skyler has completely vanished! And Captain Manzione hid this from his passengers! Hid this from his so-called guests! We may all be in danger. Was Amy abducted? We want answers! And now!"

He started to chant, the group that stood with him on stage joining in. "We want answers! No more lies! We want answers! No more lies!" Dr. Caruthers raised his arms in the air with the rhythm of the chant, encouraging everyone sitting in their seats to get up on their feet and join in.

"We want answers! No more lies." People rose everywhere in the theater, out of their seats in the orchestra, in the mezzanine, and in the balcony. Several passengers moved into the aisles. The chanting became louder and more aggressive. "We want answers! No more lies! We want answers. No more lies!"

A woman sitting in the second row, aisle seat, left side of the theater, tried to get up and collapsed, falling to the deep blue carpet, clutching her chest. The captain watched in horror and snatched the microphone back from Matthew Caruthers.

"Security, please get medical assistance here right away."

People sitting around the woman gasped in astonishment. A man yelled out, "It's the captain's fault."

A chubby gray-haired woman ran up on stage. She rushed up to the microphone. "There's more. There's more! A crewmember is missing as well! I just heard this about an hour ago from one of the waiters. The captain is concealing this, too! Now two females are missing from this ship!"

The groans from the crowd turned into chaos. Some people sat down, horrified. Some held their hands to their mouths in disbelief. Others yelled out curses. "What the fuck is going on here? Bloody hell." The chants started up again. "We want answers! No more lies! We want answers! No more lies!" During the fracas, two medical assistants rushed to the woman in the second row and helped her into a wheelchair, then rolled her out of the theater. Tensions were high. Shouts and yells from passengers, old and young.

Manzione couldn't wait any longer. He needed to talk to these people. Just as he was about to bolt to the microphone, Packo jumped onto the stage with Christian following at his side, both hoping to reason with the crowd, protect their captain. But Manzione pushed them away, moving his gaze from Packo to Christian and back to Packo, exclaiming, "Please, I must respond on my own."

Packo backed off, signaling to the crowd of passengers on stage to move back and let the captain speak. They reluctantly stepped back.

Manzione bowed his head, and with sadness in his voice, said, "I'm sorry. Yes, I did hold back this important information. Please don't blame my security officer or my hotel manager. It was entirely my own decision to hold back what's happened." He choked up, swallowing hard, and as tears fell in salty drops down his cheeks, he continued, "I was afraid to make it public. I didn't want to create a panic on board. I am concerned like you. I-I lost my wife some years ago to a violent attack. My emotions have overtaken me over the past couple of days. My wrath surfaced, causing me to make poor decisions. I couldn't deal with it so I hid it from all of you! I-I'm afraid that these two females have in fact been abducted." He broke down, sobbing. Packo held him up. The captain struggled but again spoke into the microphone: "W-we think they've both been somehow removed from the ship."

A man in the audience shouted out, "in the middle of the freaking ocean?"

"Yes, I'm afraid so. Amy Skyler was likely taken off the coast of England on the first night at sea, and the female crew member, Allison Colette, was abducted last night not long after we left Gibraltar."

"Lock him up," a voice yelled from the back of the theater. "Lock up the captain! He can't be trusted." People screamed. Some blurted out, "Yes. Yes!" Others had other ideas they offered, trying to gain attention and speak their opinion.

A tall, slender woman with red eyes walked up the three steps at the side of the stage. Her head was down, looking at the floor. She wore black stretch pants and a royal blue and gray striped sweatshirt. Her long blonde hair was tied back. Packo recognized her. It's Wendy Skyler. She made her way to the microphone.

"It's my daughter who's missing—Amy Skyler."

The crowd was stunned, everyone silent. Women shook their heads, empathizing with this poor mother.

A man with an English accent, sitting about six rows from the stage, shouted, "You're a famous actress, aren't you? I know you from that show, *The Cornwall Sagas*."

Another woman stood and spoke out: "You're my favorite actress. I love your character."

With about 1,200 passengers from the U.K. out of the 3,750 passengers onboard, many recognized Wendy Skyler. They grew up with her character, Margot Henderson. People in the audience chattered frantically with animation, thrilled to see the celebrity on board and fully sympathizing with the tragedy that had befallen her.

Wendy fought back tears, attempting to get her composure and thoughts together for the rest of what she had to say. "Y-yes, I'm Wendy Skyler, a British television actress." She looked over to the left of the stage and held out her hand. "And this is my loving husband, Russell Skyler, a pillar of strength to me as we go through this very difficult time." He took his wife's hand and gently squeezed it. Wendy continued, "Yes, our daughter is missing. But you must all understand that Captain Manzione and Officers Suarez and Stephanopolous are all helping to find Amy. They are working frantically to locate her and the missing crewmember, Ally Collette. I trust them completely. Captain Manzione has contacted the International Maritime Police, who will be on board tonight, landing in a helicopter to do a formal investigation. I urge you all not to panic but instead please assist us by keeping your ears and eyes open for any clues as to what monster took our little girl." Wendy broke down, her shoulders dropping, her stamina diminishing. She began to sob. Russell led her away from the microphone, proud of his wife, honored to be her husband.

Packo spoke. "Ladies and gentlemen, we will continue with the show." He locked eyes with the bewildered Carlos Mendano, who stood there off to the side near the curtain, his giant feathers seeming to droop. "We understand if any of you choose to leave and forego this performance. That is your decision. As your chief security officer, I pledge to work with our captain, with our hotel manager, and with the International Maritime Police to solve these two terrible crimes. We will keep you all posted and be completely open with our progress from this point on."

The shouts and yells dissipated. Many people who were about to bolt from the theater now sat down in their seats patiently waiting for the show to begin. A few dozen passengers exited the theater. Christian put his arm around the captain and walked with him down the few steps off the stage and out the back of the theater. The relatively short distance felt like an eternity for both of them.

Chapter Twenty-Five

Caged yet Sitting Pretty

Amy and Ally were now dressed in princess attire in the cage, sitting awkwardly on the two leather salon chairs, cosmetically transformed. The two Japanese women stood around them, busy administering the finishing touches to their elaborate hair creations.

Ally's hair was piled on her head in a chignon twist, held together with several small sparkling crystal barrettes, a few long blonde strands of hair hanging in curls on either side of her face. Her dress was a tight-fitted black satin sheath, with a wide white sash at the waist, a small spray of black sequins adorning its center. The slit on the dress cut high on her thigh. She wore a single strand of white pearls at her neck. Her breasts were pushed up by the wired bra and a heaving cleavage spilled out. Her snow-white skin contrasted with the dark fabric of the dress. She wore pink lace thong panties under her clothes and a push-up black lace bra. White pearl imitation diamond earrings dangled from her ears. Long, fake, black eyelashes and light blue eye shadow decorated her eyes, candy red lipstick her lips. Deep pink blush emphasized her cheekbones. The finishing touch was a pair of white glittery stiletto heels on her feet, accentuating her shapely calves. She looked like a younger, sluttier version of herself.

For some reason, the scene reminded her of when she was a little girl getting ready to do a recital at the grand piano in the sitting room of her family's Savannah plantation mansion. Only this time it wasn't her father, Randolph Colette, showcasing her musical talent. This time, it was a gang of sex traffickers on the verge of selling her body and soul to some rich bottom feeders.

Amy slumped down in her chair, rocking slightly back and forth, mumbling to herself, "Mum, Dad, "I'm so sorry. I'm so sorry."

Ally could barely make out her words even though she was sitting so close to the girl. Amy was steadily retreating inside, trying her damnedest to block out the frightening scene around her. The handcuffs were off their wrists, the leg manacles were fastened, and the cage door had been locked.

Amy wore a forest-green velvet halter dress, the straps tied around her neck in a bow. Her long red hair fell across her bare shoulders. A green gem hung from the center of her cleavage. The short dress clung to her body, a touch of spandex in the fabric. Like Ally's dress, a high slit was cut up the right side of the dress, exposing her long legs. Matching forest-green satin stilettos, a size too small, hurt her feet. Beneath the clothes, she wore pink lace matching bra and panties.

Amy began to knock her head forward and back against the back of the salon chair, still muttering, "Mummy, Daddy, I'm so sorry."

"Amy. Amy. Please try to hold it together," Ally whispered. "We don't want them to drug us."

Ally pretended to yawn and moved her hand behind her lower back, digging in the seat for her cell phone. Heiko turned her head to the cage, peering at the girl, then turned back to continue cleaning out the metal tub with the white bath towel, while the other woman started to place all the beauty equipment back into the trunk. Waiting for when both Asian women's heads would be down, and they would be fully engaged in what they were doing, Ally retrieved the cell phone, and with lightning speed, shoved it into the left cup of her push-up wire bra, tucking it under her left breast. Ally's brain ran at mach speed, as she considered her next move. She had a brief moment of pure elation as she recalled the phone's screen lit up just as she was pushing it inside her bra. The phone must have dried out since her dunk in the ocean, and maybe, just maybe, it was actually in working condition. I don't think I can manage to shut it down, but I can at least turn the sound off. She slid her hand back down inside her bra as if adjusting it for comfort, the way women across the world do every day, but instead, she searched for the silencing button on her iPhone. Good, I found it. She slid the button to the left to mute it.

Takahashi yelled out. "Heiko."

Ally jumped, thinking again that she has been found out. He said something lengthy but with lightning speed in Japanese. Shit, Ally panicked inside.

Both women nodded. *"Hai, hai"* ("Yes, yes"). Heiko half grinned, bowing her head.

Takahashi picked up a fresh martini, handed to him by one of the men behind the bar. He picked off the olive from the plastic toothpick with his teeth, savoring its pickled flavor for a moment before chewing and swallowing. The Russians followed him to the cage for an inspection of the Asian women's work. The two white girls were now exquisitely prepared for the trade.

"Bravo. Bravo," Takahashi proclaimed.

The rest of the men in the hangar clustered around the outside of the cage and peered inside like children ready for a sweet treat. Gorby could not believe the transformation of the grubby girls into stunning works of art. He'd seen it before when they did the trade of the other two girls in the Caribbean, but he was still in awe of their swift handiwork. Downing the martini and handing the empty glass to one of his men, Takahashi stared inside the cage, admiring the finished products.

"These women are incredible artists. These girls look like two sexy yet elegant princesses. The keys, Gorby. Give them to me." It was the first time he directly addressed the crass second-tier Russian.

Abruptly extracting the set of keys from Gorby's hand, Takahashi unlocked the cage, eagerly entering and then circling the two girls, more intimately examining them. We must get rid of these heavy chairs and put the girls on those tall stools, he said to himself.

He then commanded: "Get two stools from the bar. We want these darlings to appear more inviting, delicious, three-dimensional. Make our two bidders yearn to touch them. I predict that we will make spectacular money today." Takahashi shouted more instructions in Japanese.

The two muscle-bound men rushed from the bar area, each carrying a tall stool. They placed the stools inside the large cage. The two Japanese women followed behind, each taking the hand of one of the girls and pulling her up from her salon chair. Ally wanted to push Heiko away and make a break for it, but she'd never be able to get Amy out with her, and inevitably she'd be stopped anyway. Then they would be drugged unconscious or close to it. Ally stood perfectly still next to tiny Heiko, cautious to not show a hint of resistance. The men proceeded to lift the first salon chair, carrying the heavy object out of the cage and placing it in the far corner of the hangar, then retrieving the second salon chair and relocating it next to its mate.

The stools were placed in the middle of the cage about 18 inches apart. The Asian women led each girl to her own stool, so they would sit tall, fixing their hair once again. Heiko turned to Takahashi and bowed deeply in his direction, signaling she had completed her task. Takahashi entered the cage and spoke in a hushed tone directly to the girls.

"Ladies, I'd like to let you both know that if we don't sell you to one of the two bidders, you will be dead in an hour." He puffed on his slim cigarette, blowing smoke near their faces. Tears streamed down Amy's face. He looked in her direction, his eyes narrowed and fierce. "That means you better stop those tears right now, or I'll have to pull you from the bidding war and do away with you before the bidders even arrive."

Heiko rushed over with a tissue, carefully wiping the wet tears sliding down Amy's cheeks. Then she retouched them with her powder puff and added some pink blush. Ally showed no visible reaction to the Japanese man's threats, coldly staring back at him.

"I want to see a smile on your face, sweet girl." He raised his voice, standing just a couple of inches from Amy. "Let me see it then," he commanded. Her eyes meet Ally's, who nodded, silently encouraging her to cooperate. Amy's mouth trembled. She smiled, pursing her lips together. "Yes, sweet girl, a Mona Lisa face will do. That's what we want to see." He left the cage. "I can tell you, if our buyers don't like you, you're dead!"

Chapter Twenty-Six

All-Points Bulletin

Within an hour of the captain's speech at the Prism Theater, the International Maritime Police helicopter made its landing on *The Prism of the Deep Blue Sea*. Crewmembers and members of the International Maritime Police (IMP) convened in Captain Stavros Manzione's office.

Marco Pezzetti led the IMP team on this case. A countryman of the captain, Pezzetti was instantly comfortable in Manzione's presence. Outfitted in a black and tan uniform, he spoke into a large walkie-talkie, enunciating his instructions for an All-Points Bulletin (APB), carefully reading the description of the two abducted girls, which Packo had documented in detail in a mini spiral notebook usually stuffed in his jacket pocket.

The captain, still shaken by the ordeal in the theater, sat quietly and listened to the dialogue between Christian, Packo, and Pezzetti. His focus of attention right now was to find the two girls. He would sacrifice anything to have a positive outcome, getting Amy Skyler back to her family and Ally back on board the ship.

Three of Pezzetti's men stood around the table, ready to act, do whatever was required. Packo's key staff members, Hans Tinker and two other security officers, leaned against the office wall, paying close attention to everything discussed.

"We need to sit tight and wait to hear of any news as a result of this APB. My men will meet with your security staff with specific instructions on how to do a second search of the ship for clues," Pezzetti said.

Christian's cell phone beeped. Maybe it's Ilze, he thought. He needed to connect with her at the front desk, see how she was handling things, and check on any burning passenger issues. Shit, maybe there's a problem.

"Captain, please excuse me for a few minutes," he said. "I have a message on my phone and need to stop by hotel Reception and see how everything is going."

Manzione tapped Christian on the shoulder, showing his gratitude. "I understand. Go Christian, and thank you for your support earlier," he said in a whisper.

"It's a tough, stressful time, sir. Glad to be of help."

He opened the door and rushed down the promenade toward the front desk. He saw Ilze talking to a guest in the distance, a third or fourth other guest waiting in the queue to be assisted. Christian stopped half-way down the busy thoroughfare, passengers around him dressed to the nines, many perusing the shops, guitar music spilling out of the Prism Pub, men and women downing beers inside at the bar tables.

He couldn't believe what he saw on his cell phone. It was Ally's name flashing on his screen. Ally? Oh my God. There was a voice message. She's alive. He stepped into the men's restroom across from the Prism Signature Shop and anxiously listened to the garbled message.

The sound quality was poor, muffled words, some inaudible. She was whispering. It was a conversation between Ally and Amy Skyler. He pulled out a small pad and pen, replayed it from the beginning, then furiously wrote down every word he could make out. The first segment was clear. Her Southern accent made him feel warm even though the words left shivers down his spine.

He heard: "Amy, hang in there. I'm figuring out our escape." [Pause.] "Amy, Amy, can you understand me?" [Pause.] "I'm Ally Collette from the ship. Remember me?" [Long pause.] "Loo outside hangar around back corner. SRY (C) FO35. Loo? Is that what that sign says?" [Pause.] "Amy, I think we might be in England. Loo, isn't that your word for 'bathroom'?" [Long pause.] [A faint voice of another girl.] "Y-yes?" [Pause.] "I want my ... I want my mum. Please." [The girl sounded panicked, fraught with fear.]

[Ally spoke again.] "Amy, I know. I know this is bad. But please trust me. You're not hurt ..." [Word inaudible.] "They didn't ..." [Several words inaudible.] [Long pause.] "Good. We're going to get out of this. I promise. Like jack rabbits in an open meadow, we are getting outta here. " [Long pause.] "One more question Amy, did a tall R ... "[Inaudible words.] "Did he throw you ...?" [Series of inaudible words.]

The message cut off, then the phone disconnected. His mouth dropped open. Christian tried to make sense of what he just heard. She must have mistakenly phoned me. He played the voicemail over three times, double checking his documentation for accuracy.

Exiting the restroom, he raced back to the captain's office, pushing the heavy door open. "Captain, sorry to interrupt, but I have new information about the missing girls." All eyes peered at Christian, who spoke passionately. "It was Ally. She must have accidentally pressed in my number on her cell phone, maybe 'butt-called' me. I'm not sure. She obviously didn't know she was actually calling me. Or maybe she did."

He put the phone down on the conference room table, turned up the volume as high as possible, and played the accidental voicemail. Ally's twang rang out, although in a deeper tone, and parts in a subdued whisper. The men listened, straining to make out some of the more muffled words. Christian clicked off the phone and sat down at the table. "I wrote it all down word for word, everything I could decipher." He then read what he had written out loud.

The IMP leader, Marco Pezzetti, acted quickly, zealously tapping on his laptop keyboard. They all watched him.

"Tell us what you're doing now, *amigo*," Packo impatiently said.

"I'm searching for airports in the U.K., checking for smaller ones, not hubs, airfields that might inconspicuously receive small jets or prop planes emanating from Spain." Disengaging with the group, he continued typing and scrolling up and down at a ferocious pace. "Several smaller airports in the U.K., but I'm looking to see what SRY FO 35 might mean in terms of location." He beat on the keys again. "Surrey. It's Surrey! Let's see." He went back to the previous spreadsheet. "FO 35. It's got to be

Fairoaks Airport. Her phone call, whether intentional or not, was made from Fairoaks."

The captain was renewed with hope. Christian sighed with relief, and Packo laughed out loud. Manzione lit up. "So, what are we waiting for?" he said. "We need to get out there."

"Right Captain," said Pezzetti "We'll helicopter back to Gibraltar and take a jet to Fairoaks. Men, we're out of here."

Christian leapt out of his chair and called out, "Take me with you."

"Why? It doesn't make sense for you to go," Pezzetti responded.

Christian's heart beat so vehemently inside his chest he could hear it. I must be there to help rescue her, he thought.

"I have very strong feelings for Ally Collette," he exclaimed. "I love her. I need to help find her. I can't stay here enraged and powerless. You have my word. I won't get in the way."

Pezzetti looked confused.

The captain understood Christian's torment and made a plea to the IMP leader: "Let him go with you. He knows her, very well I'm hearing. He can be an asset to you."

Pezzetti shook his head. "*Va bene*" ("All right"), he said. "We'll be leaving in about 20 minutes."

Christian didn't want to waste any time, but he had to check in on Ilze. "Okay if I stop by the front desk for any urgencies before we go? I can be back here in 15 minutes."

"Yes, yes. Go. I'll be here; then we'll go to the helicopter pad."

He darted out of the office, fleeing down the promenade, forming instructions in his head to give to Ilze so she felt capable of leading the hotel staff while he was gone.

Nadia spotted him. She could see in his eyes that he was upset, anxious. She crossed the promenade and approached him. "What's wrong, Christian? Are you okay, my love? You look stressed. Ah, maybe tonight I can give you a hot oil massage." She took his hand, stroking it tenderly.

He wriggled his hand out from hers. "Nadia, I-I'm sorry but I'm involved in something important. I won't be able to see you tonight. I-I feel like maybe I misled you. I'm sorry. You're a beautiful woman, but I'm in love with someone … I-I can't explain this all now. I have to run. I'll catch up with you later."

Nadia was stunned, fuming, as she watched Christian dash away without a look back to her.

He slipped in behind the hotel reception desk. He watched Ilze gracefully finesse resolution to a passenger's complaint. She shook the man's hand.

Christian smiled. "Nice work, Ilze. Very nice. Look, there's an emergency I need to deal with, so you'll need to hold down the fort, maybe for a couple of days."

She was perplexed, but nodded in agreement, proud to be asked to substitute for him. "Yes, of course. You can count on me."

A second front desk worker, Sudhir, stood just a few feet away down the Reception counter. Christian spent a minute checking in with him, and then asked Ilze to ensure that the evening staff was set to show up. "And ask everyone to return from breaks as scheduled. Take notes on any problems for me to follow up on. And …" Ilze looked worried. "Oh, you'll be fine Ilze. You'll dazzle our guests with great service."

He was just about to dash away, but as he moved out from behind the Reception counter, he saw the small, elderly, well-dressed woman approach him. She looked sad, but her eyes still twinkled like luminous stars. "My dear, I wanted to say a few words before you rush off." He was puzzled.

"Yes, Flora, what is it?"

She put her hand on his arm, and he felt a wave of overwhelming positive energy run through his body. The same touch he'd felt when his mother held him in her arms, time after time, congratulating him on some small childhood achievement.

The old woman continued, "You need confidence, son. You are kind and you are good, and I believe that you will get everything you want. Trust me. Just be strong and remember to communicate your feelings. I believe in you."

Suddenly he felt hopeful, less frenzied. He thought about Ally and how he'd been such an ass about Nadia. He started to say thank you to the old woman, but she was suddenly gone. How did she leave so fast, with her limp and her cane?

Rushing back to the captain's office, he heard someone call out his name. "Christian, wait! Please." Verena was out of breath chasing him down the promenade. "I'm glad I caught you. I'm so worried about Ally. What could have happened to her, Christian? Was she really abducted? It's hard for me to work or do anything productive knowing that Ally is in danger. The Crab Fest and beach games are planned for tonight on the top deck. Ally was supposed to help and now …"

He took her by the shoulders. "Verena, I'm going to help find her. I may be gone for a few days."

"What do you mean? We're in the middle of the Atlantic Ocean, Christian."

"Yes, I know, but that is not an obstacle. A helicopter is waiting. We think we know the location where both girls might be."

She wanted to tell him that Nadia Zelnikov may know something about the girl but she had to check in with her lover before she mentioned her name to any of the officers. Instead, she pleaded again, "Please, Christian, help bring my friend back."

He hastened away, regretting what he just divulged to the German girl. He shouldn't have said anything about location.

Verena stood in shock. She quickly phoned Nadia. She couldn't remain quiet. She needed comfort from her lover, needed to urge her to share her conversation with Amy Skyler. No answer from Nadia. She left a voicemail:

"Nadia, it's Verena. I need to talk to you. You know from the meeting that Ally Colette has disappeared. Yes, I'm nervous. I really think you should talk to Security about your conversation with Amy the other night. Anything she may have said to you. Really Nadia, you won't get in trouble. It might help find Ally and Amy. I need to talk to you. I have an idea. I'm thinking that if you tell me what Amy said to you in the club, and what you said to her, then I can tell our head of security. I'll just pretend it was me talking to Amy, not you. Nadia, please, it would make me feel better. You had a long conversation with the girl. I saw that. I'll talk to you later. I-I love you, Nadia."

Verena hurried to the Teen Scene to begin preparation for the Crab Fest event, which was scheduled to begin in 30 minutes. The chef and his assistants were already setting up. Servers scurried around, laying out platters of food on royal blue tablecloths, then added a myriad of festive touches, creating the ambiance of being under the sea. Posters full of colorful images of mermaids, fishing boats, and crab cages, and various stand-up cardboard cutouts of a variety of ocean creatures were scattered around the area and on the tables. Verena worked swiftly preparing for the games planned between the Red, Yellow, and Blue teams. She had strategically divided the entire group into three opposing teams earlier. About forty teenagers were expected to join in the fun later. Ally was scheduled to be here with me, she thought. Looks like I'll need to handle this event on my own. My poor friend Ally—I hope you are safe.

Animated teens started to show up. She asked three of the oldest teenage girls, Sara, Charlotte, and Pita, if they might be interested in dropping off their assigned teams and instead becoming game leaders. They enthusiastically agreed, squeezing each other's hands as they jumped up and down with excitement. Verena instructed them on how to conduct the games, each girl assigned to lead one of the three teams.

During the competition planned to last for about an hour following the Crab Fest, Verena stood on the sidelines observing her three new teenage assistants perform like well-trained camp counselors. She was relieved not to have to engage directly in the games because she was so worried about her missing friend and colleague. Suddenly, she felt fingertips running down the middle of her back.

"Are you having a good time, my lovely?" Nadia whispered softly in her ear.

Startled, Verena couldn't help but jump, spinning around. She quickly turned back to watch the teams again, the Russian behind her.

"Nadia. It's you. Y-you startled me."

"What time do you finish with this?" She reached out and tickled Verena in the ribs, capriciously licking her behind the ear.

Verena tingled, excited by her lover's surprise visit, but at the same time quivering with fear that her sexuality might be detected by the teens. She would never recover with this group and she could get dismissed over such behavior. "Nadia, this is dangerous," she said. "Perhaps you shouldn't do that."

"You are such a German," Nadia teased. "Listen, my love … I'm done at the restaurant at 10 o'clock, if you're interested in having a drink in my cabin."

"I-I, well … did you get my voicemail about Ally?"

"Yes, and I think you are right. I should go to Security about that conversation with Amy Skyler. I'll do just that tomorrow morning."

"Um. *Ja.* But are you sure you should wait on this?"

"Hmm, I think maybe you're not interested in me anymore." Nadia played hard to get, turning to walk away. "I should leave."

Without turning to her, Verena called out after her, feeling aroused, anticipating what could hopefully happen between them later. "Nadia, wait! D-don't …" She caught herself from shouting. Nadia pushed her breasts against Verena's back, both of them watching the teens who were all intensely engaged in the game.

The Green team was in the lead with 28 points, the Red team on their tail with 27 and working hard to take the tournament, with this 2-point final game. Verena clutched the team medals in her hands, ready to present them to the winners.

Nadia whispered. "How about I meet you in *your* cabin? I like the way you have it decorated. Much cozier than mine."

Verena beamed, but didn't turn around. "*Ja.* I will be in my cabin at 10 o'clock waiting for you. You make me so happy, Nadia."

The Russian pecked the back of her neck and was gone. Verena's mind was torn between her concern for Ally and her lustful feelings for the ravishing Russian.

Chapter Twenty-Seven

The Jumble Untangles

The helicopter rose up from the ship, flying low beneath the smoky clouds. Christian could make out the whitecaps as the aircraft passed over the ocean en route to Marbella, just down the coast from Gibraltar. The helicopter fought the heavy gusts of wind, the craft plagued with lots of bouncing and swinging, the rain beating on the glass surrounding the rescue team. The pilot appeared to navigate the weather like an expert. This was Christian's first time in a helicopter, leaving him to sit in wonder at how normal this particular ride is for the experienced crew.

He used to dream about whirlybirds—that was what his mother would call them when he was a child. He had several toy whirlybirds, and battle-ships, and miniature ocean liners, trains, and cars. Imaginary play with toy vehicles of any shape or size was one of his preferred activities after he had an early dinner with his mother before she bustled off to her swing-shift job at the hotel. He'd sit for hours conjuring stories about traveling to places across the sea, whooshing the toys into the air and across the rug in his small room.

His mind drifted back to Ally, painfully realizing that it may be too late to rescue the woman he loves, the woman who has no idea of his feel-ings and who may have little interest in considering him as her life partner. All he could think about was having an opportunity to express his true affection for her, explain his mistakes, his inexcusable stupidity. He had been blinded like a drunken sailor foolishly focused on short-term lustful desires. Ally would likely never consider me as a possible future husband, but it doesn't stop me from wanting to save her and confess how I feel about her. As the chopper bumped along the highway of turbulent air, he thought about holding Ally in his arms.

He took his ear buds out of the backpack he grabbed from his work area, plugged them into his phone, then listened once again to Ally's unintended voicemail, anxiously seeking to decode the inaudible words. He played the segment related to the tall man over and over. Each time he heard the sound of her voice, he couldn't help but smile to himself. He listened, then re-winded, then listened again. Turning the volume up as high as it could go, he listened again, the fluttering of the helicopter blades, the wind and the roar of the rain surrounding him. Tears filled his eyes. He could sense the fear in her words, a contrast to her usually confident, sassy style.

"One more question," Ally said, "did a tall R ..." (Inaudible words.) "Did he throw you ..." (Series of inaudible words.)

He was able to understand just a bit more each time he played it back. "One more question Amy, did a tall Rush ... m ... " Is she saying the word *Russian*? Tall Russian man. Wait, the one who was staring at Nadia, trying to get her attention the night we were dancing on the pool deck. She mentioned that the guy was Russian. Christian listened again, now for the tenth time. "Did he throw ..." Shit, a tall Russian man threw Ally and most probably Amy overboard. Oh God. Both Nadia and this mystery man are Russian. Damn. Could the woman of his dreams be involved in these abductions? Are the two Russians more personally connected? Nadia was so suddenly interested in me, when she couldn't have cared less about my existence just days before. That behavior on its own should have been suspicious to me. And then she seduced me. I was the befuddled buffoon, wriggling under her thumb.

His mind drifted back to the cursory comments made by Nadia. When she slipped up and said, "He's my broth...," then gave the excuse that she was tipsy. That tall Russian *is,* in fact, her brother. The puzzle pieces snapped into place, the jumble un-jumbling. Christian tapped a quick text into his phone to Packo, but the message bounced back as "undeliverable."

When they landed at the Marbella airstrip, the weather had improved. The rain was now a light mist, the wind just a warm breeze. But thick clouds hung low, a blanket of darkness looming over the airfield. Marco Pezzetti guided the group onto a waiting jet. Christian was unable to decipher the make of the aircraft. Before takeoff, he texted Packo again, and this time with success.

Before he had departed the ship, he asked Packo for the phone number of Ally's closest relative. Packo pulled it up on the employee database and jotted down the information. The scrap of paper read, "Father, Randolph Collette." She hadn't really shared much about her family with Christian. Suddenly he felt nauseous. The plane seemed to be bouncing up and down now, his stomach turning upside down. Marco Pezzetti moved from across the aisle to sit next to Christian, clicking his seatbelt and pulling it tight across his lap.

"You okay, Christian? Rough ride, isn't it? I'm afraid we've got some bad weather going into the U.K."

"I'll survive. I'm great with boats of any size but not so good with small planes. Look at this." Christian showed him the text he just sent to Packo. "Here's what I discovered listening again to Ally's accidental voicemail."

Marco read it: "Abductors are Russians. I figured out some of the missing words on Ally's message. Abductor is extremely tall. Check crew in laundry room or engine mechanics."

"Quite the detective, Christian. As a professional sleuth, I am quite impressed."

"Thanks, but it was just perseverance on my part, and using the ear buds enabled a better audio. Marco, I have a request. I'd like to contact Ally's next of kin, notify them what's happened."

"No problem. Let's call now."

"We can do it now, during the flight? Can we be on speakerphone with her father? It would be better to have you involved too."

Marco handed him the air phone. "Go for it."

Christian took out the white slip of paper from the front pocket of his pack and punched in the number prefaced by the U.S. country code. Randolph Collette answered the phone on the second ring.

When he heard the news about his daughter, he was in shock. "Abducted? My daughter? How could this happen? I can leave for London immediately, as soon as I can get a flight. Let me have my secretary arrange it."

Pezzetti spoke out and convinced Colette to sit tight. "Wait for word from us. We'll contact you as soon as we have any news. Please, Mr. Collette, trust us to rescue your daughter."

Christian reassured Randolph of the IMP's professionalism and promised to contact him as soon as they knew anything about Ally.

"Please, save my little girl. If only … I-I wish I would have been different with her, not pushed her so much in a direction she didn't want. Please, bring her home safely," he pleaded.

Christian responded, "Sir, may I speak freely?"

"Yes, of course. About what?"

"I-I'm in love with your daughter." He feared how the man would react, but he needed to tell him.

"Son, you sound solid as a rock. I'm glad my little girl is in love with someone like you, but I'm scared to death about this situation."

"Mr. Collette, for the record, Ally is not aware that I'm in love with her."

Randolph choked up. "Son, I don't think she even knows how much *I* love her. Please, tell her when you see her." His voice dropped to a whisper. "Please."

Chapter Twenty-Eight

The Saudi vs. the Japanese

The Saudi prince sat on one sofa, the Japanese businessman on the other. Smoke hung in the air—nearly all the men in the room smoked cigarettes. Takahashi waited for the two buyers to feel comfortable, watching them finish their cocktails. A red velvet curtain hung around the cage set at the rear of the hangar. Behind the curtain, Ally and Amy sat on stools in the center of the locked cage.

Gorby stood close by the girls, a knife in his hand, as Heiko and her helper put finishing touches on them. A servant of Takahashi for almost twenty years, doing whatever tasks he desired, Heiko took pride in her work. He paid her handsomely, but more important to her was the fact that she had secretly loved him for years. But his actions often disturbed her. She was internally conflicted about her feelings for her boss and recently thought about retiring from her job. She'd often fantasized about Takahashi, imagining him admitting his love for her. Over the years, he had often given her a warm embrace, holding her in his arms sometimes for several minutes, then look into her eyes, silently acknowledging her tender love and unselfish loyalty. He didn't speak direct words of love, but his eyes would communicate all she needed to know. The hours that they spent together in the office or on business trips meant everything to her. Sometimes he'd place his hand over hers or brush her cheek with his fingertips while she typed away on the computer. She cherished those moments with him. And, throughout their relationship, he had never married, another indicator to Heiko that he considered her his true love. At least that had been her interpretation of their relationship. But lately Heiko felt more like a rejected spouse. Takahashi was suddenly spending a lot of time at work and at leisure with his pretty, very young secretary, Chiyo, who for some reason he didn't bring with him on this trip. About a month ago, Takahashi had excitedly confided in Heiko about his growing affection for Chiyo, saying even the girl's name made him giddy and feeling so much younger than his fifty-two years.

"Do you know, Heiko, that Chiyo's name actually means 'a thousand sparkles'? For the first time, I think I'm falling in love. Chiyo makes me want to dance and you know how much I have always disliked dancing."

A thousand sparkles, Heiko thought. Chiyo's just a child, a skinny girl without a brain. Heiko felt annoyed with herself and her delusions that Takahashi had romantic feelings for her. Now her heart was filled with misery. As Heiko primped Ally in these final moments before the bidding began, her heart grew heavy. She knew that like the other young female victims in South America, these two girls were destined to enter a life of indentured sex and most probably physical abuse.

Heiko looked into Ally's eyes as she repositioned the barrettes in the pretty girl's blonde hair. Ally was puzzled. It's almost as if this woman has a sincere concern for our well-being, she thought. I can see it in her eyes.

Ally heard an unfamiliar accent coming from the front of the hangar. Middle Eastern, maybe. When Gorby heard the new voice, he moved closer to the girls. Ally could smell his rank breath. He raised the knife, silently threatening them to stay quiet. Takahashi stubbed out his cigarette and rose from the sofa. Karl sat on a chair tapping his foot, anxious for the bidding war to begin.

The prince smiled as he entered with his entourage. A gust of wind brought the slanted rain inside and onto the expensive rug before the hangar door slid shut again.

"So nice to see you again, Prince Moghadam," Takahashi gushed, shaking his hand, then motioned to Karl and led them all to the back of the hangar, just outside the curtained cage. "My colleague, Karl, will run the auction. Prince Moghadam, are you ready to bid? Is there anything we can get you before we begin?"

Moghadam wore bulky robes of burgundy and dark tan, layers of linen hiding his bulging gut. Several chunky gold necklaces embedded with rubies and emeralds hung around his neck. His head was wrapped in white scarves, a braid of gold fabric surrounding the shrug. His mustache and beard were well-trimmed. He had been an impeccable dresser since he was a very young man in Dubai. Now at thirty-eight years old, his entourage kept several young women available to him at a moment's notice, some of them residing in his family compound and a few of others kept in sealed rooms in his penthouse atop his recently built flagship casino located just outside the city. He particularly enjoyed the process of selecting the girls in his harem, personally bidding on them in different corners of the world. Most of all, he appreciated the "ownership" aspect of the deals he made, keenly enjoying the fact that he was acquiring these beauties to be his personal property. Moghadam had the habit of speaking slowly and with great deliberation, his accent similar to that of British royalty, a slight smile habitually plastered on his bearded face whether he was happy or possibly seething with anger. His servants were frequently surprised by his reactions, as there were rarely any visible forewarning signs in his facial expressions.

Karl released the red velvet curtains with great flair. "*Voila* gentlemen!"

"Ah Takahashi, you have good taste, my friend," Moghadam praised, his eyes centered on the two girls as he approached the cage. "Let me feast my eyes on what you have for me in your quiver. Mmmm, my mouth is watering."

"We appreciate the compliment, Prince Moghadam. We are indeed excited to have you here." Takahashi bowed graciously and then turned to the Japanese bidder. "Murakami-san, would you like another smoke before the auction starts? Perhaps another cocktail made for you?" Takahashi spoke to his countryman in English, not wanting to exclude the Saudi.

From the elite class of Japan society, the second bidder, Tatsu Murakami, held the position of CEO of a well-known *keiretsu*, a cluster of companies forming a multi-billion-dollar Japanese conglomerate. He left his business and his aging wife at home in Shin Yokohama to jet to London and secure another lovely young girl for the cache of lovers he proudly kept in a mansion tucked away in the forest not far from Kamakura.

Today's acquisition would be his fourth purchased concubine, each of his three current girls uniquely exquisite in their own way, the youngest, a Central American from Columbia, just thirteen years old. Then there was the fourteen-year-old beauty from Peru and the oldest, now sixteen, coming from El Salvador. His physical coupling with the girls had served as a satisfying coping mechanism, a successful method for dealing with the numerous high-pressure business scenarios he's had to face over the recent years.

After a long workweek, having struggled with his Board of Directors, or having negotiated a deal with a strategic customer, barely sleeping most nights, he looked forward to his women. Every Friday night at about 9 o'clock, his limousine driver would drive him out to his twenty-two-roomed mansion in the country. Upon arrival, he'd first swallow a little blue pill served to him on a small silver tray with a small cup of water. Then he'd don his colorful robe and walk outside to his small temple, where he'd pray alone for 30 minutes, sitting on his zabuton facing his beloved Buddha. Then he'd be served two cups of hot sake before walking back across the garden, entering the mansion, and climbing the staircase, to enjoy one of his women in every position possible all night long, releasing his pent-up stress with the selected beauty that waited for him in bed. Sometimes he'd stay at the mansion for a second night, sending a message to his wife in the city that he had a business deal to attend to or that he was golfing at some resort with an important customer and wouldn't be home until Sunday. He'd choose a second girl for his Saturday night date. Most often it would be the thirteen-year-old, the youngest. Sometimes she would look frightened, but always be obedient and grant him whatever he wished. The young girls were his form of geisha, but unlike geishas, they were incarcerated on the property, free only to roam the balconies and small garden area, which was surrounded by chained gates and guarded by vicious pit bulls.

Occasionally a girl would appear to be subdued by drugs, her body limp yet her mind aware of what was happening to her. He never inquired as to what his servants may have injected the girls with before he screwed them. He didn't care. Sometimes a girl would be fully conscious and drug-free before the sexual act, but she didn't dare resist his affections, fearing that she would immediately be drugged and then not feel anything for hours, possibly for days. Recently, he felt as though his life was charmed.

But today Murakami was impatient, eager to acquire the most beautiful of the two white girls up for bid, then swiftly jump on his jet and head back to Japan, the sweet candy in tow. He was irritated that Takahashi seemed to be coddling the smelly Saudi and not paying more attention to him. He expected special service from his fellow countryman.

The girls were perched on tall stools just inside the cage, each with a chain around her right ankle attached to the leg of the tall metal stool, both wrists in handcuffs. Ally felt incensed and was tempted to bolt from the stool, but she knew that if she moved the wrong way, she would fall to the stone floor with a thud, bringing the heavy stool down on top of her.

Karl held two wooden paddles, giving one to each of the buyers. Takahashi nodded for him to begin the bidding war.

Karl announced, "Gentlemen, we are starting with an opening bid of 450,000 pounds for each girl. Let's kick off with the red-haired girl and leave the tempestuous blonde for later."

The two men signaled with their paddles in the air as Karl raised the price to the next level time after time. Amy was successfully purchased by the Saudi prince for 875,000 pounds. Takahashi smacked his lips with delight, winking over at Karl. Amy sat in shock, taking in what was happening in this cold gray airplane hangar. Her life was over. She was dying inside.

Karl started up the second round of bidding. "My friends, the blonde will be even more action for you in bed. I can tell." He laughed. "As before, the starting bid is 450,000 pounds. Do I hear 50,000 more?"

Murakami raised his paddle. Takahashi dragged on his cigarette. The Saudi quickly responded, swatting his paddle in the air. This went on for several minutes, the bidding rising higher and higher. Murakami was annoyed at the Saudi, who has brought the bid up to 975,000 pounds, and then quickly to one million. The Japanese bidder was disgusted, throwing his paddle on the cement floor. It wobbled, danced for a few moments, and finally stopped with a clatter.

Karl smiled and shouted, "Prince Moghadam takes the blonde at one million pounds. Congratulations!"

The Saudi grinned back, satisfied at the acquisition and his ability to outbid his opponent.

Anger erupted in the hangar. Murakami took a pistol from his suit jacket pocket. Damn, Ally thought, as she eyed Amy, who looked wide-eyed and frozen with fear. Now we're all going to die, Ally thought. Takahashi looked up in shock, himself trying to keep his cool, but inside he was startled by the production of a weapon at the close of a bidding war. He must somehow get Murakami to back down, while still salvaging the man's dignity. He wanted to preserve their relationship, salvage the potential for future business opportunities with him.

"Murakami-san, this girl is not worth it." Takahashi spoke softly and respectfully. He moved closer to the disgruntled bidder, raising his voice just a little. "This blonde, she's too slutty for your taste, Murakami-san. You can easily see that. I can see that you require a more sophisticated kind of girl. More elegant. An Eastern European girl would be perfect for you. I can get you two or three of them within the next month. Trust me. Leave these two substandard products to the Saudi to add to his harem."

Murakami hesitated, but then placed the pistol back in his jacket pocket.

Takahashi snapped his fingers to a member of his entourage. "A whiskey for Murakami-san."

Murakami moved toward him and whispered in his ear. They shook hands and the Japanese businessman left accompanied by his group of men, each one of them wearing dark aviator sunglasses. They scurried out of the side door at the back of the hangar.

The Saudi perked up. "I'd like to feel the flesh my purchases, if you don't mind, just to be sure."

Takahashi turned to the prince. "Be my guest, Prince Moghadam. Feel free to touch either one. As featured, they are supple girls with the softest skin."

Ally looked over at Amy, whose face was now streaming with tears. Ally pushed her leg out of the slit of her dress, arched her back, hoping to entice the prince to touch only her. He noticed her unspoken invitation, laughed, and moved inside the cage to Ally. Standing over her, he felt her bare arms, running his manicured fingers from her shoulders down to her manacled wrists and back up again slowly. He reached his hand under her dress and pushed the hem up high on her thighs. He knelt down and peeked under the fabric of the dress.

"Pink lace. Nice touch." He crept his fingers up inside her panties. She jerked away from him, almost falling off the stool, kicking him in his jaw. "Ouch! Oh, she is a feisty one. That will need to be tamed out of her." He smelt his fingers. "Oh yes, but it will be worth it. I can tell." He kissed her neck. "Don't worry butterfly, I have a nice garden for you to explore."

He pressed his hand to the front of his pants and moved closer to Ally, rubbing his crotch on her bare leg so she could feel him already getting excited. She spit on the floor, barely missing his shiny black shoes.

The prince jumped back. He looked into her eyes. "The taming will be tougher on you than on me. You know that." He reached into her cleavage, into her bra, and pinched her left breast hard. She wanted to scratch his eyes out.

"Asshole," she screamed at him.

Takahashi suddenly clapped his hands. "Okay, are we ready to leave, get the girls into your SUV and off to your homeland. I think we'll need to drug the blonde for you."

"Yes, I agree, drug her just enough to take off that edge. I want my way with her on the plane to Dubai, but I want her to know what's happening. Get the Range Rover ready, Nadir."

Takahashi looked over at Heiko who stood silently by the girls. "Heiko, give her this drug." He took out a vial from his pocket. "These pills, two of them. These will put her in a fog for you, Prince Moghadam." He spoke in English to Heiko, loud enough so all the men could hear him. "We don't want to use some Russian injection technique and risk the girl having a bad reaction. Who knows what poison sits in those dirty needles. No, let's be more civil." He looked over at the Saudi. "We want to be very careful with your precious cargo and ensure they are both in perfect shape for your arrival in Dubai."

Karl sneered, fully feeling the sting of Takahashi's insults to his culture, but holding back acting out his emotions. Who cares, he thought, we're walking away with a fortune. Fifty percent of the take, that's what we get. Let the Japanese control freak win this unimportant battle. Karl looked over at Gorby and warned him with a stern glare not to retaliate. He could see his colleague boiling over and starting to move toward Takahashi. Gorby backed down, veering off to sit on the sofa, keeping his distance from Takahashi so he didn't slug him.

The Saudi snapped his fingers at one of his men, obediently picked up two briefcases sitting on the rug at the front of the hangar, and placed them down between Takahashi and Karl. He knelt and unlocked each case with a click. He raised the lids and revealed bundles of British hundred-pound notes.

The prince instructed him: "Count out 1,850,000 pounds. A lot of money, but I think I'll have some left over," he chuckled. "Yes, I would have spent more if needed. These girls are perfect to house in my casino penthouse in Dubai. I will enjoy them. I love owning young white flesh."

Heiko handed Ally a cup of water. She then carefully placed two tiny pills inside Ally's mouth, aiming for the tip of her tongue. But once she met eyes with the pretty blonde, feeling the girl's silent plea, she shoved the two pills back into the pocket of her overalls. Ally pretended to swallow the pills before Heiko backed away. The men were focused on the money in the briefcases. Heiko shuffled over to Takahashi and demurely said something in Japanese, confirming that Ally had indeed swallowed the white pills.

"Good," he responded for the Saudi's benefit. "The girl will be groggy in just a few minutes."

The Saudi beamed with happiness over his purchases. He directed one of his men to get the Range Rover ready to leave. The hangar door slid open. Ally was still befuddled by Heiko's kind gesture but didn't know what her next step would be, and there was no way she could get to the cell phone, which remained buried in the cushion of the salon chair. The only consolation was that at least both she and Amy had been acquired by the same buyer and were leaving this place together.

Chapter Twenty-Nine

D e c e i t

Nadia knocked on Verena's cabin door. A bottle of cognac was tucked inside her large designer leather purse. As the door was opened by a grinning Verena, Nadia pulled out the bottle, shaking it playfully in the air. "For you, my love. I want you to try our special Ruskie version of cognac. Do you have two glasses?"

"*Ja.* Come in. Nobody saw you knock, did they?"

"*Nyet.* Nobody. I made sure of that." She refocused on the bottle. "I adore this cognac, but I need your expert opinion. Germans are such aficionados of the finest alcohol."

Behind her back, Nadia held a rolled-up drawing of a dog. She pulled it out, removed the rubber band, and held it up for Verena to see. The penciled sketch was of a black and white princess spaniel, sprawled out on a large gray cushion, something she had an artistically gifted waiter draw just outside the kitchen while on his break that morning. She had to listen to him talk about his six years at the Art Institute in Amsterdam, his eyes glancing up at Nadia, hopeful that she would be impressed with his talent, maybe enough to let him buy her a drink later tonight.

Verena stood looking at the sketch. "Oh, Nadia, it's wonderful. You didn't draw this yourself, did you?"

Nadia handed her a glass of cognac. "*Da.* This is a sketch of my dog, Koda."

"You are not only beautiful but also have an artistic gift. Oh my God, this drink *is* indeed very smooth." She finished the rest of the glass. "I love it." The sensation of the warm liquid sliding down into her belly made her head feel light almost immediately. Nadia poured more cognac. They sat and talked for several minutes as Nadia watched Verena get drunk.

"Verena, you know what I'd like to do? I'd really like to sketch you. Capture all of your curves, your smile, your lovely aura. Would you mind being my subject? Do you have some paper and a lead pencil?"

"You want to sketch *me,* right now?"

"*Da.* While we enjoy our special drink together. Trust me, I will create a masterpiece." She laughed with abandon.

"*Ja* Nadia, if you want to do that. I will sit here." Verena stumbled and then moved to the chair.

"Before I begin, can you strip down to your underwear, please?" Nadia purred.

"Nadia? Really?" Verena giggled.

The Russian nodded. "Yes, it must be natural, how you appear when you are relaxing in your own space."

Verena shook her head, puzzled, but at the same time, excited about their evening together. She opened the top drawer of her desk and took out a few sheets of paper. Searching around for a pencil, she found one in the side drawer. She handed both to Nadia. Verena turned away and removed her T-shirt and jeans, letting them fall to the carpet. Then facing Nadia, she stood in her white cotton underwear and beige bra, feeling somewhat awkward. She reached for her glass and took another sip of the cognac, then sat on the edge of her bed.

Nadia removed the barrette from her hair as her long dark hair cascaded over her shoulders. "You can sketch me too, while I draw you. *Da?*"

"But, Nadia, I don't really know how to draw. I have absolutely no artistic ability."

Nadia moved to the bed placing her fingers on Verena's lips. "Shh, *Fraulein.* For me, will you do this, please?"

"Okay, *ja,* I'll try it."

"Wait Verena, before you start sketching me, you must sign your name at the bottom of the paper as if you are a famous artist. If you sign it, then it is likely that you will be able to draw me as beautiful as I am." She smiled, puckering her lips and pleading with her big eyes.

Verena shrugged her shoulders, happy to humor her lover. She felt fuzzy with the drink, but as instructed, she rose and walked over to the desk to sign her name across the bottom of the sheet of paper. She laughed, beaming at her lover. "I am already getting inspired to draw."

"Beautiful handwriting. I'm sure your artwork will be as lovely. It will be fun. Uh, oh Verena, can you pour me a bit more cognac?"

"*Ja,* sure."

Verena turned back to the desk, reaching for the cognac. Nadia grabbed her from behind with a brutal force, quickly wrapping a long black scarf around the girl's face, covering her eyes, completely startling Verena.

"Let's play a game first. *Da?*"

She threw the German down on the bed, face first into her pillow, then retrieved another long black scarf from her blazer pocket and tied the girl's wrists behind her. With a third scarf, she pulled Verena's ankles together and tugged on the fabric, tightening it to ensure her legs were completely restricted.

Stunned, Verena struggled to speak. "W-what … what are you doing?"

"Never mind me."

Nadia quickly snatched the scarf from around her eyes and wrapped it across her mouth, gagging her. Astounded, Verena tried to scream, but only muted grunting noises escaped.

"You are one stupid girl, Verena. I would say a complete waste of female energy, just like your pathetic friend, Ally. You should have minded your own fucking business, *da?*"

Verena struggled, desperate to break out of the knotted scarves, but it was impossible. She turned her head, watching Nadia as she flitted around the small room, grabbing the desk chair, then pushing Verena down onto the floor and pulling the top sheet away from the bed, then the fitted sheet, twisting them up, weaving them into a makeshift rope. Nadia stepped onto the chair, reached up under the foam ceiling tiles, and wrapped the sheeted rope around the metal ceiling frame, knotting it at the end to form a noose, which now hung from the ceiling. Verena flailed in distress on the floor, her eyes looking up at Nadia, fully comprehending the preparations being made. Verena began to pray. Oh God, save me. Save me. Don't let this happen.

Nadia placed a second chair next to the chair directly under the noose. She picked up the barely dressed girl and hiked her up onto the other desk chair, then hoisted her body up into the air just a couple of inches from the seat cushion. With one hand, Nadia wrapped the noose around Verena's neck. Nadia then jumped up onto the other chair next to Verena.

"You despicable dyke. You're a disgrace," she whispered in her ear. "It will be hard to choke that oversized neck of yours, but I am determined in my pursuits."

Verena exuded her last vestige of energy, hopelessly attempting to keep her tiptoes touching the chair beneath her. The braided cotton sheet tightened around her neck. She heard the desk chair fall to the floor. Verena hung, dangling from the ceiling, her body twirling one way and then the other. The pressure around her throat was too much to fight. Her world went black.

Nadia picked up the sheet of paper that had fallen from the bed during the process of preparing to take Verena's life. She pulled out a folded white envelope from her purse that contained a glue stick and pieces of paper with words cut out from magazines. Lining up the words carefully on the desk blotter, she began to glue each word onto the paper just above Verena's signature. When she finished, she read the three short sentences aloud: "I AM FINISHED WITH THIS WORLD. TOO MUCH PAIN. FORGIVE ME, DEAR GOD."

In her mind, she pretended that it wasn't Verena, but instead her own father who she just hung. It was her bastard of a father that she just murdered.

Wiping the unwanted tears from her eyes, she removed a white dust cloth from her handbag and painstakingly wiped down her prints from everywhere she could remember having touched, moving from left to right across the cabin. She washed the glass she personally drank from and replaced it on the doily sitting on the dresser. She placed the bottle of cognac on the desk with Verena's glass and positioned the suicide note next to the half-finished drink. She untied the three scarves from the dead girl's body, stuffed them into her pocket, and grabbed the sketch of the dog, pushing it into her leather handbag. She wiped everything down a second time, scanning the room for anything she might have missed. Opening the cabin door slightly, she peered down the corridor to see if anyone was about. Nobody was out there. She wiped the door handle on both sides with the white cloth and rushed down the long passageway to her own cabin on the same deck at the other end of the ship. I had to do it, she told herself. I couldn't chance the girl going to Security or getting word to the captain.

As soon as she entered her cabin, she picked up the small crystal-framed photograph of Verena's cat, stuffed it in her handbag, and rushed out the door, taking the elevator to Deck 4. She walked quickly to the back of the ship, opening the heavy door to the outside. The wind was blowing hard over the Atlantic Ocean. The water looked rough in the late afternoon light, like bubbling liquid steel, whitecaps as far as the eye could see. The setting sun peeked out slightly from behind the dark gray clouds. Nadia stretched her body out over the wooden railing, took the framed photo from her leather handbag, and thrust it overboard, watching it hit the water below her.

Chapter Thirty

Packo's Pain

Packo stepped out of the shower, the first one he's had in well over 24 hours, having been ensconced in the mystery of the disappearing girls. The green light on his cell phone blinked on his bedside table. It was a text from Christian: "Abductors are Russians. I figured out some of the missing words on Ally's message. Abductor is extremely tall. Check crew in laundry room or engine mechanics."

Packo picked up the item he found that morning on the top of lifeboat #7, wedged in between its white and orange painted hull, where it attached to the bright orange roof. The small object was a worn metal key fob that must have fallen from the deck just above from the running track area. Some letters were etched in red in the oval piece of metal. Packo could make out two of the letters: a capital "C" and the last letter, a capital "P". "*Dios mio*," he exclaimed. It could mean Russia, the old-time version, CCCP. There was a small chunk of metal missing from the round hole that must have held the piece to the keychain. Could this fob be from the abductor's keychain?

"*Mierda!* Fucking Russians! I don't trust them." He threw on his clothes, tucking in his white shirt, noticing he had missed a belt loop on his trousers. Not worth the time to correct it, he ran a comb through his curly black hair, without using the hairdryer. He was determined to quickly get up to his office computer so he could peruse the list of crewmembers for any male Russian nationals. He rushed from his cabin.

Staring at his screen, he marked off the five names appearing to be Russians. Three were waiters, one a specialty restaurant hostess, and the fifth one was a laundry room worker. He scanned the personal information for each of the Russian men in the Human Resources database. Bingo! Leopold Zelnikov was a very tall man. He read aloud, "Height: 6' 5", Weight: 240 pounds, Age: 25, Hair color: Brown, Eyes: Brown." *Si, I've seen this hombre around the ship.* How can anyone miss him? He's a monster of a man. Dark, bushy eyebrows, Packo recalled. Going back to the other four Russian names, he realized that the one female listed was twenty-six-year-old Nadia. He studied her photograph. It was the beguiling woman Christian was holding around the waist, the delicious vixen who was nibbling on the Greek's ear, just as Packo had opened the office door. He brought up Nadia's information on his computer. Nadia Zelnikov. His eyes zoned in on the last name: Zelnikov. Was she related to the laundry worker, the perpetrator?

Packo phoned the head of housekeeping.

"Housekeeping, Leena Garcia," she answered. "How can I be of service?"

"Leena, it's Officer Suarez. I have an important and very confidential question for you."

"Yes, what is it?" Since the captain's meeting that afternoon, Leena had kept her eyes and ears open with her hospitality staff, reminding them all to look for any clues that may be related to Amy Skyler's disappearance.

"Is Leopold Zelnikov working in the laundry room right now? Is he on duty?"

"Zelnikov? Hold on a minute, I need to look at the staff schedule. Let's see, um, yes, Officer Suarez. He started his shift two hours ago. He should be on Deck 9 in the aft laundry room. Why? Should I get him and bring him to you?"

"No. Don't say a word to him. It's critical. I need to talk to him and I don't want him to have any signal ahead of time. *Comprendes,* Leena?"

He leapt up the staircase, three flights to Deck 9, and then ran to the back of the ship, his handgun in his pants pocket. Nobody was supposed to have guns on cruise ships. That's what passengers were told. No firearms anywhere. But the truth was that he and the captain both had guns.

He carried it everywhere he went, and he knew that the captain took his with him whenever he sensed potential danger. It was an unspoken practice. Laundry room. Laundry room. *Mierda.* Where the hell is it? Finally, he saw an open door. He could hear two men talking.

With his hand on his weapon, he turned into the doorway, yelling out, "Leopold Zelnikov, hands on your head. Drop to the floor!"

Disappointment in his eyes, he saw two short Asian men at work, but no Zelnikov in sight. Startled, the men jumped at Packo's entrance, dropping the loads of laundry they'd been carrying and kneeling on the floor. One man put his arms up; the other dropped his head down. "Zelnikov, where is he?"

The one with his arms up spoke. "Leo, h-he just left, took an early break, said he'd be back in 20 minutes. He said he had to find something he lost when he went for a run early this morning. H-he said he was going to look in a staff restroom."

Packo felt his fury rising. "If he comes back, don't tell him I was here. Got it? If you do, I'll find out, and you'll be facing the captain tonight," he grumbled.

The two men nodded, and then stood up. Packo moved quickly, stopping at one staff restroom after another, checking all nine men's toilets. No Leopold. Maybe the Russian went back to the laundry room. It's been about 15 minutes since I left the two men. A thought hit him. He froze on the staircase. The Asian said that Leopold went for a run earlier today. The running track was on Deck 6. I need to check there, he thought.

Packo pivoted and raced down the staircase, heading for the track. The sun had set and the running track was dimly lit. Signs hanging from the overhang encouraged passengers to keep running. One sign read, "Burn off the buffet—SMILE!" Another read, "Catch me if you can!" The track was empty. Most passengers were at dinner or enjoying the early evening entertainment around the ship. He could hear the rain falling on the ocean, the wind howling. Although the exercise area was well-protected, the rain blew in, wetting his face, as he stealthily tiptoed down the white lines of the track, hoping to find Zelnikov.

He rounded the corner and spotted an unusually tall man, his back to Packo. The man held a mini flashlight and seemed to be frantically searching for something on the wooden deck floor. Packo stepped behind a white metal column, out of sight, as the man straightened up, looking flustered and discouraged. Packo watched him scratch his head and then bend down again, the tiny flashlight close to the floor. Packo stepped up behind him, one hand on the gun in his pocket and the worn-down CCCP key fob held out in the other.

"Did you happen to lose this from your keychain, *amigo*?" He held the metal oval in front of Leopold's face.

Alarmed, Leo acted quickly. He dropped the flashlight and produced something from his pocket, holding it in the dim light by his side. The shadows marred the clear definition of what he was holding, but Packo had an idea that it was a knife or another weapon. He moved closer to Zelnikov. Leo kicked him in the stomach with direct force and karate-like intention, his long muscular leg hitting Packo in his chest, taking him down to the floor.

He lay there, next to the deck chair, the same chair that Amy Skyler sat in before she was ruthlessly tossed overboard. Packo rolled onto his stomach, trying to get his legs under him and his hand back on the gun. But Leo was determined. He lunged at him. A switchblade was in the Russian's hand. Packo picked up the chair and threw it into his opponent's face. He hit Leo on his nose and the blood started flowing. Got him. Good. Packo started to get his physical confidence back. But Leo didn't stop coming toward him. However, in the process, his knife shot off the deck, down into the ocean. But the Russian didn't miss a beat, picking up Packo with all his strength, leaning over the wooden railing and tossing the Spaniard down into the dark ocean, just like he did with Amy Skyler.

Packo felt his body plunging. He desperately held out his arms, hoping to grab onto something, Anything. He reached for a rope that hung out from Deck 5 and grasped it, attempting to pull himself in. But the rope snapped. He fell further, slamming down onto the roof of a lifeboat just above Deck 4. His back felt like it was broken, but he could still move. He saw Leo's face peering down at him. Then Leo disappeared, probably coming down to finish him off. Packo's ankle felt crushed. He could sense it crack, something tearing as he hit the metal lifeboat with a thud. He was sure that his head was bleeding, too. He could see the blood smeared across the bright orange painted surface. His clothes were soaking wet, the rain pelting down. He spotted the worn metal key fob, on the rooftop, just inches away from him. He reached out and grabbed it, stuffing it into his pants pocket.

Crawling down awkwardly to the deck floor below the lifeboat, Packo attempted to stand up on his feet, knowing at any moment the Russian would come shooting through the automatic door to the deck outside. He limped over to the door, managed to trigger it to open, and staggered inside, now out of the rain. He spotted the sign for the men's restroom, quickly pulling the door open and finding a stall where he could hide. Hiking his body up onto the toilet seat, so his feet were not visible to anyone entering the bathroom, Packo winced in pain. His ankle throbbed. Thank God, my cell phone is still in my pants pocket, he thought.

He phoned the captain, whispering, "It's Packo. I'm in the aft Men's Restroom, Deck 4. The girls' abductor is a Russian crewmember, Leopold Zelnikov. Get here now. He's coming after me."

The captain dialed 911 and connected with the nightshift security supervisor, Hans Tinker. "Get Security to Deck 4, Men's Restroom, aft. We have a criminal, Leopold Zelnikov, a crewmember coming to attack Officer Suarez. Stop him. I'll meet you there. *Pronto! Pronto!*"

Packo heard the door fly open. Somebody entered. The stall door flung open, the lock breaking off from the shear brute force exerted by the intruder. Leo grabbed Packo by the neck as the head of security reached into his pocket and brandished Sissy Caruthers' taser. He pushed the instrument onto Leopold Zelnikov's testicles, pressing the button down with all his strength. Leo fell to the floor in pain, knocking his head against the stall's gray metal door. Captain Manzione stormed into the restroom, two security men flanking him.

"Cuff him immediately," Manzione shouted.

The security supervisor, Hans Tinker, grabbed the struggling man's wrists and cuffed him. Packo tried to sit up, still on the cold floor by the toilet seat, exhausted, looking up at the captain.

"So *amigo,* did you stop for an espresso on the way over here?"

They both smiled. The captain chuckled out loud, kneeling down by the wet, bleeding Packo. Leo swore repeatedly in Russian as he rolled around on the tiled floor half outside the toilet stall, still writhing in pain from the sting of the taser.

Manzione called out, "Tinker, take him to the lock-up. And you," he pointed to the second security man, "get me a wheelchair for Officer Suarez."

The men escorted the still dazed, weakened Leopold out of the restroom. Dark red liquid was smeared on the restroom floor.

"Your head, it's bad. You're spewing blood," the captain said, examining Packo's head laceration more closely.

"It's f-fine," Packo muttered, unable to hide the pain behind his words. "The real damage is to my fucking ankle. I think it's sprained, maybe broken."

Hans Tinker burst through the door. "Captain, Officer Suarez, we have big trouble."

Packo cringed in pain, his ankle pulsing. "What is it, man?"

"A crewmember, Verena Keppler, hung herself in her cabin. She's dead."

"What? *Mierda!* I need to get to her cabin, see what's happened."

The captain placed his hand on Packo's shoulder. "There's no reason to hurry. Did you hear him? The woman is already dead."

Packo pulled himself up and limped out of the stall and over to the sink, checking the damage to his body in the mirror. He turned on the tap, hung his head in the sink, and let the cold tap water run on his bleeding head wound.

"Let's go. I don't know if the hanging is related, but we must find Nadia Zelnikov immediately. She's either the sister or wife of Leopold Zelnikov, the Russian who abducted the girls."

Manzione came to his senses, jumping up, ready for action. "You can't do anything right now, Packo. Your ankle is hurt badly and you're bleeding from your head. You probably need stitches."

"That won't stop me. I'm going to halt this tirade of terror. I have a sneaking feeling that this Nadia woman is the mastermind behind these abductions and that Leopold is just a pawn." Packo shook his fist, determined to get her. "I could see it in her eyes when Christian was caressing her. When she looked over at me, there was evil in her smile. I tried to ignore it at the time but—"

"What? What do you mean? Christian, our hotel manager, was with her?" The captain was baffled.

"*Si*. A long story. She's the hostess in the Crystal Dining Experience. Let's go." Packo hobbled out of the restroom, the captain helping him to the elevator. "She's dangerous, Captain. We need to be careful."

Chapter Thirty-One

The Search for the Abductors

Racing out of the elevator, they stopped at the restaurant. Nobody stood at the podium at the hostess station.

"She must be seating guests," Packo said.

The captain nodded to several passengers as they passed by, most in a quandary as to whether to smile or not, still reacting to the earlier scene at the theater. Several shot worried glances at Packo, who had bloody stains splattered down his white shirt.

Manzione pulled Packo away from the restaurant entrance. "Packo," he said sternly, "I'm still captain of this ship, and I command you to sit on that bench over there out of sight." He pointed to a wooden bench just outside the sliding glass doors. "I will take care of this. I have my gun. Give me the taser."

Packo handed the taser to the captain, who shoved it into his white jacket pocket. Packo's ankle was throbbing. He could barely stand, let alone walk. The captain helped him over to the bench and turned to leave. Packo tugged at his arm. He then pulled out his phone. "Here's what she looks like." He flashed a photo that he had downloaded from the online personnel file on his computer.

The captain opened his eyes wide, surprised at her beauty. *"Amigo, be careful and keep your hands to yourself."*

They both grinned, bonding as men and as colleagues.

The captain hurried to the hostess station, still no Nadia in sight. Where is she? A petite young woman with big blue eyes and curvaceous hips slid in behind the podium, graciously greeting a couple waiting to be seated. Manzione approached them and made eye contact with the blue-eyed hostess.

"Excuse me, but may I have a word with you?"

At first the man and woman seemed annoyed, and then realized it was Captain Manzione interrupting their seating. They had felt sorry for him in the theater just hours ago.

The hostess looked confused as to what to do, but obeyed her superior. She addressed the couple. "Please pardon me for just a moment."

The captain took her aside. "You're not Nadia Zelnikov, are you? I thought she was the hostess here."

"Sorry sir." The young woman spoke with an upper-crust English accent. "I'm taking her place tonight. I guess she's under the weather. I got a call at about 4 o'clock to get over here to substitute for her."

The two men walked over to Nadia's cabin, Manzione leading the way, Packo limping behind, but keeping up. Outside the door, Packo handed the card key to the captain and placed his hand on the gun in his pocket. Once the plastic card passed through the slot and the green light blinked, Manzione turned the handle and burst inside.

"Nobody here. Damn that woman!" he exclaimed.

Packo quickly moved around to check possible places where she might be hiding. "Where the hell is she?"

The captain sat down on the single bed, noting the forbidden candle sitting on the bedside table. Anything enabling a potential flame was not permitted on the ship. He closed his eyes in annoyance, wishing Nadia were here for him to interrogate, and then take into custody. He was at a loss for ideas on where she might be, what she might be doing. "What now, Packo? Where should we search for her?"

Packo shook his head, then looked around the room again, hoping for any clue that might help them. He opened the bathroom door and saw a pair of black bikini lace underwear and a similar-style brassiere hanging on a makeshift clothesline in the shower. He sorted through the cosmetics bag that sat on the counter by the sink. Nothing strange or unusual. Hobbling out of the bathroom, he checked the desk again. Maybe something on her laptop? He turned it on and saw that it was password-protected. *Mierda!*

Wedged in the bottom right corner of the wall mirror was a black-and-white photograph on glossy but yellowed paper. He pulled the half-ripped photo from the mirror and looked at it closely. Although the photo had been taken in poor light, he could clearly see a stunning, slender preteen girl sitting on a bench next to a poorly dressed, bedraggled middle-aged woman. The two were huddled together affectionately, most probably mother and daughter. They both looked cold, wearing dark wool coats, gloves, and thick scarves wrapped around their necks. The tired-looking woman wore a fur hat. The girl wore a striped knit cap, her long, raven black hair falling in curls below her shoulders. She was holding onto her mother's arm with both of her gloved hands, half-smiling for the camera. The mother wore a proud grin.

"Look at this. It's Nadia Zelnikov when she was barely a teenager. This must be her mother with her. The girl was a beauty even as a child."

He passed the faded photo to the captain, who studied it with curiosity, and for a moment imagined what his wife and daughter might look like now if they were still both alive. Manzione let the photo fall to the floor as he got up from the bed.

"Come on man, we need to continue our search for Nadia."

"Right, in just a moment, sir." Packo opened the wardrobe, sticking his hands in each pocket of both jackets hanging next to an array of dresses of various styles and colors. He pulled out a scrap of white paper from the longer coat and saw some scribbling in pencil. "Bingo," he yelled out. He read it aloud: "Leo - Ami Skyla. Trac. 11:30." He handed the note to the captain, saying, "The Russian temptress might be ravishing, but she can't spell in English worth a damn."

"So, is Leopold her husband, boyfriend, or brother? What's your guess, Packo?"

"I don't give a shit *how* they're related or even *if* they're related. I want to catch that woman, and the sooner the better. Let's search the ship. I'm going to call in my security team."

He whipped out his phone and sent a text to Hans Tinker. Manzione bent down, retrieving the black-and-white photograph from the blue carpet. He stared into the young girl's coal-black eyes.

Packo jammed his phone back into his pants pocket. "I told him to meet me at my office with as many security staff as he can gather in 5 minutes." He wondered why the captain was still staring at the photograph. "What's up? Did I miss something there?"

"She was a beautiful young girl, Packo. How in the hell did she fall so low?"

"Hmm. I wish I could see it that way, but I can't. Let's go."

Packo stumbled out through the cabin door with the captain. The crewmember next door was just exiting his cabin. It was Conner McIntosh, one of the bar staff who worked in the lounge just outside the main dining room, a young Irishman from Dublin.

"Hey Conner," Packo said.

Conner looked up, startled to see these two officers coming out of Nadia's cabin.

"*Amigo,* have you seen Nadia, your neighbor, anywhere around in the last hour?"

"Well, yes I have. Around 30 minutes ago. To be honest, she looked drunk, in bad shape, not her usual flawless composure. Why? What's going on?"

"Any idea where she was headed?"

"N-no, not really. But I kidded her a bit and asked her if maybe she'd had one too many. She just smirked at me. I remember that look. Then, slurring her words, she said that she needed another cognac. She had a cigarette between her lips, but it wasn't lit. She knows the rules. That was the end of our conversation, probably more words than she's ever said to me. Then I entered my cabin ready for a short kip. I'm off to my next shift now."

Packo tapped him on the back. "Of course, you better get going, Conner. If you see her, don't give any heads-up that we were here. It's official business. Okay, *amigo*?"

"Got it." Conner whisked down the hallway, wondering why the captain would be in Nadia's cabin with the head of security. Could it have something to do with the missing girls he talked about at the meeting?

Chapter Thirty-Two

Goodbye Papa

The ship rocked from side to side. Packo felt his cell phone vibrate in his pocket as he rushed down the corridor with the captain. Passengers walked by them, barely noticing the two men. Men, women, and children were holding onto the wooden railing along the walls. Others leaned against stable objects like bar tops, sofas, and tables as they tried to get to their next destination. Some guests looked as pale as ghosts, their Dramamine patches not effective; others were nauseous and had lost their equilibrium.

Packo latched onto the edge of the espresso bar counter and glanced at the text he just received. It was from Ari, the Starlight Piano Bar keyboardist, who had written, "Send security staff. Passenger problem."

"*Mierda!*" he exclaimed, and showed the text to the captain.

"Never mind that for now, Packo. We have other fish to fry."

"We're passing right through that lounge anyway, Captain. I can quickly check it out."

Manzione felt a sudden surge of energy. He had no need to hold onto anything for balance or support as they maneuvered down the promenade with the rocky seesaw motion of the vessel. The captain had his sea legs, having mastered the tumultuous ups and downs of the ocean a long time ago. This would allow him to be solely focused on apprehending the abductors. At the same time, he felt dismayed and ashamed about the poor quality of his decisions. He knew that this was likely his last sail on *The Prism of the Deep Blue Sea* or for that matter on any other Millennium Cruise Lines ship.

As they entered the Piano Bar, Packo realized that Ari was playing his all-time personal favorite, "Fly Me to the Moon." The bar was just about empty. Guests were off doing other things. Now between early dinner and late dinner, the second show was scheduled to get under way in the theater in just 15 minutes. The casino should be filling up too. Many passengers were likely hanging out in their staterooms clutching their pillows until these squalls subsided.

When Louis, the bartender, saw the captain and Packo enter the Piano Bar, Ari looked up from his keyboard and rolled his eyes toward a woman sitting at a table in the corner.

She slammed down her drink on the table, just having downed a double shot of Stoli Vodka. Two other shot glasses sat on the table filled to the brim with more vodka. She looked down, staring at her own reflection in the polished tabletop as she rocked her head back and forth.

The captain's eyes almost doubled in size. "It's her, the Russian," he whispered.

Packo wasted no time, rapidly moving to the corner table, as he gestured to Ari to keep playing his song. She picked up a sharp, short-handled kitchen knife from the seat next to her and looked directly at Packo, her eyes swollen, bloodshot. Her hair, in a French knot earlier today, now dangled loosely, half up, half down, long stray curls falling in her face. The ship rocked more furiously. Nadia cackled as Packo lost his footing, his injured ankle giving out. He pulled himself up, regaining his balance, and fixed his eyes on the knife in her hand.

"I can shoot you, Nadia Zelnikov. I have a .45 pistol in my pocket," he threatened her, knowing that he didn't want to resort to this with passengers likely within earshot.

"Da! Da," she screamed at him. "Get it over with then or shall I save you the trouble?" She pointed the tip of the knife to her own neck, aiming for the jugular. She chuckled to herself, then spoke out in a low register. "The fact is I want to die." Her elegance had vanished, her perfect posture a distant memory. Her mascara was smudged under her eyes, her face gaunt, resembling a horror film character. "I-I didn't have to kill her. I always knew that Leo would fuck it up, my stupid brother." She broke down sobbing, the hand holding the knife shaking.

The captain stood away, still near the entrance to the bar. He backed out the way they came in, devising a plan to come up from behind her on the other side, through the alternate entrance.

Nadia's eyes glazed over. In her mind, she was back in the cabin with Verena, observing herself committing murder. She refocused on Packo now before her. "The truth is, I enjoyed hanging the German slut," she confessed. "I liked it! *Da*. I *liked* it," she repeated as if bragging. She quieted down, swallowed another shot of vodka, and whispered, a faint smile emerging, "Her legs, did you see them dangling there?" Nadia waved the knife in the air replicating the dangle, then laughed hysterically.

Ari abruptly stopped playing the piano and slithered out of the bar. She twisted her face, her expression like a woman gone mad. She gripped the knife in her hand, feeling the sensation of the thick black handle, the tip of the blade now denting the skin on her neck.

"That Verena, she had stumpy tree trunks for legs. I hated touching her, but I had to do it," she said, her voice quivering. "I despised myself for touching her. Just like my papa, I violated the young girl, told her that I loved her." She yanked the knife away, lowering it, to put it down.

"*Dos vedonya, Papa.*" Telling her father goodbye, Nadia spit on the table, raised the last shot of vodka in her free hand, gulped it down, and plunged the knife into her neck. Her head fell back. Her mouth curled in a satisfied grin. Blood gushed out onto the table and down her clothes. She closed her eyes, and then slowly opened them again, seeming to savor her own moment of death.

The captain shot around from the other bar entrance where Ari just exited. He stood horrified for a few moments, viewing the gory tableau. As he moved to Packo, he felt like he was immersed in a surreal dream.

He shook his head, staring at the corpse. "It was her tragic destiny," he said.

The ship jolted, rocking from side to side. Packo's ankle gave out. He fell to the gold- star-studded black carpeting. The captain knelt. "Let's get you to the doctor, my friend."

Chapter Thirty-Three

A New Life Together

Ally rocked her head back and forth, pretending to have been subdued by the drug. Was it some kind of date rape drug? She was guessing that was what they'd given her or something similar. *What would I be like with this drug inside me? How would my body react? Shit, what if we can't get out of this?*

The monster-sized Saudi guard scooped Ally up in his arms. She felt something fall out from the bottom of her dress and down to the hangar's cement floor. *Fuck, it's my phone.* Nobody noticed the thud with the sound of the men talking and laughing and the noise of the pouring rain. The man holding her accidentally kicked the cell phone with his boot, sending it off to the side wall. He showed no sign of noticing, but Heiko quickly eyed the phone and shuffled over to pick it up. Ally wanted to hug the woman. The man carried Ally out of the hangar to the prince's Range Rover. As he shoved her into the back seat of the car, although feigning having been drugged, she managed to turn her head to see another Saudi guard holding Amy firmly by the arm and leading her outside to the SUV. From the other back door, he pushed Amy into the seat beside her.

"You lucky girls," Karl shouted out to them as the rain continued to pelt down, the sky darkening. "You've been purchased by a Saudi Arabian prince. Thank your lucky stars. I should have you both kiss my Ruskie ass for that."

The men laughed at Karl's joke. Through the car window, Ally could see them carousing together. Even Takahashi chuckled, standing just outside the hangar next to Karl. He raised the collar of his black raincoat, to protect himself from the rain, dragging on another cigarette.

The prince came out of the hangar and stood next to Karl and Takahashi. One of his guards held up a black umbrella to cover him. He shook Karl's hand and then did the same with Takahashi. Heiko rushed up next to her boss, arriving a little late, and opened a large plaid umbrella over his head.

Slumped down in the car like a ragdoll, Ally commended herself on her acting skills. They think I'm drugged. Now I can be creative. I have no cell phone anymore to help us. Shit. Her eyes moved to the compartment between the two front seats just in front of her. She spotted a metal cigarette lighter sitting next to a pack of cigarettes. Must be the driver's. While the men outside were cajoling and congratulating each other, Ally reached out for the lighter. Testing the lighter, the flame glowed for a millisecond. She smiled to herself. Looking up into Amy's vacant eyes, she took the girl's hand and gently squeezed it.

"Amy, I'm not drugged, just pretending. Amy, listen to me. When I say go, we must go. I want you to push that door open and run like hell."

Amy sat there stoically with her hands in her lap. Ally thought she saw Amy's head nod slightly in understanding, but she wasn't sure. The girl was clearly traumatized. Amy's eyes blinked fast several times, her attempt to warn Ally that one of the men was looking over at the car, checking on the girls. Amy touched Ally's shoulder. Ally instantly reverted back to her limp ragdoll position. She could hear the Saudi prince chattering away to his guards in Arabic and then speak in English to Takahashi. The men drifted back inside the hangar to say their goodbyes as the rain fell harder. They seemed to still be laughing and joking and enjoying a final cigarette before departing. Holy magnolias, those men can smoke, Ally thought, pleased for any delay in their departure. The mood of this international gang of thugs seemed to have lightened now that the auction was over and the trade was done.

After what seemed like forever to Ally, the Saudi Arabian driver got into the SUV and prepared the vehicle for the journey. First he turned on the headlights and windshield wipers, then picked up some paperwork and read it. Her head down on the leather seat, Ally looked up and saw the thick wrapped fabric of his white Arabic head cover. The noise of the rain and the windshield wipers, Ally thought, would help her carry out her plan. The prince opened the other door and sat down in the front passenger seat. He looked back at the girls for an instant, nodding his head in satisfaction, and turned forward, looking down at his cell phone. The driver then put the car in drive.

Ally quietly pressed down on the lighter and saw the yellow flame. She bolted upright and raised her hand in the air, lighting the back of the driver's head scarf first and moving the flame to the prince's head covering. The fire took hold. Angry orange flickers of light spread around the heads of the two men, and then enveloped their arms and hands, which flung every which way in desperation. They yelled out in agony as the flames engulfed the front seat and the dashboard.

Ally pushed Amy to get out of the car fast, screaming, "Go, Amy. Get out. Run!"

Amy hesitated, then thrust the car door open. Amy jumped out and Ally followed, but quickly took the lead, grabbing Amy's hand, pulling her away, catching a fleeting glimpse of the SUV being consumed in flames. The girls could hear the burning men's screams intensify as they rushed away. They didn't look back again, but Ally could imagine the shocked expression on Takahashi's face and the utter disdain of the startled Russians.

They kept their hands linked as they ran for their lives, the day quickly turning into night. Ally eyed the closest hangar, but continued to hold onto Amy and run like hell, looking for a better place to hide, a hangar further away, knowing that she's risking them being easily seen as they run on the open airfield. She must get them somewhere inside, as fast as she can, but somewhere less obvious. The rain beat down, their pretty dresses now plastered to their wet bodies, their carefully prepared coifs now dripping mops around their smeared, carefully made-up faces. Their high heels were slowing them down. Ally pulled Amy close to the side door of one hangar and stopped. She pushed the door.

"We're not going inside this one, but take off your shoes, Amy. Leave them here by this door just like I'm doing." Amy looked confused and tripped on the tarmac, and then obediently removed her shoes. "You're okay, Amy. We're going to find another place to hide, a hangar further away." Ally reached up to her neck and yanked on the string of pearls. The pearls scattered all over the wet ground, pearls falling everywhere around the door. "Good. They'll think we're in here. This should throw off those imbeciles. Let's go. Our feet will get wet, but this way, we can run faster."

They turned a corner along the perimeter of the airfield. "This one, let's try the side door." Ally pushed it open. Amy followed her inside. The smell reminded Ally of a Savannah vegetable garden. Fragrant. She closed her eyes for an instant. Her father's face flashed before her as she remembered him touching her nose with a ball of cotton when she was eight years old. She wiggled her nose and they both laughed. He wore his wide-brimmed straw hat that contrasted with his suit and tie.

Ally opened her eyes. She saw that the hangar was almost completely filled with large wooden slatted crates, allowing the girls to make out the contents of each box. Several contained red tomatoes, while other crates were filled to the brim with bananas and some with what looked like mangoes. Although the hangar was dimly lit inside, she could see that each crate was marked with bold black letters. Ally walked around, gazing at the contents of each crate. Thinking. Thinking. Some crates were marked with "Honduras>U.K.>Russia." Others were marked with "Costa Rica>U.K.>Russia." She moved back to Amy, who hovered by the door where they had entered. Amy's body had stiffened, her face looked petrified. With a moment to pause, Amy was conscious of the danger and started to panic, her anxiety now in full bloom.

"Amy, come and sit down by me. I have an idea. Maybe you can help me." She led Amy to the crate closest to the door. Amy crouched on the hangar's cold gray stone floor. Having spotted an old toolbox sitting on a shelf at the back wall, Ally said, "Ahh good. Tools."

She rushed over to the open metal toolbox and plowed through the assortment of tools. A half dozen empty coke cans sat on the shelf by the toolbox. Not far away on the shelf sat four cans unopened. Ally grabbed a screwdriver, not a Philips-styled tool but a long flat-tipped screwdriver. God, how do I even know the difference? I don't remember anyone teaching me that. In the other hand, she held an unopened can of coke. Turning to head back to Amy, she could see the girl huddled on the floor, shivering in fear like a bedraggled, lost, wet puppy. Me too, Ally admitted to herself. It's only a matter of time until our angry captors will be on our tail, after watching those two slimy Arabs burn to a crisp in the car. It will be Gorby and Karl bursting through the hangar door, ready to brutally silence us with a bullet to the head or a knife in the throat. Damn it, Ally cringed. We're like two lambs awaiting their inevitable pathetic slaughter. No, we've got to fight back, she reminded herself.

She noticed the thunderous noise of the increasingly heavy rain now pelting down on the metal hangar rooftop. Geez, it's like we're trapped in a giant tin can. As she approached Amy, she could see the girl rocking back and forth, silently sobbing. Ally started to pry open some of the wooden slats on a crate filled with bananas. "Yes. Got it," she yelled out and reached in to grab a few bananas. She quickly peeled one and threw the banana skin against the side door where they entered earlier. The peel hit the door and fell to the floor. She peeled another and did the same routine, then another and another, scattering about twenty banana peels. Amy stopped rocking and looked up at Ally, who continued to peel and throw banana skins, covering the area around the door.

"What are you doing, Ally?" Amy asked.

Ally opened a coke can and ran over to the banana peels scattered across the stone floor. She poured the coke out, dribbling it across the skins. Amy's eyes opened wide. Then it clicked. She suddenly understood Ally's plan.

"Good aim, huh? I hit the door every time," Ally gloated as she returned to retrieve another unopened coke can. She popped it open. "Here, have a drink and a bite of banana. Then you can help me. We've got to fill more space between us and the door with wet banana peels."

Amy nodded and took a sip of the coke. She smiled up at Ally, who stood over her. Ally handed her a couple of bananas. Amy started peeling, taking a bite of the sweet banana, and threw the peel toward the pile of skins.

"Wow, girl. Amy, you've got some arm there! Good aim."

Ally popped the third and fourth cans of coke and hurriedly poured the liquid over the mounting banana peels.

"Slick! Very slick," she yelled out, raising her arms in the air like she just scored a goal. "Yeah! Those pigs are going to leap like lizards and land on their asses, if I have my way."

As Amy continued the peel and toss process, Ally picked up the screwdriver and jammed it between the wooden slats of a crate filled with tomatoes. "Let's use these tomatoes as combat ammunition. When those guys come through the door, we'll yell at the top of our lungs like we're on the attack and seeking to take down the enemy. We'll hurl as many tomatoes as we possibly can at their heads and chests. It doesn't matter, just bombard them. Are you ready for this?" She piled the tomatoes around them and crouched down next to the young girl. Amy nodded in response. "Listen, I know it's a weak plan, but it's all we've got." She took Amy's hand, squeezing it. They sat in silence, both holding a tomato in hand. The sound of the rain seemed to soothe them. "The rain," Ally added, "it's an asset to us. The wetter their shoes, the more slippery the surface, the harder they'll fall. Wait. Wait! One more thing we need." Ally rose and scooted back over to the toolbox, retrieving a large hammer. She darted back to Amy and handed her the hammer. "Here, you keep this weapon by your side, just in case. I'll use the screwdriver as my weapon. Go for the chest, if you use it. Oh my God, someone's at the door." Ally could hear a Russian accent just outside.

"Fucking girls!" Gorby said as he opened the door. "Chickadees, are you in here? We're going to fucking kill you both!" The two men didn't look down. They stepped inside and slipped, sliding like oysters down a beer-coated throat, both crashing to the hard stone floor. Ally could hear the crack of Gorby's head on the cement. Karl's gun fired as he slipped, then tried to regain his balance. Amy froze up when she heard the bang of the bullet escaping from his gun.

Ally yelled out, "Throw the tomatoes now. Throw them!" They went into action, the tomatoes hitting the one who tried to stand. Down on the floor, Gorby was not moving. Karl was holding his left leg as if in extreme pain. He's hit! Ally realized that Karl shot himself while skidding on the wet banana peels. The tomatoes smacked him in the face, in the chest. He was down on the floor. He put all the energy he had left into reaching for his gun, noticing that Gorby's head was spurting blood, which now ran across the banana peels under and around his comrade's torso. The tomatoes kept coming as Karl edged closer and closer to his gun.

Just about to touch it, he shouted, "You're dead now little girl." Picking it up, he pointed it at Amy.

"No!" Ally grabbed the hammer from Amy's side and rushed over to Karl, banging the metal head into each of his legs, his pistol dropping to the floor.

He reached out with his other hand to grab Ally by the hair. She turned quickly and smashed the hammer into his forehead and then down on his nose as he wriggled freakishly, trying to fight back, almost getting his grip on the pistol again. Raising the hammer high in the air, she thrust it down on his skull once and then again. Amy screamed out in terror. Karl fell back on the banana peels, his arms flailing at his side, blood pouring out from his head. Then he went limp. Ally dropped the hammer and kicked the pistol across the floor. In shock, she stopped abruptly for just a moment, staring down at the silenced Russians.

"You're the victims now, guys," she said.

"You saved me, Ally. You saved me," Amy cried out. Ally ran over to Amy, knelt down by her side, and then cradled the quivering young girl in her arms, shielding her eyes from the two lifeless, bloodied men. "You saved me," Amy whispered. "Thank you."

The door at the front of the hangar sprang open. Several uniformed men came running in, flashlights beaming, navigating around the dozens of wooden crates.

"Ally. Ally!"

She could hear Christian's voice.

"Hello," another male voice called out.

Christian saw her sitting there, her arms wrapped around Amy Skyler. They looked like two sisters comforting each other in the midst of a family crisis. Her bright blue eyes gazed up at him.

"Do you like fruit salad?" Ally asked. Despite the blood and the chaos, she hadn't given up on teasing him. "We've got it all: bananas, mangoes," she said.

Marco Pezzetti rushed over to the girls and placed heavy green blankets around their shoulders. But Ally's eyes remained on the man she loves. Marco's mouth gaped open, taking in the rest of the horrific scene. He raised his eyebrows, moving closer to the Russians sprawled out on red-soaked banana skins, taking in what appeared to be two dead bodies. Perplexed by the scattered banana peels and the squashed tomatoes, he noticed the hammer on the cement floor near the thinner man's body. He put it together in an instant.

Shaking his head in disbelief, he looked over at the girls. "Very impressive ladies," he said. "Quite a bizarre strategy, though the best defense I've seen devised on short notice." Then he said to Amy: "Ready to go back?" He helped the petrified girl to her feet.

Christian reached for Ally's hand and gently pulled her up, taking the woman he admires and adores into his arms. "Guess you didn't need me to protect you," he said. "I only hope that you need me to love you."

"You love me? *You* love me?"

She couldn't believe what she was hearing. He nodded.

"Are you sure it's not the fact that I've impressed you with my ninja warrior combat abilities or maybe it's this sexy outfit?" She gestured for him to behold her bloodied clothes and smeared makeup. "And what about that tall, voluptuous Russian back on the ship who really 'vants' you?"

"That was a big mistake, one that I will painfully regret for the rest of my life. She was actually behind this whole mess."

"Yes, I figured that one out."

"I love *you*, Ally Collette. I've loved you for a long time, but I was too blind to see it. I've made some stupid decisions, and—"

"Shh, a bee's gotta buzz before it finds *real* honey," she soothed his concerns and looked up at him. "I love you madly, Mr. Stephanopolous."

He beamed. "What would you think of a honeymoon on a cruise? You know that little old lady who frequently travels on this cruise ship, that insightful and magical woman you pointed out to me—she could be our maid of honor." Christian led Ally out into the rain, into the night, headed for their new life together. "By the way, your father loves you, too, and told me so just this morning. He's waiting to hear from you."

The End

About the Author

Linda S. Gunther lives in Aptos, California. After growing up in New York City and then attending Columbia University graduate school in Counseling Psychology, Linda was given the opportunity to spend a summer in London, England. Deciding to take a giant leap and start a new life in the U.K., she married an Englishman, gave birth to her son, attended graduate school in psychotherapy, and taught primary school. After six years, Linda returned to California and began her career in Human Resources, also completing an MBA. Linda has held key positions in several Silicon Valley companies. Also an actress, she has performed in numerous theatre productions. She studied with the British American Drama Academy and Yale School of Drama at Oxford University. Linda's passion for travel and learning fuels her fire to create vivid fictional characters and unforgettable storylines. She has written two other romantic suspense novels, *Ten Steps From The Hotel Inglaterra* and *Endangered Witness.* Visit Linda's website at lindasgunther.com.

www.ingramcontent.com/pod-product-compliance
Lightning Source LLC
Chambersburg PA
CBHW020636260626
47157CB00008B/2774